P9-CBJ-844

THE KALIGARH FAULT

The
Kaligarh Fault

by
PAUL ROADARMEL

HARPER & ROW, PUBLISHERS
New York, Hagerstown, San Francisco, London

Frontispiece by Howard Asch.

THE KALIGARH FAULT. Copyright © 1979 by Paul Roadarmel. All rights reserved. Printed in the United States of America. No part of this book may be used or reproduced in any manner whatsoever without written permission except in the case of brief quotations embodied in critical articles and reviews. For information address Harper & Row, Publishers, Inc., 10 East 53rd Street, New York, N.Y. 10022. Published simultaneously in Canada by Fitzhenry & Whiteside Limited, Toronto.

FIRST EDITION

Designer: Eve Kirch

Copyeditor: Bernard B. Skydell

Library of Congress Cataloging in Publication Data

Roadarmel, Paul.
  The Kaligarh Fault.
  Novel.
  I. Title.
PZ4.R6286Kal [PS3568.016]   813'.5'4   78–13900
ISBN 0–06–013600–6

79 80 81 82 83 10 9 8 7 6 5 4 3 2 1

THE KALIGARH FAULT

one

Bottles and bodies were a way of life on the island, a way of life that had somehow come to center itself around Tommy Berren's place. "La Casa Confuso," they called it, a whitewashed jumble of a house up in the cliffs along the eastern shoreline.

They liked to arrive en masse, cheering and overwhelming him at the door or infiltrating over the veranda, around on the ocean side, and going straight for his liquor supply.

Berren usually took their intrusions good-naturedly, and there were even times when he found himself enjoying their background buzz of indolence. It was lightweight company, true enough, an underculture of European dropouts. But in a way, they were just caught up in their own kind of exile, like he was, trying too hard to get away from something and falling into a never-ending game of forlorn silliness.

It was the game that made the difference. Berren could

play it for only so long before sneaking away. He was sitting cross-legged on the veranda wall that night, with the noise and the lights behind him and the Mediterranean out there in the dark. He'd been musing about time and distance, and the great sea swells out beyond the surf rolling silently past the island in the gloom.

There was a blast of music as someone stepped outside and closed the glass-paneled doors again. Whoever it was wavered drunkenly for a moment, then skillfully negotiated a straight line across the flagstones to the wall beside Berren.

"That you, Tommy?"

"Huh?" Berren knew the voice. "Oh, hi, Edgar."

" 'Nother one o' your winners," Edgar said, stifling a belch. "Bunch o' real dips in there, bunch o' washouts. Even the goddamn host is out here hiding."

"Hey, man . . ." A lighter flickered in the shadows and revealed a shaggy-headed young man pinching a tiny joint between his fingernails, trying to get a puff without setting off his beard. "Hey, I mean . . . I heard that, ya know?" The lighter went out and he hissed in a deep breath between his teeth. "I mean, how can you . . . ya know?" He was angry at the drunk but not sure why, so he tried another puff. "Rude, man . . ." he finally said. "Good old Tommy, know what I mean?"

Edgar was tottering a bit and had to grab the stonework. ". . . rest my case," he said.

There was a gale of masculine howling from inside and some girls were laughing too loudly.

"What's going on back in there?" Berren asked.

"Oh, Anita's doing her striptease thing again. Real trooper, that girl."

2

"Sure is," Berren agreed, trying to get a look from where he sat.

Somebody was down on the drive pumping the kick-starter of a motorscooter and the doors slammed on the nearest Fiat. In spite of the entertainment, it began to look like things were breaking up.

"Coming with us, Tommy?"

"Where to?"

"Going out to molest the natives," someone shouted from the drive. "Come on."

They'd grown restless with their own company and were regrouping in smaller clusters, heading off to look for their amusement elsewhere.

"Come along, Tommy. We're going to Paco's."

"Sorry," Berren called back. "Really. Gotta finish an article on Barcelona or my agent's going to cut off our booze."

"*Ciao*, Tommy."

"Bye-bye."

"Yah, see ya," Berren said to no one in particular. He watched the last couple trying to jump-start a whirring and sputtering motorscooter down the drive.

"Push, push!" the girl was urging.

"Number two gear—please."

"Got it. There it goes."

"Wait!" cried the man.

"*Ciao*, Tommy."

"Wait, wait!"

When their lights disappeared into the first of the steep curves, Berren stretched and lay back on the stone wall to listen to the night. There were only a few hours left until daylight and it was no good trying to sleep.

He had been living here for almost a year now, putting the pieces of his life together again. And yet he could still wake up in a sweat, hopelessly lost in the dark, unable to remember where he was, whose bed, what part of the world. Once it had been enough to know that Anna was asleep beside him, but now there was only the long wait for morning to settle him down again.

He put his hands behind his head for a cushion.

A sense of place, that's what Jason had called it. He'd told Berren once that that's what he got from his little mountain village. A core of stability after all that wandering around.

Nothing was left of the life they'd had in India. There were still some research grants around then, and quiet nights like this in the Punjabi foothills. There were things worth achieving and some adventure in the trying.

But, what the hell. Jason was probably right to take Anna and for them to go off on their own like that, things were such a mess between them. In the end it had cost Berren everything, and God only knows what good any of it could really have done.

If only he could regain that sense of place, he was sure he'd feel whole again, he was sure he'd be safe.

But for someone like Berren, the real scale of life is much larger than the day-to-day details of the island. It is a world of power and greed with currents and eddies that can hold a man in hazard or draw him into its much greater designs.

There was no way he could know it, but for Berren it had all begun again, months earlier and half the globe away.

The snow atop the highest peaks had turned to bronze with the setting sun. The sky held the twilight glow a while longer and then the tiny Himalayan village was lost in the valley's darkness.

There was a cold draft seeping through the wooden slats that covered the window. The old man poked at the slats a few times, then gave it up. He lit the wick of a small oil lamp with the flame of another that burned nearby and placed the lamp in a niche in the wall beside a soot-blackened clay figurine.

It was time again. Past time; she should be ready by now. The *puja* was an ordeal and it took longer each night, leaving her more exhausted with every attempt. She was so old, he thought, and yet it was the only way.

He listened for the sound of her approach while behind him, deeper in the shadows of the room, a few of the village elders still hunkered against the wall. Some were mumbling the droning chant begun by others several days earlier. They had kept a long vigil over the emaciated figure of their young foreign friend, who lay there in the stink of his festering wound.

The rockslide had shattered the leg and all the medicinal procedures had been followed—the old woman had seen to that. She'd had the leg pulled straight and bound. She'd cleaned and covered the ugly open gashes and salved his bruises every day. He should have healed by now, she'd said, but he wouldn't lie still. He had attracted a demon by his delirious thrashing and it was poisoning him.

When the blackening and swelling came, the old woman made several long lacerations near the fracture, then wrapped the leg in moldy, broadleafed herbs she'd gathered from a thicket near the rim of the valley. Now there was nothing to be done except the magic.

An earthen jug of rice liquor was passed among the somber men, enticing even the most exhausted among them to rejoin the mindless chant. When the jug reached the old man, he spared a portion of his ration to dampen a clean rag which he dabbed at the invalid's glistening face.

The young man had always looked so much like one of them, but now his skin had lost its brownness; it had become pale and clammy from the long confinement. The old mountain man knew nothing of the coloring of foreigners. It seemed unnatural and frightening to see such black hair and eyes against that pallid skin.

The invalid pushed restlessly against the blanket. He was trying to speak.

The old man continued dabbing with the rag, feeling helpless and clumsy as he tried to soothe him.

"*Shanta*, Ja-son. *Shantahuna*," he whispered, trying to quiet him, for in his delirium Jason sometimes cried out in his own strange language, clutching the blanket and cursing his stupidity and the rock that had betrayed him. The old man covered the cracked lips with the rag in time to stifle the cry. Even now the soldiers could be passing, and sounds carry a long way on a quiet mountain night.

The plank door scraped over the threshold and a grave young boy entered, urging a heavily bundled sweaty figure over the sill. The old woman was ready.

She was a horrible apparition, dressed in brightly colored rags and bent almost double. Her face was painted garishly with dark lines of mystical design and red blotches of gummed *peprica* beneath her eyes and in the hollows of her cheeks, and her breath was foul from the herbal drugs she had been chewing.

The chanting stopped. The villagers all stared. She was even more frightful this time, and several of the men shrank back against the wall as if the demon already possessed her.

Someone picked up the jug and, with some hesitation, the chant began again. She stood with her feet wide apart, weaving back and forth. Her eyes were glassy and unfocused until they fastened on Jason's pale face, then her swaying body picked up the rhythm of the maddening chant. Moaning softly, she staggered to Jason's side and knelt close to him. Her face held a crazed and twisted expression as if she were on the verge of hysteria.

She took his head in her hands. Her eyes rolled back, her consciousness entering into his delirium with him, searching there with the drug and the power of the trance, calling and coaxing the demon, drawing it out into her own, more healthy body.

Jason was writhing with her cadence, mimicking the words and sounds that were teasing him toward the surface, when there was a hoarse shout from the nearest end of the village compound. After a moment of shocked silence the alarm came again, this time from in front of the house, as the neighbor who had been keeping watch fled past them down the path.

There was a commotion outside, more shouting, then a pounding on the outer door. The room was already a swirl of activity. Only the old woman, still in her trance, and the invalid, on whom all of her senses still focused, continued the *puja*. Then the boy swept her aside and leaped over the cot. He clamped a hand over Jason's mouth and supported his head as the villagers lifted the sagging body through the doorway into the back storeroom.

The intruders had battered their way through the barred door and when one of the elders put himself in their way, the first one through grabbed him by the shirt and pummeled him with an open fist, driving him ahead of them toward the others in the back room.

There were four soldiers in dirty, threadbare fatigues. They swaggered about the room, carrying their carbines with a casual arrogance, inspecting the villagers who stood bunched together, wringing their hands and staring at their feet.

The soldiers were festooned with lethal hardware clipped to bandoleers and webbed belts that were hung from their waists or thrown over their shoulders.

Their leader turned to watch the old woman with bemused interest. The *puja* took an awful toll on those who practiced it, and to interrupt it like this . . . even now her head was rolling back and forth, and she was beginning to mumble again. She was caught between two worlds and could not comprehend what was happening.

With an ugly grin, the soldier took her face in his free hand and squeezed her reddened cheeks roughly until her mouth opened. Her breath was still sour from the drug and he screwed up his face at the offensive smell.

"Deko," he sneered, twisting her face toward his laughing men. *"Ye gunja wallah hain."* More laughter as the men set about rummaging through the house, overturning the *charpoi* cots and emptying the few metal boxes they found under them, sniffing, then pouring the contents from the various clay vessels that lined the shelf in the corner.

"Yaha hain!" One of the soldiers came in from the anteroom holding a jug of rice liquor like a trophy. The leader lost interest in his tormenting. He threw the old woman to the floor and reached for the jug. The soldiers gathered loudly around him as he shook it to determine its level. He took a loud gulp and wiped his mouth on his sleeve while the villagers stood gaping at one another. That was all the soldiers were after; they were just out foraging for liquor. They took the jug with

them when they left, passing it among themselves as they made their way out.

None of the villagers moved until they heard the laughter dying away beyond the walls of the compound. It was the old woman who broke the spell. She'd struck her head in the fall and large droplets of blood streaked her forehead and spattered on the earthen floor as she struggled to get to her feet. She was blinking furiously, working her face as she tried to free herself from the trance. She ignored the protests of the men and pushed her way ahead of them into the storeroom.

A pile of heavy hemp grain bags had been dragged away from the wall. The invalid lay with the boy on the floor behind it under a dusty pile of empties. The boy's hands were still clasped over Jason's mouth as if he were not yet sure the danger had passed. When he removed his hands, he did so with great care, for the lamp had been brought in and it was apparent from Jason's eyes that he had regained a measure of consciousness. The pain must have been awful, but the only sound he made was the dry gasping of air through his clinched teeth. His eyes had been fixed on the tiny flame from the lamp until the old woman bent close. He flinched at the sight of the dark blood and tried to lift his hand to her face.

"Anna," he managed to say. "My God, you're hurt, too." The old woman gave the boy a puzzled look, but Jason gripped his arm and pulled him closer. "See her, Tommy? Do you see what we've done to our Anna?" The boy looked up at the others and tapped his forehead. Delirious again. Jason couldn't hold his head up any longer. He let it fall back against the boy. "Now," he said as his eyes pressed shut. "Now we'll all die."

two

It wasn't the kind of morning he needed. A thick gray haze rose out of the surface of the sea a few miles out, leaving the island more isolated than ever. The sun was little more than a dim oval, squatting on the rim of the horizon.

By now its first rays should have reached the tops of the weathered cliffs on either side. And that marbled black face of the Mediterranean should be dazzling with sunshine, cluttering his senses and melting away the gentle melancholy that always followed the oppressive merriment of these late-night parties.

Berren glanced back at the arched doorway of his living room. The litter had spilled out onto the stones of the veranda. He winced at the thought of the mess that was waiting for him inside and leaned out over the stone wall again.

"Hell with it," he mumbled, and gave himself some more time to brood over his coffee and watch the surge and ebb of the dark water against the beach below.

He'd been letting things get on his nerves last night, but he was feeling better now. His eyelids seemed less heavy and that familiar hollow feeling was easing. He leaned out slightly, the edge of the wall sharp against the center of his chest, until he could see the cluster of whitewashed houses that spilled down the southern hillside to the beached fishing boats swaying easily beside the quay.

No signs of life yet. Modern times had come to the island, he thought. Electric lights extend the day, and now everybody has to sleep later.

He pushed back the hood of his baggy sweatshirt, then swept aside the thick mop of brown hair that fell over one eye. Free of the hood's shadow, the coloring of his eyes seemed strangely out of place against the dark tan of his face. It was as if, like the faded sweatshirt, the hot sun had bleached them to that disturbing shade of pale blue.

Berren had a boyish face: There was something about the fullness of the cheeks and mouth, something that made the other features seem open, unassuming, and ready for an excuse to burst into a show of quick, almost childish exuberance.

And yet his skin showed some seams where it was drawn a little too tightly over his angular jaw, and the creases that were beginning to etch back from the corners of his eyes were deep enough, now, to remain even in a kinder light, as if he were forever squinting into the sun.

He pulled another swallow from the bottom of the mug, hoping to bolster himself for the chores ahead, and scowled at the result. Worst damn coffee when it got cold, he thought, and flung the remainder over the side.

He shuffled back inside and was making his way through the debris when he stumbled over one of the playmates the others had gone off and forgotten. She was curled up on a furry throw rug and wearing nothing but one of Berren's old, oversized cardigans. Her long legs were drawn up to her chin and the white V where her bikini had been showed how new she was to the island's bathing customs.

She slept with her hand clutching the sweater tight to her throat, but one willful little breast managed to peek out from the opening left by a long-lost button. Crowning the greenish wool sweater was a mop of curly red hair that hid everything beneath it except the freckled nose of its owner.

Berren lingered indecisively for a moment, then crouched beside the girl. The view from the lower angle was even more appealing and, on impulse, he bent forward, intending to pat her on her somewhat bony behind. Then for some reason he thought the better of it and squeezed her thigh lightly instead.

"Anita?" he whispered. There was no reaction. She may have heard him, for there was a catch in the rhythm of her slow breathing. Other than that, she ignored the intrusion. "Anita." He realized there was no reason to whisper; for that matter, there was no reason to wake her, either; but there was something about this morning, and he thought he might enjoy her company.

"Anita!"

This time her head responded by moving just enough for the curls to fall away from her face. One eye stuttered open.

"Tommy?"

"Yes."

"What time is it?" She tried to tug the sweater down a little. She wasn't being coy, but her nakedness didn't seem like as much of an event now that she was sobering up.

"Six or so."

"And what are *we* doing up at this hour?" She emphasized

the word "we" to remind him that her awakening was not of her own choice.

"I'm not much of a sleeper," he said, "and I thought you'd like to join me for some kind of breakfast."

Her face went passive for a moment while she considered the invitation, then she wrinkled her nose in consent. She rolled over on her back and arched in a lazy stretch. Her puffy eyes were squeezed shut, but she was not unpleasantly aware of Berren's gaze following the frontier of the cardigan as it retreated up her waist.

With her arms still thrust back, she ventured a glance to gauge his reaction and caught a glimpse of something behind him. She tried to blink it away, but it was really there. She jerked herself upright. In a single motion she drew her knees to her chest, grabbed the hem of the shapeless cardigan, and plunged it to her ankles, retrieving her modesty under its green woolen tent.

"Who's that?"

Berren twisted around, startled by her first frightened look, and saw the shape immediately. The sunlight had reached the opposite corner of the room and revealed, first, a pair of shiny black shoes and the creased blue cuffs above them. Berren stumbled to one knee, upsetting the coffee table as he pushed himself up from the floor.

"Now, now, Dr. Berren. Don't let's be rash." There was an exaggerated, almost mocking, calm to the intruder's voice that checked whatever Berren's next move might have been. "I'm really quite harmless. Much more so, I dare say, than that scrubby lot that spent most of the night here."

Berren was on his feet, hunched forward with his weight on his toes, ready for what, he didn't know.

"Good heavens, look at you." The irritating voice went on

as if the whole thing were a joke. "If I hadn't spoken up just then, you might have jumped me. Now do I look so awfully dangerous?"

Berren was amazed that he had failed to see him there. Even the gloom of a few minutes earlier would have done little to hide this pale creature with his pressed white shirt.

"I know," the intruder said, "ready for the worst, and all that, eh? Well, that's understandable. You've obviously spent too much time among . . . the heathen." He was watching the girl.

"What the hell are you doing here?" Berren growled.

"Doing? I was just waiting. That's what I do, you see. I wait for people, and when the proper time comes, I tell them things they are supposed to hear." The man hadn't moved the whole time. He just sat there, delivering his lines through an unrelenting smirk. "In this case, I have several things to tell you, uh, in private."

"In private?" Berren was furious. "Apparently you don't know what the word means. You just walk into . . ."

"Ahhh, I see." The man's mouth opened a little this time. "You and the girl were . . . and I interrupted. That's unfortunate. Nevertheless, I feel introductions should wait," he gave a vaguely contemptuous wave toward the girl, "until your little friend leaves."

Berren's reply would have been coarse, but Anita needed only the suggestion. She struggled to her feet, still tugging at the sweater to hide what she could, and looked from one door to the other, apparently trying to recall where she had left her clothes.

"Aha," she said, and ran stiff-legged from the room.

The stranger was wearing the wrong head. It was too large for his slight frame and its weight must have been too great for a neck to hold, so it rested directly atop his narrow torso. What hair remained on it was trimmed close to the scalp and oiled to flatten it in place.

He seemed unnaturally stiff and upright, an uncomfortable-looking posture reinforced by his starched shirt and his cardboard-stiff collar, closed tight at the throat by what Berren assumed was the "old School tie." A dark blue jacket of indeterminate style hung tidily over the back of the straight chair beside the one in which its owner sat.

The whole situation was ridiculous. Berren realized, sheepishly, that but for the girl he would have seen most of this the minute he came in from the veranda, and he hated the man all the more for making him feel like a fool.

Berren decided it was his turn to be condescending. Let him sit. Whatever business somebody like this might have, it could wait until Berren was good and ready to hear about it. So he left him there, crossing the room with a loose sandal scuffing awkwardly over the planks of the floor, and squeezed into the cubbyhole of his kitchen.

He was still fuming while he fumbled through the mess, ignoring the glasses that his elbow tipped, and their disgusting contents of liquor and cigarette butts that spilled over the counter. He removed the grounds basket from the percolator and tossed it into the tin basin he used for a sink. He took the pot back into the living room with the cold leftover brew sloshing about inside, and plunked it down noisily on the make-shift bar. He plugged the cord into a waist-high socket and leaned back against the wall with his arms folded.

Berren eyed the intruder belligerently. He was sure he wasn't going to like this, just as he was sure he wasn't going to like the reheated coffee. He had just sent off the copy for the airline brochure his agency on the continent had set up for him, and he had been looking forward to a week of simple island pleasures as soon as the Barcelona thing for his biweekly tourist column was done.

One of the simple island pleasures he had been considering opened the door she had retreated behind. Having gathered up her clothing and her dignity, she affected a superior attitude as she clattered toward the front door.

"*Ciao*, Tommy, and say good-bye to your friend."

As she made her exit, Berren noticed that her skirt was only slightly longer than the sweater had been.

It was a time-honored principle on the island that postponing an unpleasantness was the next best thing to avoiding it, so when the girl had gone Berren turned his attention back to the coffeepot. A few bubbles were steaming to the surface and he snatched the plug from the socket before it could scorch. He poured out a mugful, ignoring his instinct for hospitality, and slurped a little off the surface. The aromatic steam filled his lungs and seemed to loosen the congestion brought on by a night of chain smoking someone else's Gauloises.

The place was a real mess, and the intruder's tidy figure sitting aloof amid the refuse made it look even worse. His short-sleeved shirt was the only concession he appeared to have made to the Mediterranean sun. He was probably angry that his skin had refused to submit to his sense of propriety and had burned anyhow.

Berren's slurping grew louder with each swallow, a disagreeable noise to the intruder who made a face and began to fidget. He looked around the room for a way to get the interview started.

"Not very much on security, are you, old man?"

Berren ignored him.

"That is to say, with guests such as those you had here last night, you should be more careful."

"You mean," Berren spoke into his coffee mug, "I should be more selective about my friends? Lock the doors . . . ?"

"Yes, that sort of thing."

" . . . count the silverware?" Berren set the mug down.

"Oh, I hardly . . . "

"Count them as they leave? Be sure some sneak isn't left behind, hiding himself away in my house?"

"Now, now."

"Okay." Berren's self-restraint was beginning to slip. "Let's have it."

"Have it?"

"I mean, that's a real cute act. Great entrance—lots of drama. Satisfied? Now, I've got a long day at the typewriter coming up, so I want you to tell me, in short, simple sentences, who you are and what you want. Then I want you out of here."

"See here, old man, I didn't mean to upset you."

"Of course you meant to upset me. You thought a bit of flair would serve your purpose. It just never occurred to you that I'd get mad, too—mad enough to kick your ass out of here if you don't start talking."

"Oh, very well." The intruder didn't sound particularly worried. "My name is Parker. I have a lengthy title, but it isn't important. I'm really only a messenger."

"Very modest," Berren injected. "But a messenger would always claim the official title. What's more, messengers use phones and knock on doors. You're from the Guild, aren't you?"

"Of course."

"That being the case, messenger boy, you can give them a

message for me." Berren searched the intruder's eyes for a flicker of reaction. There was none. "Go back and tell them to find some other sucker. They've got nothing more to say to me."

"You don't mean that, Dr. Berren," Parker said. "You really want to know what this is all about, don't you? You see, although we've never met, I've managed to learn a great deal about you. It was quite easy to do so, what with all that work you've published: your doctoral dissertation, all that work in India. And, of course, the Guild has files . . .

"The most impressive thing was your overwhelming curiosity. I mean, 'Origins of Parsee Funeral Customs'—really! You're curious about everything.

"And I know the Guild doesn't consider you a 'sucker.' No, indeed. If they did, your relationship with them would have ended long ago."

"It did, mister."

"Oh, dear." Parker curled a finger over his upper lip, perplexed that his presentation was going awry. "It appears that we are getting ahead of ourselves. Very well, perhaps now is the time. First of all, Tommy—may I call you Tommy?"

"No."

"Of course not. Well then, Dr. Berren; you must understand that a news service like the Guild, whose very stock in trade is the *selective* allocation of information, would find it relatively easy to foster certain, shall we say, misapprehensions for you to live under."

"Misapprehensions?"

"Yes. You see, while you undoubtedly believe you left the Guild's employ after that unfortunate Indian CID affair, the fact of the matter is that you haven't really been on your own since you first joined our ranks."

Berren must have started to say something, but the man continued without pause.

"Your agency—the one that makes such lucrative use of those tourist pieces you've been writing this year—is actually a subsidiary of the Guild. You may find that hard to accept, and yet, after all, we live in an age of conglomerates, so there it is. You were allowed to think you were rid of us, while actually you never left our employ at all."

Berren looked as if he'd been struck in the face. He gaped at the intruder for a full minute, then, with great care, he put the coffee mug down. His stomach was churning, and for the first time that morning the house stank with the smokings and spillings of the party. He eased himself around from behind the bar and walked slowly from the house out onto the veranda.

So that's where he really was, he thought grimly. Well, to hell with them. There were other sanctuaries; he could just split, leave it all behind. New grants in aid, new studies to lose himself in. The chairs of anthropology at several of the more liberal universities were his for the asking. But he'd said all that before and he'd ended up here. He hadn't moved at all.

It was a new twist, to be sure, and yet it was the same elusive antagonist as always, hounding and using him as cynically as ever. Simpler men called it "the System" and saw it as an almost mythical pyramid with each level crushing the one under it.

Berren knew better. To him it was a vast tangle of conflicting power, a myriad of purposeless detail, where cause and effect were often as inscrutable as the objectives that put them in play.

"Your participation is requested once again . . ." That's

what this toady was here to say. Thomas Everett Berren, Ph.D. Always within reach, ready for one more round.

Who said he wasn't a sucker?

"Rather a pleasant view you have here."

Parker had joined him on the veranda, keeping a discreet distance from Berren's side as if to avoid any familiarity that might be unwanted. He was aware of his role as the bearer of unsettling news, so he just stood silently for a while, looking out over the water, careful to keep his spotless white shirt well away from the wall.

"Cummings wants to see you," he said at last.

"Huh?" Berren was watching a tiny white bird that was strutting along the water's edge.

"Cummings. Surely you remember him. He wants you in London, and by tomorrow night."

"What for?"

"One might assume that he wants your affiliation to resume its active role again." He eyed Berren carefully. "I was told to mention that it involves someone named Jason Josefs."

Berren started. Of course it involved Jason. If there had been some sort of scheme to all of this, then it would have had to involve them all.

"And what about the girl? What about Anna?"

"I know nothing about a girl. I was specifically told that should you be less than interested in leaving this . . . this heathen backwater I was to mention this fellow Josefs."

Berren flared angrily at the man's shallowness but checked himself. "This 'heathen backwater,' " he said, "has had a stable civilization dating back to the Phoenicians."

"I'm sure," Parker said with a patronizing shrug. "Well, you'll be happy to know I shan't be traveling with you. I push on in"—he checked his watch—"an hour and thirty-five minutes for Morocco."

"Morocco," he repeated. "God, what next? Straightforward business there, though. Most of my work is like that; just everyday stuff, you know."

Berren grunted an acknowledgment. He turned and went back into the disheveled living room. Parker followed him and gathered up his suit coat. He held it up while he brushed absently at a few imagined wrinkles with his free hand. Then he stopped. Still examining the fabric, he said: "I say, you are going? I mean, you haven't really said, have you?"

Berren watched him and said nothing.

"We assumed," the man continued, "that you might be a bit put off at the news—the agency and all that. To be quite frank I had been prepared for the worst.

"But you know, you didn't seem to have much of a response at all, certainly not enough to predict your intention, don't you see?"

Berren knew he would go. Whatever was happening, it had taken him and the two people who meant the most to him and twisted their relationship into two years of deceit and regret. Of course he would go, and this time somebody was sure as hell going to tell him what it was all about.

"Chalk it up to your persuasive charm," Berren said, coldly.

Parker waited for a second before he realized he had his answer. "Right," he said. He glanced about the room, still a little uncertain. "Right," he said again, then turned and walked briskly out the front door.

Berren returned to the bar and found the plug to the percolator. He didn't plug it in; he just stared down at it for a long time as if he'd forgotten what it was for.

"Shit," he said.

three

A front was moving in over the channel. All along a line that curved north and east of the big Boeing's flight path, huge cumulus clouds billowed toward the stratosphere, their peaks a bright creamy fluff where they rose out of their own shadows. Against such a background, the lumbering jet hardly seemed to be moving.

Berren's mood was foul and getting worse as London crept closer. To deal with somebody like Cummings, he needed to pull himself together; work it all out beforehand. But everything was wrong, from that hair-raising liftoff at the very edge of the sea to the flight's only little bottle of bourbon going to the greasy fellow across the aisle. Yes, scotch would do, as usual. "Just a finger of water, *por favor.*"

The tiny bottle was delivered with a plastic tumbler brimming with water. Decorum denied him his first impulse, so there was nothing but to drink most of it before adding the whisky.

After all that, he had to force himself to sink deeper into his seat and, between sips, concentrate on inducing his knotted nerves to relax. Yoga with a scotch chaser, he thought. What am I coming to?

The jet was rolling down the rain-puddled runway, braking against one set of landing gears and arching slowly around toward Heathrow's terminal before Berren gave up his strategies. He'd been trying to plot them out for hours but they had slipped away with the tedium of the journey. Like debates conceived against his fellow academicians, they would never have amounted to anything more than conversations with himself.

Some of the passengers were already in the aisle, gathering up their belongings, while the announcement requesting them not to do so was still in its Spanish translation, but Berren just refolded his jacket over his arm and looked out at another of London's dismal autumn late afternoons. He was wondering what he used to think was so special about this city.

The preliminaries were strained. Cummings's years with the colonial service had left him with an abiding dislike for the pleasantries he'd been forced to recite when he was merely a functionary. Since then he had managed to arrange a position for himself that would allow him to minimize such necessities, and he didn't like bothering with them now.

His office, hushed with thick draperies and deep-cushioned leather chairs, held in its stolid furnishings an atmosphere of confident authority where, in the quiet, each word and motion seemed isolated and amplified.

Cummings was an imposing figure, an impression for which the environment of his office was in no small way responsible. Despite his age, he'd managed to maintain an acceptable waistline and a care for his diction as unusual as a legible signature for a man of his station. He wore a neat silvery mustache to make up for his thinning hair, and worried sometimes about the reddening capillaries that were beginning to show close to the surface of his nose where they might give the impression of an alcoholic habit.

Impressions were important to Cummings, and he used the combination of his office and his person to its fullest advantage. Within this domain his normal course of action would have been to come straight to the point and be done with it, better or worse.

But the young man who sat before his desk, comfortably rumpled in his turtleneck and corduroy jacket, presented him with an unknown commodity. Each time he looked over at Berren's face, he found the steady gaze of those cold blue eyes a little unsettling.

But, however awkward, these little rituals must be adhered to, and so he continued rummaging through the heavy wooden cabinet, although he'd known before he started that there was no bourbon.

" 'Fraid we're not equipped to satisfy your American tastes; will a scotch whisky do?"

"Fine," said Berren.

"Ice?"

"No thanks. I've lost the habit."

"Mmmm, s'pose you have," Cummings said, and handed him the glass.

Berren, who had been sitting slightly sprawled in the deep club chair, corrected his posture long enough to drink the scotch down to a safer level, then settled back again and continued his inspection of the room.

Its paneling was of fine-crafted squares of warm black wood

that ran from the floor to an elaborate crown molding at the ceiling. Most of the wall space was taken up by arrangements of photographs and framed awards naming "International Journalists Guild" in large scrollwork lettering. Behind the desk was a wall-sized bookcase of the same dark wood and full of surprisingly undecorative books.

The cold light that drifted in from the rainy afternoon outside was supplemented by several brass lamps with translucent green shades. Hanging in a shallow recess in the wall, lit by its own exhibition lamp, was a large Mercator map of the world, very precise and very up to date.

The drinks did little to relieve the long silence. Cummings glared at his watch one last time.

"There's someone else who's supposed to join us," he said. "A rather eccentric fellow, a temporary member of our organization. Well, consultant, actually. He's a brilliant man, but he has an irritating disregard for punctuality."

Cummings punched the button on his intercom. "Any word from Beal, Miss Fenner?"

There wasn't, so Cummings began without him. "So, Dr. Berren, first off I'd like to apologize for having Parker present you with the facts in such an awkward way. We had intended originally to ease you back into things with a little more, uh, consideration; should we have needed you, that is.

"Yes, well, it all sounded good in the scheme of things. As it turned out, recent events changed all that. We knew you would be concerned about your friend, Jason Josefs, so we felt we could be more, well, frank."

"The 'scheme of things,'" Berren said. "What an apt turn of phrase. And I assume this scheme was initiated sometime before my supposed dismissal."

"Yes, quite right. Nasty business, that," Cummings tried a

look of paternal benevolence, "but it had to be done, as you'll see."

"Had to be done." Berren planted both feet on the carpet. "You let them steal six months of work, all the evidence, all the photos . . . "

"Impound," Cummings corrected with exaggerated calm. "The work was impounded."

"Bullshit! The government of India doesn't condone official censorship any more than we do."

"Right; any more than we do." The point was made so Cummings didn't linger. "Now suppose we had arranged publication of your investigation," he said. "How long would you and Josefs have been allowed to stay? How long before those on the receiving end of those Relief Fund rakeoffs would have arranged for your permanent silence?"

He met Berren's cold stare for a moment, then turned away, rubbing a pair of stubby fingers into the soft flesh of his jowls, as if intent on something beyond the heavily draped window. The rain was starting again, and the wind was swaying the boughs of the oak tree outside.

"By now," Cummings said, still staring out the window, "you must have assumed that we do not always limit our endeavors to today's stricter notions of journalism. Oh, we maintain a solid reputation in our field; I'm sure you checked that out before you came to work for us." He looked over at Berren for confirmation.

"But, in fact, we sometimes fulfill what one might call a secondary function—an, uh, activist role." He considered for a moment, but the phrase seemed correct enough so he continued.

"We have at our disposal certain talents. Talents that would be difficult to find and more difficult to coordinate under any other organization. I sha'nt bore you with details of its origins. It's sufficient to say that over the years several agencies concerned with specific problems of, uh, international security have recognized our organization's advantages. Just as a practical matter—application of resources, that sort of thing—they found it was to their advantage to allocate funds to the Guild and let us carry out certain investigations, rather than recruiting and arranging cover for agents of their own for short-term assignments."

"Like a secretarial pool," Berren suggested.

"Something like that." The sarcasm had been lost on Cummings. "A few years ago, some of our people attended your lectures at the Lucerne Conference. Not surprising, after that, that the Eurasian Council should retract their offer to you and Mr. Josefs to coordinate the Schweitzer Chair of Anthropology. After all, academia is still a card-carrying member of the system, no matter what it professes, and your rather nihilistic attitudes were not what they wanted to hear." Cummings managed a chuckle. He wished he'd been there while the decision was being made. "We, on the other hand, found them refreshingly honest."

"So," Berren added cynically, "because you admired our honesty, you recruited us to write the 'truth' about the Bihar famine."

Cummings let a barely audible grunt escape as he reached for his blackened and well-chewed pipe. This was the hard part.

"No, not exactly. Because you were pragmatic and experienced and because you were almost broke, we recruited Josefs for something quite different. You just went along for cover."

He'd said it wrong so he hurried on.

"Look, the Bihar thing was solid newsy stuff. The problem

is you took it all so seriously and so, when it began to look as if Josefs was on to something, we decided that the potential publicity your work would arouse would certainly compromise his situation. Then, of course, when he disappeared we had to act with utmost care. We couldn't tell you what it was all about so we just put a word in the right ear about how unpleasant your series would be to a few officials and allowed the Indian government to remove you from the scene."

"And had them destroy the evidence, too?"

"They needed no such suggestion. They were happy to do it on their own."

"I'll bet," Berren said. "Now, I suppose, you're going to tell me what all this is about so I'll tell you why Jason took off like he did."

"Oh, we know why he, uh, 'took off,' " Cummings said. "Or, at least we know that he was on to something, something important enough to force him to leave the cover your work provided and disappear.

"At first we didn't think too much about it, but months later we still hadn't heard from him, and there was nothing we could do about it. If he'd decided to melt into the crowd with that—how shall we say—camouflage of his, he was beyond any chance of contact."

Berren looked at Cummings with amazement. My God, he thought, I'd forgotten. This man sits behind a desk in London. He couldn't have known. How easy it is to leave out a word, an episode, and misunderstand everything that had happened.

four

Camouflage. A hell of a way to put it, Berren thought, but it figures. Jason Josefs was remarkable in many ways, but the one that was most important to the Guild was his appearance.

His looks were the legacy of his Armenian Jewish ancestors; it had colored him dark as a gypsy and carved his face with the stark Semitic features so much like those of the people of central and northwest India. Given a week of glaring sun and the dry summer winds sanding away at his skin, and even his closest *farenge* friends could miss his presence in a crowded bazaar or in a shuffling throng of pilgrims.

Jason had a particularly effective method of field research that made the most of his appearance and his linguistic talent. The village-level people took him for one of their own and were open and at ease with his constant questioning. He had teamed up with Berren on several involved studies, and with their success had come a disaffection for the self-indulgent world of academia. It had all come to a head at the symposium on "Anthropology in a Changing World" in New York.

"Professorial hacks," Jason had said, shouting over the din of a Second Avenue singles bar as he'd vied for the attention of the bartender. "Any claims they have on professional integrity are based on tenure and their own longevity. Bourbon, wasn't it?"

"Right." Berren gestured with his glass and spilled some on the floor. "Out to document the esoteric. If I have to sit through any more platitudes on 'relevance,' I'll . . . "

"You didn't sit through the last bunch."

"Well, somebody had to warn them," Berren said. "One of those idiots is liable to go out and trip over the real world."

Jason had been trading glances with a blonde at the end of the bar. "Yah, well, issues and answers may be good for the soul, but who do we lie to for our next grant in aid?"

Jason was always the practical one, one of the reasons that as a team they were greater than the sum of the two parts.

It had been like that until Bihar. Then Jason was on his own.

Well, Berren thought bitterly, not entirely on his own.

"And what about Anna?"

"Anna? Oh yes, the girl," Cummings replied. "She wasn't in on any of it. We didn't want to involve anyone we didn't have to, and frankly she seemed a bit too unstable, what with her unfortunate habit and all."

"You knew about that, too, huh?" Berren said. "Well, did you also know that Jason and I got her out of it? Did you bother to put that in your file? . . . Anyhow, we were *all* a 'bit too unstable' in Bihar."

"Mmmm, no doubt." Cummings didn't want to talk about

it. "Well, what's happened is this: We've come upon some information that shows that your friend Josefs is in trouble."

"Yah? Well, that's tough shit, isn't it?"

Cummings was stunned. "See here, Tommy, I mean very big trouble. Now, I don't know what happened between you two in Bihar, but you must understand . . . "

"We *three* in Bihar," Berren corrected angrily. "And I'll tell you what happened. We had to sit there and watch an inept and corrupt system magnify a problem into a disaster. Life and death and all that suffering, and we had to eat and sleep right in the middle of it. It tore us apart. No, it tore *me* apart. When it got to be too much for my good friend Jason, he took *my* girl and split"—his hand swept the air—"for sunnier climes.

"The only thing I had left was my story." He stared coldly at the tweedy gentleman behind the desk. "And you know what happened to that."

Before Cummings could say anything, the door crashed open and a disheveled man in large round spectacles entered the room with giant strides that nearly upset the lamp on the table next to Berren.

"Mr. Cummings, I'm so sorry. I . . . " he started to say, but the buzz of the intercom interrupted. Cummings gave a silent curse and leaned across the desk to push the reply button.

"What is it?"

"Dr. Beal is . . . "

"We *know*, Miss Fenner."

"You see, I've just gotten a new . . . and I couldn't . . . " Beal dropped a battered, old briefcase into a chair and was leaning over, rummaging inside. "Well, you see, I just overlooked the time."

"Yes, well. You're here now. I suppose that's all that matters,"

Cummings said, and took him by the arm as if to guide him away from the briefcase. "Dr. Frederick Beal, this is Dr. Thomas Berren."

Beal adjusted his ridiculous glasses to show it was their fault he hadn't noticed the other guest. His face lit up in genuine pleasure.

"How d'ya do," he said.

Berren stood and shook the hand he offered. "Hi."

Beal swept off his tan raincoat, which was long overdue at the cleaners, and threw it over a chair. His jacket was ill-fitting but of recent vintage, and his shirt was a fresh light blue with its collar buttoned securely. The narrow tie matched them both, but it was a poor choice for such a skinny man.

Berren thought he must be married. And a good thing, too. No telling how he'd look if someone weren't taking care of him.

"Dr. Beal has been lent to us by the United Nations Commission on Narcotics and Drugs. He's an expert on narcotics and their trafficking, and he's been working with Interpol as a temporary adviser for the last few years."

"Narcotics!" Berren interrupted.

Cummings held up his hand. "Now, listen up. We've a lot to learn. I've asked Dr. Beal here to give us some background into the latest patterns in heroin trafficking."

"You did?" Beal looked as if he'd lost something. "I thought you were interested in pharmacology? Surely, Doctor . . . "

Cummings nodded at Berren. "Anthropologist."

"Oh? Oh, I'm sure that must be interesting. I'm a chemist m'self, not sure how I got into all this." He sat on the arm of the club chair opposite Berren and launched himself into his subject as if he were reciting a tract from the encyclopedia.

"Heroin, diacetylmorphine hydrochloride. Developed by the

Bayer Company of Germany in 1898 as a cure for addiction to morphine, which was . . ."

"Dr. Beal," Cummings suggested, "I'm sure we're most interested in all this, but could we be more, uh, relevant?"

"Relevant," Beal acknowledged. "Of course." He pursed his lips thoughtfully, now that his recitation had been interrupted and he didn't know where to pick it up again. "What would you like to know?"

"Smuggling," Cummings suggested.

"Oh, yes, fascinating, really, but we'd have to start back with the opium—that all right?"

"Please," Cummings nodded impatiently.

"Well then," and his voice became a lecturer's drone again. "Opium originates from a wide range of geographical sources. Most of them in the Middle East and Asia. This is partially due to favorable climate and soil conditions, but mostly because it's a highly labor-intensive crop and labor is cheap in these areas.

"Some opium goes into pharmaceutical manufacture, and some, of course, is sold to local opium addicts. But not including these markets, Interpol estimates 1,200 to 1,300 tons, that's 90 percent of the world's yearly crop, elude the police completely."

Beal lowered his eyes from the spot on the ceiling where his attention had been fixed while he talked. "Mind you, this is only the opium. It still must be turned into morphine, and from that into diacet . . . sorry, into heroin. So its flow is interrupted at certain places whose locations and lack of police activity make them amenable to what are referred to as 'factories'—processing laboratories, really.

"Now, like most international commodities, the opium trade tends to follow traditional trade routes, east to west—a line of least resistance through opium-producing countries where surveillance is nil—toward the Mediterranean ports where technology has always made large-scale covert processing possible. Places like Beirut, Naples, Genoa, and especially toward Marseille. Now, in the past couple of years since '68, a series of events has begun to interrupt that traditional trade pattern. For one thing, the American heroin epidemic spread back to Europe, forcing the French into some halfhearted efforts at intercepting the Marseille shipments. At the same time, the Turks were generously induced to cooperate by the Americans, which meant that they pretty much ignored their own crop but tightened down on smugglers trying to cross their borders.

"Then there was a series of Middle East military actions and secular fighting to disrupt the traffic further—all of this," Beal was wagging his finger enthusiastically, "all of this, and yet the only real change in the market has been a serious shortage in *legal* opium products. Apparently we have been left with the same old question: Where in heaven's name is it all coming from?"

Cummings had lit up his pipe and the room was filling with a cheesy fragrance. "Mmmm," he said and removed the pipe from his teeth. "Dr. Beal, may I add something here?"

"Yes, of course. I need a drink anyhow."

"Sorry, help yourself. The scotch is in that crystal thing there."

"No, no," Beal said brightly. "Just some tonic water will do nicely."

Cummings made a face and went on. "For a number of years we've been watching the growing network of opium traffickers operating in Southeast Asia. Nothing new about that, of course, but with that absurd war everything's blown out of proportion. There are even reports of armed skirmishes being fought over crop and transport rights under the very noses of the more conventional combatants.

"Oh, yes," Beal interrupted. "That would probably be some of Chiang Kai-shek's old 93rd Kuomintang Division. It's mostly their show, you know. They were the ones the Reds drove south into Cambodia, Laos, and Thailand where the poppies grow. They had built-in organization and discipline, and pretty soon they had a wonderful new market: the U.S. Army.

"They had help, of course. In fact the CIA had been buying aid or neutrality from any element they could, including the mercenary efforts of the hill tribes whose chief crop was opium. Before long they were up to their necks in the whole system— subsidizing, transporting, even buying some of the stuff up and shipping it off to God-knows-where.

"Finally, the CIA found it expedient to simply turn its back so that the Chinese could skip the middleman and start processing the heroin, what they call the 'G.I. formula,' in their own 'factories.' The system was ugly but tidy, that is until the basic character of the war changed. First the Allies pushed into the Cambodian countryside, driving the Communists deeper into the drug makers' sanctuary. Cambodia and Laos have become confused battlefields, lines of supply are cut off—all very unstable.

"And now the Paris peace talks are bearing fruit and the Americans are beginning to pull out. Do you see what that means?" Beal was getting excited again. "The market is leaving the supply. Now the heroin must find a way to follow the G.I. addict home, so they're back in the business of large-scale international smuggling.

"Furthermore, the factories are being jeopardized. They need a fairly permanent base, and with the war as confused as it is, they don't know how safe an area will be from one day to the next."

"I thought," Berren interrupted, "these 'factories' are pretty simple operations. Why don't they just move on?"

"Aha," Cummings answered, "you've been listening to the French explanation: bathroom factories, laboratories in the backs of vans, always on the move—pumping out packets of heroin like soft ice cream. That's all nonsense, just an excuse for their lack of effort."

"Quite right," Beal added. "Making heroin is an exacting process. One must first produce the opium alkaloid—morphine—then treat it with acetic acid and acetic anhydride, a process that produces a noxious and explosive gas as the morphine cooks. There is a leeway of five degrees to boiling point, and if it is exceeded, the fumes ignite and the whole lab can go up like napalm.

"So you can see, to go into that business you'd better be damn well equipped and have a stable site to work in." And he took a gulp of his tonic water as if he meant it.

"As for our part in all this . . . " Cummings left his perch on the corner of his desk and went over to the map. He tapped his finger at a spot that looked like western Cambodia. "There's this trail, you see, like the Ho Chi Minh Trail, with tributaries that stem from every obscure area of Southeast Asia. All of them join up along this hidden main trunk heading approximately"—he paused to look back at Berren—"northwest.

"Consider for a moment the political situations all along this line." With that he lifted his pipe, using its soggy stem as a baton, and began to trace a line close to the southern border of China.

"A state of war throughout South Vietnam, no effective

central government in Laos, and the Shans in Burma fighting the Rangoon government, leaving the interior open to the Communist Chinese to train India's Naxel Barri and Naga hostiles, who, in turn, keep things stirred up in India's northeastern districts.

"All this would be just a jumble of facts except for one thing they all have in common. The trail passes to the north of each of these troubled areas, yet south of the Chinese border, an area well beyond the threat of the policing power of these governments.

"Now, along the Himalayan frontier areas, here," Cummings's pipe stem left a brown streak on the map's surface, "through Assam, Sikkim, and these others, the situation is ideal for the smugglers.

"Since their war in 1962, India and China have been concentrating their armies along these borders, each convinced the other is about to invade. You can see how jittery they are just by the frequency of the shelling incidents while you were there. And they haven't let up.

"To keep these incidents from happening too often and escalating out of control, an unofficial 'demilitarized zone' has been developed between the two armies, sort of a no man's land!

"What information we have indicates that the trail runs through this no man's land safely out of reach of either side. Since this sanctuary extends no farther west than Himachel Pradesh, then the trail's objective must be hiding in the mountains somewhere east of there."

"Somewhere east includes 150 miles worth of mountains," Berren reminded him. "And what's this objective?"

Cummings struck a straight match and rekindled his forgotten pipe. "That," he said, "is what Josefs was to find out."

"Now he's disappeared, so you still don't know," Berren said.

"Yes and no. He pumped enough rumors out of your contacts in the Bihar underworld to tell us what to look for, but not where. He must have gone off to look into that himself, and that's the last we heard."

"When was that?"

"A little more than a year ago, just after he left you in Bihar."

"A year ago! Anything might have happened since then. He might be dead."

"We have reason to think otherwise," Cummings said. "Anyhow, he's gone off like this before, hasn't he?"

"Yah, but a year . . . "

"Tommy," Cummings had seated himself on the edge of his desk. "You said yourself it's a 150-mile stretch of mountains, and what he's looking for is very small, but it's the key to the smugglers' whole plan. He's looking for a factory.

"If they can refine it up there on a large scale, reduce its bulk to tiny packets of pure heroin, it would be child's play to smuggle it through the more closely guarded terrain of Jammu and Kashmir and out of any of a dozen ports along the Arabian Sea. Get at that factory, and the whole operation will be bottled up. It'll take years to set it up again."

Berren drained his glass. "Sure," he said. "I hope you're going to tell me why you don't just tell the Indian government and let them march in there and wipe out the whole thing."

"The reason's obvious," Cummings said. "As I mentioned, the truce between India and China is precarious, to say the least. Any unusual border activities, especially within that no man's land, could be misconstrued as a hostile act, and they might find themselves in a shooting war again.

"So, of course, they've decided to let a sleeping dog lie. Officially, none of this exists, and so far they've refused any

Western efforts even to get them to look into the matter, let alone instigate a police action.

"Who could blame them? We have little enough proof ourselves. We can't even prove there *is* a trail, so why should they listen to a story about a factory? If we could"—Cummings leaned closer—"if we could prove it, we'd be able to mobilize Indian public opinion and let them force their government to take action. 'Foreign elements,' 'exploitation,' 'the CIA'—the Jan Sangh and the other opposition would have a field day."

"And that's where Jason went," Berren said. "Up to get your proof for you."

"That's it," Cummings said.

"Did he take Anna with him?"

"Apparently not." Cummings turned away. He was embarrassed by the need to consider personal relationships. "Whatever their . . . " there must be a better way to put this, " . . . their 'arrangement,' it must have been a temporary one. Records show she renewed her visa a month ago in New Delhi."

A temporary arrangement. Berren decided he deserved that. His eyes blinked shut against a sudden pang of guilt. God, he'd treated her terribly.

" . . . cut 30 percent of the traffic," Cummings was saying.

"All right," Berren interrupted. "Okay. What do you want? What is it?" There was a hint of resignation in his voice that he didn't intend.

Cummings stopped and tucked the pipe into his breast pocket. He returned to the desk chair, which squeaked loudly as he sat down.

"I want," Cummings looked over at Beal who was scribbling notes in the margins of some papers he'd pulled from his briefcase, "we want you to meet someone. An ally we have recently acquired who can help us enormously. He's a publisher of some influence in both India and the Mideast. And since you'll be acting with the discretion of our agent, he wants to meet you face to face before you reach India, so we've arranged for a stopover in Istanbul." Cummings coughed slightly into his fist. "Seems to think of it as a neutral corner, so to speak."

"Istanbul!" Berren muttered. "Thinks of that place as neutral, does he?"

But Cummings wasn't finished. "Nevertheless, he's someone we can't say no to. I understand security is a phobia with this fellow, and if he feels that Turkey is somehow safer, then that's where we'll meet him. Frankly, if he wanted you to meet him in Buenos Aires, we'd send you there, and we'd do it because he's Indian and using his newspapers will probably be the only way to stir up public sentiment in his country.

"We'd about given Josefs up for lost when we heard from Mr. Sharma, this publisher fellow, who told us that he had somehow caught wind of the heroin conspiracy and our 'involvement' in it. He's apparently very upset about the whole thing, and offered to ally his resources with ours.

"His resources must be rather good, because it was he who informed us that Josefs's cover, as you Americans say, has been blown. He's in grave danger, Tommy, and there's no way to let him know. It seems the enemy doesn't know who or where he is, exactly, but they do know he exists and they've guessed why he's there. To them he's a time bomb, hidden away up in the mountains, and they must be desperate to find and dispose of him."

"And you want me to go up there and get him out," Berren said.

"Yes, and get hard evidence. Take your camera along. We'll

need more than just his personal observations."

Berren's eyes narrowed. "Is it Jason you want, or just the evidence?"

"We can skip the moral issue," Cummings said coldly. "At this point, Josefs and the evidence are one and the same."

That was met with silence, so he played another card.

"Of course," he added, "there will be the option available under your initial contract with us. You'll have full rights to any story, and . . ."

"You didn't need that," Berren said flatly. "I'll go."

five

There was a book lying open on the heavy oak desk, its pages rustling nervously with the breeze from the half-open window. Berren let his foot slide off the end of the desk to the floor and massaged the knee which had stiffened up from its prolonged stretch.

Beyond the tall windows, dusk was settling in over Istanbul. Across the harbor a darkening skyline of domes and minarets marked the heights above the oily silhouettes of a few tenders that were still plying the waterway.

The draft had finally flicked over a few pages. He reached over to save his place, then thought better of it. Why bother? Eighty pages and he couldn't remember a word of it. If he'd known it was going to be this kind of a wait, he'd have dug up a couple of Agatha Christie mysteries in that Piccadilly bookstore, instead of this damn *Tantric Metaphores* thing.

Berren was getting angry. He didn't like waiting, nor the

idea of dealing with a businessman who apparently wanted the kind of security that came from being left anonymous. Istanbul was very understanding about that sort of thing; like Beirut it was less a marketplace than an arena where shadowy financial empires shape the lives of millions from a few discreet suites overlooking the Golden Horn.

This Sharma guy probably operated like that, Berren thought. He was no *deshi* merchant for whom time was the element of life most easily ignored. No, indeed! In this town he'd be another of those media-age potentates, the kind who'd let his callers cool their heels so they'd know his attention was not lightly bestowed.

Berren got to his feet and paced around the musty, heavily draped room until he found himself at the window again.

Anna had been with him the last time he'd been here. The same hotel, too. He wondered if they'd known that when they arranged this rendezvous. After all, they'd known about her "habit." In fact Cummings probably had used it on Jason to con him into all this in the first place. So they'd found a use for her after all. Berren shook his head cynically. Of course they'd known about her renewed visa. How else could they be sure of pulling good old Tommy out of the reserves?

"Cummings, you bastard," Berren said aloud and banged his fist against the window frame. The mileage that son-of-a-bitch got!

His attention had gravitated to the outside world again, and he was absorbed in watching the great puffs of white smoke that poured from the funnels of a small ship when there was a quiet tapping at the door. He didn't hear it at first, but the second time it was a little louder.

"Yes?"

Instead of a reply there was a third series of taps, a little louder, a little more impatient.

Berren snubbed his cigarette in an ashtray he passed as he went to the door and opened it a few inches. A small dark figure stood in the ill-lit hallway. He wore a frayed but spotless pinstriped jacket whose outdated bulkiness made him seem even smaller.

The door had opened too suddenly, and had caught the man in a furtive glance down the empty corridor toward the elevator cage. When he realized the door was opened, he swiveled around, snatching the wilted cloth cap from his head at the same time.

"Mistah Barrings?" The question was a loud stage whisper.

"Berren," was the correction. "What do you want?"

Instead of answering, the little man squirmed quickly under the arm Berren was leaning on, and was inside the room before anything could be done to stop him.

Berren had no time to be irritated, for he was immediately disarmed by an open grin, full of large white teeth. The little man braced his shoulders back and thrust his hand out straight so that Berren took the offering without thinking and was rewarded with two exact pumps.

"So pleased to meet you, Mistah Barrings." The grin had so frozen his other features that the greeting sounded more like a recording than a voice. "I am Kemal Supka. I am sent here to you, acting as your guide. You are wishing too soon to meet Mistah P. K. Sharma, yes?"

Seeing that his only reply was Berren's blank stare, an anxious line appeared above his eyebrows.

"Mistah Sharma," he explained, "maker of the newspaper of Hindustan."

"Oh, *that* Mr. Sharma."

"I am sent to this place by this Mistah Sharma," the little Turk continued, "because I am a trusty fellow, and very important to his organization. We go to him when you are ready, yes?"

"All right."

"And you are ready now, yes?"

"Yep, I guess so."

The meeting was going to be a chore, anyhow, and Berren wanted to be done with it. He rarely enjoyed the company of wealthy Indian businessmen. Most of them acted as if their wealth were due them as a matter of course, a deference to their superiority. It was an assumption that invariably left them pompous and rather dull. He had a feeling that this little conference was going to be insufferably tedious.

He was wrong.

The process of exiting from the hotel was an experience in itself. Kemal was bent on double-timing their pace, as if he were convinced that at any moment something would happen to snatch his prize away. He stuck so close to the American's side that Berren was sure that at any minute his guide would clutch him with one of those childlike hands and steer him physically past the intersecting hallways.

The elevator presented a problem. Kemal, perhaps a connoisseur of such devices, obviously didn't like this one. He tested his weight on the platform and rattled its flimsy iron filigree cage before motioning Berren aboard.

Berren was fascinated by the guide's antics. He'd met this kind in a hundred different cities and had long admired them as spirited denizens of the middle ground, who clung by their wits to the fringes of a secure world they could never be a part of. He made it a point, as he always did, of treating Supka's comic dignity with appropriate seriousness.

When they reached the street, Supka pointed at the exact spot where Berren was to stand while he stepped from the curb in search of a taxi.

The first ignored his *Sieg heil* salute. The second, a 1949 vintage Dodge, swerved in front of the oncoming line and screeched to a stop. Kemal stuck his head inside the window and began negotiations. Something was said in anger, and the taxi sped away, almost knocking Kemal off his spindly legs. He righted himself quickly, rescued his baggy cap from the pavement, and slapped it against his pants leg.

"Mistah Barrings," he announced, "that man is a bugger."

He barely had time to replace the cap when another opportunity presented itself. This time the negotiations proved successful and he hustled Berren inside, jumped into the back seat beside him, and slammed the door. Then he slammed it again to make sure. Only when he was satisfied did he give the order, and the immaculate Kaiser-Frazer sped off over the hill and into the darkening square.

The evening traffic was thinning as they raced out of the city and gained the highway that rounded the base of the wind-carved hills bordering the northwest shore of the Bosphorus. The taxi slowed occasionally to maneuver through the streets of the smaller towns, their cafes now lit for the evening's business.

The last of the day's packet steamers, ablaze with tiny lights, disengaged itself from the Asian shoreline across the water and began gliding toward its berth below the city. As Berren turned to watch he noted again the big Mercedes that had pulled in behind them while the taxi was twisting through the last town.

Supka was also aware of the automobile that was following and he drew himself up in watchful attention, glancing back now and then to check its progress. At last he leaned forward and ordered the driver off the road onto an overview facing the sea. The dark-colored Mercedes swept in beside them.

"Please to change automobiles here, Mistah Barrings," Supka said through his grin. Then he leaped out and rounded the car, too late to help Berren open his door.

"I am so sorry for this inconvenience, but these are our orders. Mistah Sharma is a most careful man."

Berren assured him that it was quite all right, and the grin returned. Their new driver was a huge man, with hands so beefy that, even wrapped around the wheel, they showed no knuckles. Yet he handled the machine with unexpected deftness along a swift, smooth course northward.

They sped on for what seemed a long time before they swung off the highway and followed a gently sloping drive until they slowed to a stop before a high iron gate. Another man, at least as large as the driver and dressed in a black leather coat, lumbered into the glare of the headlights and shaded his eyes as if to be sure of the car's identity. When he was satisfied he pulled back on a heavy iron cross-latch with a clank.

The gate was a clumsy, pseudo-Gothic affair, part of a ramshackle network of crossbraced iron pickets and short spans of shiny cyclone fencing where the original fence had been beyond repair.

Behind it was a somber, empty-looking Georgian mansion with the driveway leading directly below its facade and through the arches of a sharply peaked portico. The grounds between were narrow and brightly lit in the cold glare of several pole-mounted P.A.R. lamps. The effect was the desolate look of a European train station as one might pass it in the dead of night.

This time Berren allowed Kemal to win his race for the

door handle. He slammed the door twice after him and composed himself as the Mercedes pulled away. Then he patted at his oily hair and arranged his rubbery face into a more formal expression.

"Come with me, please, Mistah Barrings," he said, and led the way inside.

The interior was not unlit, as it had seemed from outside. The tall, arched windows were shuttered, Asian style, from the inside, and locked so securely that no light could escape.

Supka led the American up three flights of staircase that once must have been the focal point of the house. Its heavy marble banisters and turned balustrade, built in a more luxurious era, now contrasted sharply with the sparse furnishings and vast, empty hallways. The monotonous expanse was relieved occasionally by low archways to which oddly incongruous double doors had recently been added. The effect was to section the hallway off into a number of smaller chambers and it was in the last of these chambers that they found the room that Supka was seeking.

"Please to wait here, Mistah Barrings," he said, touching his elbow as he gestured him inside. "Mr. Sharma himself will come to you." Kemal turned to leave, then hesitated as if he had something to say. But he changed his mind and left Berren alone in the room.

Unlike the rest of the mansion, at least what Berren had seen of it, the room was well furnished, in the elegance one associates with Turkish gentry. In the center, several wingback chairs, upholstered in crimson velveteen, were angled carefully around an ornately carved mahogany conference table. The luxury of the grouping was enhanced by the round carpet of a Persian design unfamiliar to Berren.

The ceiling, sculptured in floral patterns around the edges, seemed a long way away, and its height was matched by the tall windows that ran along two walls, hidden almost entirely behind old-fashioned tasseled drapes.

The rest of the room was a bit more Spartan, compared to the conference area. Berren imagined the design was due to the priorities of a man whose interest span was limited to whatever business emanated from around the table.

He found the thought oppressive. He also found the atmosphere oppressive. There was a mildewed stuffiness to the room that was made even more uncomfortable by the faint, leafy smell which Berren recognized as *bidis*, the Indian village cigarette. The combination was making the wait seem longer than it actually was, and he decided he could use a little air.

Let's see, what would be the front of the house, he thought. He went to one of the windows and drew back the curtains. He was surprised to find that even here, on the third floor, the same interior shutters barricaded the room against the night.

Berren turned the lock and pulled the shutter back. No place for a claustrophobic, he thought. He opened the French doors behind, then stepped out onto the iron balcony that overlooked the lights, twinkling along the coast. This was better. There was moon enough to see the soft shapes of the hillocks that made up the expansive lawn beyond the fence.

Directly below, the less friendly glare of the P.A.R. lights divided the cement and the few yards of enclosed lawn into blue-white circles.

Something at the far end of the drive caught his attention. He watched as two figures rounded the corner into view.

It was the driver and the man in the leather coat. They walked with a careful watchman's pace, each behind a pack of three Doberman pinschers straining in frightful silence at their leashes. There was no conversation; each man was scrutinizing the area with great care, guiding, yet being guided by, his glossy, black-faced charges. It was an eerie sight. Men that size planting their heels with each step to brace themselves against the dogs' potential, and all as quiet as death.

Berren decided to withdraw.

Above the balcony, another figure who had been watching Berren from the roof behind the eaves also pulled silently back from the sight of the approaching men. He crouched low until they passed, then pushed the cloth cap back from his face and returned to the edge of the roof.

six

Berren had stepped back into the room in time to hear a sound from down the hall. There were footsteps for an interval, then a pause, and a metallic click. The pattern of sounds repeated itself, closer each time. The symmetry intrigued him: each interval the same, each series of sounds a little louder.

Finally he recognized it—first the footsteps, eight or ten of them, then a pause, and this time the creak of a hinge followed by a mechanical click and then the footsteps again.

Of course. Whoever it was had been stopping at each of the portals to close and lock the doors as he passed through. The footsteps stopped outside the room and waited for a short time, as if listening, then the door opened, and Sharma entered the room.

Like Shakespeare's Cassius, Sharma wore a lean and hungry look. His piercing black eyes were set deep in their dark sockets in dramatic contrast with his fair skin. His nose was a large, hooked caricature one might expect to find in a Baghdad bazaar.

He wore a suit of slender, conservative styling whose color was of such a muted shade it could hardly be called a color at all, just a gray that changed from a warm to cool, according to the light.

"Dr. Berren," he stated, and turned his attention to the door he had just come through. Using both hands, he pushed it closed and twisted its lock.

"We are happy to see you could join us."

If he was, his expression didn't show it. It remained grave as he inspected the American, then motioned him to a chair.

"Your trip was pleasant?"

"Fine," said Berren. "I always enjoy this city."

"You didn't mind our little—precautions?"

"Not at all. Quite understandable," he lied.

"Good," Sharma said. "Then let us, as they say, 'get over to business.' Since we have learned of this problem that has developed in the sacred mountains of my country . . ." As Sharma launched into what was bound to be a totally unnecessary speech, his real attention seemed focused on the open French doors. He assumed a casual air, yet as he spoke, he moved steadily toward them.

". . . we have become anxious to help your organization. . . ." he closed the doors and shutters. ". . . in any way we can." He twisted the lock and turned back to his guest.

"Of course we are using the editorial 'we,' for we are a humble man, although we rule a large industrial complex—similar, we think, to your Mr. Howard Hughes."

Berren accepted this as his cue.

"Yes, of course," he said. "I've heard of you many times."

Sharma seemed satisfied, and went on.

"Indeed. Well, we wish to emphasize that this venture we are embarked upon is between you and ourselves—alone. That is why we must be ever mindful of our security." Sharma obviously enjoyed applying his baritone voice to the more sonorous phrases he found to use. "And why we have a rule in our house against the opening of windows. By opening this one, you have set off our little alarm." He held up a hand to fend off the required apology.

"Of course, how were you to know? But you see, there are spies everywhere." His eyes checked the room quickly, as if he might catch one in the act to prove it. "We have many enemies, Dr. Berren, many enemies.

"But enough! There will be more to say on this subject when we have more thoroughly explained our relationship."

Sharma tapped at the side of his large nose with his finger while he searched for the point where he had left off.

"For many years we have watched the tragedy of opiate drugs grow around the world. Fortunately, our own wise peoples have spared themselves this affliction, but that does not mean that we can be less vigilant, no indeed. . . ." Sharma's attention returned to the shutters he had just locked. Without breaking stride in his speech he returned to them and tested the lock, then began a methodical inspection of each of the windows, checking behind each set of drapes to see if the security of the room was complete.

Berren decided that all this was more than caution. The man had a screw loose.

"And so we must maintain our defense," he was saying, "against this most evil of Western influences.

"Furthermore, it is obvious that the trade and transport of these illicit products is an infringement of our nation's sovereignty. These mountains, which we are constantly forced to defend, must be kept free of these powerful groups with their illegal and self-serving intentions."

At last he had finished with the last of the windows and turned back to Berren. "The Himalayas are the very soul of Mother India." He raised a bony finger for emphasis. "These criminal elements are desecrating their sanctity!"

It was a better-than-average finale, Berren thought, and he was obliged to respond. "Quite right, Mr. Sharma," he said. "But surely a man of your worldly stature has a less spiritual, more practical, motivation . . . as well," he added as an afterthought.

Sharma's manner shifted slightly. A half smile creased one side of his face for an instant, and then was gone. Instead of answering, he settled back into the dark velveteen armchair opposite Berren and sat for a moment in silence, tapping the side of his nose absently as he reexamined his visitor.

"Let us be friends, Dr. Berren," he announced at last. "And as such, we may be most frank. We can see this is best for men like ourselves. The little speech we have just now given would do well as our newspapers' central editorial thrust: not crude enough for the masses, perhaps, but with some 'showy' bits of evidence, well-orchestrated headlines . . ." For a moment Sharma seemed lost in his plans; then he cleared his throat as if starting again. "The truth, as we both know, is that our 'sacred' mountains are full of thieves, dacoits, and smugglers. So," he shrugged, "it has always been. It would be nice, of course, to rid them of all these villains, but we have another reason to aid your organization and whomever it represents."

Something made him glance once again toward the shuttered French doors. He paused to listen for a confirming sound. Apparently he heard none, so he continued. "You are no doubt aware of the atrocious political situation imposed by the ruling Congress party. Without pressing the point, let us simply state that we are unalterably opposed to the present government, which has so badly mismanaged since the day of our independence.

"For years we have supported financially a number of opposition parties whose strength is based on embarrassing the Congress party and its policies in any way we can."

"So," Berren suggested, "this heroin thing must seem another golden opportunity. What you're after is something to wave at the Prime Minister. If nothing happens, you can damn her government for inaction, and if the Chinese get sucked in, you can blame her for the war. That's just lovely," Berren added. "A risk like that for a Parliamentary seat or two."

"Oh, much more than a mere seat or two, we can assure you," Sharma said. "And the end suits us both, does it not?" Sharma cocked an eyebrow and waited, but Berren had nothing to say. So he leaned forward, his voice hardly more than a sibilant whisper. "But before our humble powers of persuasion can be brought to bear, you see, we must have hard evidence to show. The sort of thing that the masses will react to. The sort of thing your friend, Mr. Jason Josefs, must have by now."

He tugged a white handkerchief from his jacket and dabbed at his glistening brow. Berren found that he had been carried along by the Indian's enthusiasm, and now that there was a lull he noticed the stuffiness of the room, too.

"Don't you think we'd be more comfortable if we . . ." He indicated the window.

"No!" The reply was abrupt. "No," Sharma repeated, in a more subdued tone. "It must be that we haven't cautioned you adequately about security. We will explain more fully.

"We are sure you must understand that it is a subject of paramount importance. All of this must seem a totally Indian effort. Any hint of foreign aid in the discovery of this menace, and all of our efforts will be dismissed as foreign adventurism. Our countrymen are extremely nationalistic, at least where defense is concerned, and your word, no matter how well documented, will never be accepted by the government or the masses. Nor will ours, if they suggest you are the source.

"So you can see that our meeting must never—we repeat—*never* be found out. Even here, in this great city, far from our homeland, there is the chance of being spied upon.

"You must understand that a man of our position . . . well, with prominence comes risk. And so it is," he touched his nose with his handkerchief, "that we meet here alone.

"We have received many threats. We were even in attendance on the Mahatma at his prayer meeting when the assassin . . . but that does not concern you."

Sharma had been speaking more to himself than to his guest. Now his attention returned.

"It is necessary for you to know only that we will never meet again. You must find your friend and bring him to safety along with whatever evidence he has. To help you and to transmit the information back to us, you will be met by one of our people."

Berren jerked himself upright in his chair. "Wait a minute . . ." but Sharma held up his hand.

"He is our Southeast Asian correspondent and was chosen for his . . ."

"I don't want anyone tagging along."

". . . for his resourcefulness." Sharma would allow no interruption. "It is entirely possible that you will need his, um, physical help. Times are difficult in our country, and a foreigner, even one who knows it as well as you, is not always safe. And, since your part in this must remain anonymous, he will transmit whatever evidence you find through our bureau in Vientiane, Laos. More practically, if something happens to you, we will want to know where you left off. We do not wish to lose you as your Guild lost Mr. Josefs, isn't it?

"Oh, you'll get on fine," he insisted. "He is an Englishman with our bureau in Vientiane . . ."

"Christ, that tears it," Berren blurted. "First Cummings . . ."

"Please, Dr. Berren." Sharma was looking down his long nose at Berren, requesting calm with a graceful wave. "We have told you that Mr. Michaelson is resourceful. More to the point, you'll find that he, shall we say, knows how to handle people. We think you will find that an important asset."

"But . . ."

Any further objections were cut off by a sharp rap at the door.

"A moment, please," and Sharma rose and went to the door. He didn't open it; he just put his ear to the upper panel.

"Yes?"

From where he sat, Berren couldn't make out what was said, but Sharma was plainly upset. He unlocked the door and spoke quickly to whoever it was on the other side. Then he turned to his guest. "Please be at ease, Dr. Berren. Something has happened that I must attend to." And with that he was gone.

Their footsteps hurried down the hall; doors were unlocked at intervals and then there was silence.

Berren was staring at the door, trying to imagine what could make a man like Sharma move so quickly, when a barely perceptible sound reached his ear. He looked around, but couldn't quite place its source. He listened for a moment, and was about to dismiss it when he heard it again. It came from behind the shutters that hid the French doors, a flapping sound against the glass. A bird, or, in this house, maybe a bat.

No, there it was again; three soft, flapping sounds in succession.

Alarm be damned, it was a signal of some kind. Berren got up and went to the shutters. He undid the lock and drew them apart just in time to see a hand reaching out to strike at the windowpane with its tightly clutched cloth cap.

Berren immediately pulled the doors wide, and there, balanced with one foot on the railing of the balcony and the other wedged into the ornamental brickwork, stood Kemal.

"Mistah Barrings," his voice was a hoarse, frightened whisper. "I am listening to whole thing—what that man Sharma say to you." Kemal's painful English was losing out to his haste and fear.

"My God, man, you'll fall," Berren said, and reached out for the little Turk's hand.

"No, no, sah. They kill me in there. Listen to me, I thought you are with those men. Listen, they lie to you. Sharma say . . . they . . ."

Before he could say anything that made sense, there came the sound of running feet rounding the far corner of the building. The driver and the man in the leather coat were racing toward them down the drive. They had just passed through the first pool of light when one of them looked up and saw Kemal. He called the discovery to the other man, and both paused for a second before they turned to the front door. They shouldered it open, and disappeared inside.

Frantically, Kemal lurched back onto the brickwork as a hand grabbed Berren's arm and yanked him forcefully back into the room. Sharma shut off the balcony again while another of his giants held Berren from behind.

The entire event had lasted only a few seconds, and ended with Berren having no idea what to make of it.

"All right, okay," he said angrily. "Tell your man here to give me back my arm, Sharma. Then I think I should know what that was all about."

"As we mentioned before, Dr. Berren, there are spies and traitors everywhere." A smug smile spread from the shadow beneath his nose. He was pleased that his suspicions had been confirmed. "Though we are particularly annoyed to find such deviousness in Mr. Supka. He was a trusted employee.

"As for Mr. Amin here, he wishes assurance that you will remain calm. When we have that, he will doubtless release you. In the meantime, let us offer you a drink. Yes, of course, alcohol is just the thing, we have been lacking in hospitality. Naturally we cannot join you, but please feel free . . ."

Sharma moved to a heavy cabinet nearby and opened it to an array of unopened bottles.

"While you are a guest in our house, you must consider that events outside are not your concern, nor can you influence them. You would be a scotch whisky drinker, isn't it?"

"Bourbon." Berren said it without thinking. He was listening for some hint of further action outside, but heard none. It was as if nothing at all had happened.

"Amin," Sharma said sharply, "why is there no bourbon whisky?"

Amin loosened his grip enough to bow apologetically.

"Okay, then. Scotch," Berren said, since that was just what Sharma was pouring anyhow.

Sharma held the glass with the tips of his fingers and far

away from his person, as if he were bringing Socrates his hemlock. Before Berren could take it from him, there were sounds of a scuffle on the roof above.

A second more and there was a loud, guttural scream that ended with an abrupt crash.

Berren wrenched his arm free of Amin's grasp and burst through the shutters to the balcony.

It was the cap he saw first, a small pile of cloth lying beneath the edge of the portico where pieces of roofing slate still clattered to the ground.

From the dark portico roof a figure slid slowly into the level of light from the nearest P.A.R.'s, gartered stockings extended from crumpled pants legs, pulling more pieces of roofing along as the limp form drooped over the eaves and dropped to the pavement.

"Kemal!" Berren darted a glance at Sharma. "It's your man, Supka."

"Oh, my," Sharma replied.

"He's . . . no. See there, I saw him move."

The body was a frail, broken heap, and yet the head rolled, as if unable to call out its agony. Somehow Kemal managed to flop himself over and raise to one arm. With an enormous effort he began to drag his body forward.

Berren shoved himself away from the iron rail toward the room and collided with Amin, who had stepped sideways to block him.

"Look out, you . . ." But Amin didn't move. "Sharma, we've . . . tell your . . ." Sharma ignored him. His eyes were on the heavy, shadowy figure standing up on the roof line above the portico with one arm extended toward the opposite end of the mansion.

Suddenly a silent black wave swirled around the far corner and down the drive.

"Jesus, the dogs!" Berren couldn't tear his eyes from the sight. "Behind you, man!" he shouted. "My God, Sharma, call them off!"

"I cannot."

Berren flung himself at Amin, flailing at the immovable bulk to get to the door.

Kemal saw the dogs. His arms began pumping frantically, dragging himself toward the gate.

The pack moved as one, legs a blur of motion, glistening, sleek bodies level to the ground as they hurtled down on their victim. There was an instant when Kemal must have known that all was lost. He looked up toward the balcony where Berren was still struggling, and uttered a thin wail of horror as the pack struck.

Berren turned at the sound and the snarling fury that followed and saw the man in leather trot over from the doorway to enter the fray. Kicking and shouting, he heaved the dogs out of the way, striking with his fists at the bloody muzzles of those that refused to let go. When he had inspected the body, he stood and gave an unnecessary gesture of finality.

"Oh! Oh, how dreadful." Sharma was the first to speak. "A terrible accident."

"Accident?" Berren was still immobilized by the sight below.

"Indeed, a most regrettable accident. Poor Mr. Supka must have fallen while trying to spy on our conversation." He searched the face of his guest for a clue to his reaction. "Come inside, Dr. Berren. There is nothing we can . . ."

"Accident!" Berren turned on him in anger. "This Amin, this gorilla of yours, holds me here. I could have . . ."

"Could have what, Dr. Berren?" Sharma asked evenly.

"Could have gotten through a few of my security doors? Could have reached the drive too late to help? And to help a spy? Amin was only protecting you. The dogs can be handled only by their trainers. They would have turned on you, isn't it? Come inside now and have your drink. Amin?" Sharma nodded to his bodyguard, who pressed Berren back into the room. "Here. Here is your whisky. Drink it down, we will make another. That's it.

"We will see that the trainers are reprimanded for letting the dogs become escaped. However, you must remember that you yourself caught him in the act of spying on our delicate conversation. Think of the continual suffering if our enterprise were endangered; of your friend Mr. Josefs." Sharma shrugged. "Now, of course, Mr. Supka can do no damage."

"Almost providential." Berren was regaining his composure.

"The irony did not escape us," Sharma replied, and for a second Berren thought he saw a smile flicker across his face. He took the glass from Berren's still shaky hand and poured him another less than generous measure.

"Drink this," Sharma ordered. "As you Americans say, 'One for the trail.' Now then, you are not to worry about this incident. We shall postpone contacting the authorities until you are gone. No doubt they would detain you as a material witness."

Sharma went on talking as they made their way to the door, but Berren wasn't paying much attention. He was thinking about the little Turk and what he was worth compared to the Sharmas of the world, while at the same time trying to make himself believe what Sharma had said. And yet, hadn't Kemal risked his life to tell him something? No. That was part of it. It must have been. His eavesdropping had been discovered and he was probably trying to enlist Berren in his escape.

Berren had himself pretty well convinced until they reached the door and stepped out under the portico.

". . . Mr. Michaelson will find you when you reach New Delhi, and . . ." Sharma was leading the way to the car, but Berren had been stopped by the sight of the dogs still fighting over the body. Sharma glanced back and saw that he had lagged behind. He signaled for the car and returned to Berren.

Berren was pale with nausea. The leather-jacketed keeper had lost interest in trying to control his pack and Berren could see one of the dogs, hunched and growling away from the others. It seemed to be eating something.

"Remember, please, your mission and your friend," Sharma said. "We will take care of Mr. Supka."

The use of the corpse's name triggered something in Berren's mind and he turned on Sharma in a rage. "For God's sake!" He had the Indian by his narrow lapels and yanked him to his toes. "Whatever he's done deserves better than that. Get those fucking dogs away from him!"

Sharma only stared down at the fists that were crushing his jacket. "Dr. Berren." He was annoyed. "There is no need; and we do not like to be touched." He removed Berren's hands.

The car was there, the door open.

He's right, Berren thought. There is no need, and he collapsed into the back seat of the car. He'd seen worse.

seven

Gas fires were burning in the oil fields several miles below the airliner, a strange sight in the midst of all that moonlit wasteland. The other passengers probably hadn't noticed. They were either asleep or dazed with boredom. Berren seemed alone in his wakefulness, his mind alert despite its meandering.

He had spent the hours before the flight sipping black Turkish coffee down to its muddy grounds, trying to wipe the image of the little Turk from his thoughts.

He caught the eye of the sleepy stewardess and asked for a refill of coffee. When it came, he held it in both hands below his face, inhaling the bitter aroma between sips, trying to concentrate on the business of sifting through what he had so that he could work up some kind of plan.

When he finally took another sip of coffee, it had turned cold and left him with a sour, tinny taste. An hour of total concentration had slipped by and he was left with only one way to begin, and that was with Anna. If she had renewed her visa in New Delhi she might still be there. Where else did she have to go? Damn, he thought, where else did she have to go?

So, it had all come full circle. It would have been better if he hadn't found out about all this. Better to think of her with Jason, better his loss of pride than the thought of her alone again, as she'd been when they'd first met. He remembered thinking at the time that she was the alonest girl . . .

He tried to force his thoughts to rejoin him aboard the Air India flight, but they seemed to have wings of their own. It had been a long time since he'd let himself think about Anna, and a longer time since the memories were free of the pain.

And, of course, she was laughing, for that was his favorite picture of her. God, how she could laugh. It was always the trickle and then the flood. Or, when she tried to hold it back, it would spill over in a perfect pattern of tuneless ho-ho-ho's.

"Tommy. Tommy, wake up. C'mon, big fella. Roll over and say hello."

Berren opened his eyes to the blur of green tentacles she had been brushing at his face.

"Botany ain't my line," he mumbled sleepily.

The clump of grass was tickling his nose, the stiffest of its leaves poked into his nostrils, forcing him to move his head to avoid sneezing.

"Tommy!" She feigned exasperation, then peevishly swept the fronds across his face.

"That's right, woman." Berren rolled into action. "Beat me, flay me." He grabbed the fist that held the grass and pretended to gnaw on its knuckles. "I love it." She pulled away, laughing, as he followed his target, rolling over and sprawling with her down the slope of the lawn.

"Tommy! People are watching."

"Quite right, madam," Berren said, and sat up stiffly, posing in mock severity. He took the girl's hand and helped her to sit up beside him.

"Such a thing as propriety."

He watched her quietly as she adjusted her hair. So did several lounging Indian students nearby, who had interpreted their play as something much more than that, and whose jokes about them had not yet died away. It was Sunday morning, and, as usual on Sunday morning, she had not tied it back into that damned bun thing. Berren loved her for that long brown hair and for the slender oval face it framed when it hung loose over her shoulders.

It had been a Sunday when they'd first met, too. Cooler than this one, with air so clear he had been able to see the network of paths on the hillside miles away as he and Jason waited in the courtyard of the District Health Center.

"Well," Jason said, "Shanti picked a good day to get sick."

"He's been sick for weeks," Berren said. "Did you see the yellow in his eyes?"

"Yah." Jason glanced back at the office where a line of villagers squatted under the adobe porch. "We should have seen it sooner."

They waited for another half hour before the doctor came out, motioned for them, then refolded his hands over his oversized belly until they stood before him. He tucked his head back each time he spoke, deepening the creases of his triple chin.

"You may take your boy now. He has amoebic hepatitis."

"He's not our boy," Berren replied angrily. "And what do

you mean, we can take him? He's in bad shape."

"Yes, he is," the doctor said. "But it's not contagious, so you must take him. There's no room for him here."

"What do you mean, no room?" Berren exploded.

"Doctor, sahib." Jason stepped between them. *"Suniyay."*

"Speak English," the doctor said abruptly.

"All right. I see a number of empty *charpois* back there with the others. We could let him stay in one of them."

"Those cots are for patients who are less seriously ill. For amoebic hepatitis a bed in a ward is clearly proscribed. And," he said, "there is none."

"There's a bed in my room, Doctor." Standing in the office doorway was a tall, handsomely beautiful girl in a white Western style dress. "We'll put him there."

"But—but, that will not do, sister," the doctor sputtered.

"Sure it will," she said matter-of-factly. "I can sleep with the other sisters." And before any more could be said, she had set the process in action with a few orders to a passing pajama-clad attendant.

The doctor had nothing more to say. He stamped back into his surgery, waving impatiently to the next in line, who was hesitating at the door.

"Listen," Berren said to the girl, "I really appreciate this. You American?"

"Canadian." And she turned to oversee the attendants who were half dragging poor Shanti between them down the porch. Berren followed along, trying to think of something more to say.

"You've got the local language down pretty good. Been here long?"

"Forever," Anna said, without looking back.

"You made a big hit with that one, I see," Jason said later as they followed the trail back to their site.

"Yep," Berren said, "as usual. Did you see how haggard she looked?"

"Before or after you made a pass at her?"

"No. I mean she's got a lot on her mind."

"No doubt," Jason said. "She's probably got her hands full in that butcher's shop. By the way, before you decide to spend a lot of time down there easing her burden, let me remind you that you're the writer around here. If that abstract isn't in by the fifteenth of next month, we can kiss off the rest of our grant."

"Hmmm? Oh, yah."

He found the time. Shanti had to be looked after, and in the Indian way, Berren played the part of the family he didn't have, bringing food to supplement the hospital's meager rations, changes of bedding, and gossip from the village.

The patient was slow to recover. Berren searched his grizzled, old face each visit for signs of a healthier pallor, but the jaundice hung on.

Anna was there each time, fussing over Shanti's charts or just ducking into her room for a few moments' peace. Gradually she got used to Berren being around and passed a few words with him when politeness required it. For the most part, however, she showed him the same cold reserve she showed the others who surrounded her. And every time Berren thought she seemed a little more frayed than the last. Her huge brown eyes were often wet and jumpy, and sometimes he noticed her biting fiercely at her lower lip.

One day he returned to the room after an absence of several days to find her sitting below the barred window staring straight ahead and shivering violently. He crossed the room quickly and knelt in front of her.

"You okay, lady?" She nodded. "No, you're not. You're sick. Just look, you're shaking like a leaf." He reached over to feel her forehead, but she brushed his hand aside.

"No," she said, "I'm just tired."

"Listen, nurse, sister, or whatever. Foreigners like us kind of mind each other's business. There's a bond of some kind between people with similar roots. Now you may have some reason for not caring much about me, but I care about you, and it doesn't take a psychologist to see where you're heading. You're too important around here to drive yourself into a nervous breakdown. These people need you whole. My friend Shanti here would have died if you hadn't . . ."

"Your friend *has* died, Dr. Berren."

"Oh, Jesus."

"A few minutes before you came in."

"Oh. Oh, Jesus. Poor old Shanti."

"And I was sitting here wondering, I was wondering if he had any family."

"No. Not around here." Berren was gazing down at the weathered, old face, brown against the pillow, shocked that he hadn't seen its slack-jawed mask of death before. "I'll bring some villagers down. We'll take care of him."

"It's not that," she said, avoiding his eyes. "Will they, will any of them do that awful shrieking thing . . ."

"No, there's no family."

". . . where they cry and moan and tear at themselves . . ." She was going on as if he hadn't spoken, confused and distracted, as if she were nearing the edge of hysteria.

"No, they won't."

"Good. That's good, because I don't think I can—I mean, they do it every time."

"They have to. It's part of their *Mrityu puja*." Berren took her arms. "It's a purge for their grief; it's always been their way."

"It's a terrible, horrid sound." Tears burst from her eyes, and still she looked away from him. "And it's worse each time—like it was all too horrible." She was shivering again and trying to pull away. "Like life and grief were too awful to bear and they were screaming for themselves." She broke free and ran for the door. "For all of us."

It was some time before he found her again. He'd taken care of the hospital details concerning the disposal of the body and was talking with a village acquaintance who was hunkering in the courtyard with the other families, waiting for news from the evening rounds. It was getting late, and a few cook fires were being stoked around the compound when she appeared on the porch across the way.

She paid no attention to his approach. She was leaning against a pillar, her arms folded in front of her, watching the groups of people in the courtyard.

"Feeling better?"

"Much," she nodded.

"It's getting chilly," Berren said, and lifted the jacket he had slung over his back. "Want this?"

She shook her head. "It's very peaceful," she said at last. "There's a kind of serenity to the everyday life of these people, isn't there?"

"For some of them," he said, and watched her for a moment before he spoke again. "You certainly recover quickly. An hour ago I thought you were going 'round the bend."

Anna looked down at her feet. "Yes, well, I have my ways," she replied. Then she changed the subject. "You're right. I mean about us foreigners. I guess I haven't been very nice to you, have I?"

"Just a little frostbite," Berren smiled. "I'll survive."

"It's just that I've been going through a lot lately, and it seems to get harder every time."

"Culture shock, you know, usually comes and goes," he suggested. Then he cleared his throat as he always did when he broached the subject. "If it's more than that, then it's best to know when to go home."

"Home," she repeated. "I guess I don't really have one. I always thought this would be home. After all, I was born in the Punjab."

"Really?" It was the last thing Berren would have expected.

"My parents were with a medical mission not far from Patiala. They tried to stay on after the British left, and were killed in the communal massacres in '47."

"I'm sorry."

"It's all right. It was a long time ago, and I was hardly more than a baby." She shifted nervously as she spoke, as if uncomfortable at having committed herself to finish the story. "I was brought up in Quebec. The relatives took turns, passing me around, paying for things. So I guess I got to believe that my real home was here where my parents had been.

"So—here I am. And you must know what it's like. Just a daily grind of futility. Kids die of tetanus, the flu. Medicine gets 'lost.' There's a jeep here. It's supposed to be an ambulance, but the good doctor won't let it be used for anything but visiting his relatives."

"There're other things, though," Berren ventured. "Some pretty fine things about this country that you won't find anywhere else." She was still looking out over the courtyard so he peeked around to get a look at her eyes. "I could show you some."

She turned away. "I took some leave a while back. I was

supposed to meet some C.U.S.O. friends in Bombay."

"And?"

"It was a disaster. I took a side trip to visit the place where they told me in Canada my parents were buried. Only"—she broke off and pressed her face against the pillar—"only they weren't. No grave, no marker. There was this man who'd seen it all and told me what happened." Berren stood helpless behind her as she began to sob. "They'd been ambushed, cut up with swords, hundreds of them. The man said the sight had addled his son—and then they burned the bodies." She turned to Berren, her eyes darting about as if looking for something to keep herself from saying more.

"It was horrible. I got sick and then I ran away from the man. I got to Bombay, I don't even remember the trip, and I couldn't find my friends—and there was nobody and I ended up in this place—the Blue something—full of these freaky Westerners."

"Yah. The Blue Raja. That cesspool."

"And it was an awful place. There was this German guy, they called him 'the Doctor.'"

"Hey, listen. You don't have to tell me this." He pulled her close to him and held her there. "Just relax now, and . . ."

"I was there for a month."

"Oh."

She was trembling again. Tears were streaming down her face.

"Here," he said when the worst was over. "Take this jacket." This time she accepted it, but as she stretched her arm awkwardly to get into the sleeve, he dropped it and grabbed her elbow.

"This one of the 'ways' you were talking about?" She tried to jerk away and he tightened his grip, his thumb clamped harshly over the crook of her arm. Above it was a line of ugly, purpling blemishes. "Was that your German 'Doctor's' prescription?"

"You'd better go now," she said evenly.

"They know about this here?"

"Some do. They understand."

"Do they understand you're killing yourself? Do you? What is it, skag? Or do you have access to that special stuff that medical people are pumping into themselves these days?"

"Of course I know what's happening." She stared at him defiantly. "I don't need this lecture. I'm taking care of myself."

Berren was suddenly ashamed of himself. Of course she knew what was happening. It was like arguing with a suicidal.

"Sorry," he said, and adjusted the jacket over her shoulder. "I really am."

"Please go." She was sorry, too.

"Are you really?"

"Really what?"

"Are you taking care of yourself?"

She nodded uncertainly. "When all this started, I was just holding on day to day. At first it got me through the day, like some reward or something. Then it got me going, and then I knew what I was really doing. So now it's a little less, and a little less, except . . ." She glanced around the compound then returned with a look that he'd never forget. "I think it's all going to drive me mad."

"Are you determined to do it alone? I mean, you may be right." She didn't reply, so he took the notebook out of the breast pocket of the jacket that was still draped around her. He wrote something, then tore the sheet out and folded it into the pocket.

"That's an address in the Chandi Chawk in Delhi. Jason

and I will be there after the fifteenth. We have some good friends there who will help. Understand? If you can't do it your way, just get sick leave and come down." He didn't expect any response, so he left her there, leaning against the pillar as before. He paused only when he reached the path, and he called back, "And bring the jacket."

Berren lay on his side, propped against one elbow, trying to decide whether to mention the grass stains on the back of her new *cameze*. Anna was still checking for a few elusive strands of hair, patting them into place, when she found them. Her full lower lip covered the one above it as if she were concentrating on some very important operation.

"You look real good, lady," he said. "Your eyes are big and brown again. How many times do I have to warn you about that?"

She shot him a chastening look. "You go into that *Kama Sutra* routine and this time we'll get arrested."

"Farthest thing from my mind," he said. "Or one of them. Say, you're the doctor around here. What have you got for this hangover?"

"I'm a nurse, not a doctor," she said, "and your hangover is your own doing, so you can just cure it yourself, too."

"Drunkard, heal thyself, eh? Heartless bitch." He groaned and eased himself lower to the ground. "Anyhow, you can't kid me. You're the real doctor up there."

She didn't answer, so he looked up into her face and saw the familiar cloudy sign of an unpleasant distraction. "Shouldn't have brought it up, right?"

"Right."

"But things are better for you up there now, aren't they?"

"Things are better," she said, "for me. Now let's drop the

subject. I'm going to enjoy this leave while I can. Roll over."

He obeyed gratefully as she moved herself to his side and began to massage the knotted muscles at the base of his neck.

"Listen, big fella, where did you two go last night?"

"I dunno, lady. It's all a complete blank."

"C'mon, you can tell me, I'm a big girl." To prove it she found a tiny spot that shot a burst of pain all the way down his spine.

"Awk!" he jumped. "You win. But it was your own fault. You could have joined us, but you were too tired."

She leaned close and pecked him wetly on the ear.

"Dummy," she said, "couldn't you take the hint?"

Berren groaned again.

"Well, I'll tell you," he began. "Jon and I decided to go off again on our time-honored search for Gunga Din."

"Gunga Din! Kipling's water boy?"

"The same, only we were thinking more of the one in the old Cary Grant movie. It's become our own little odyssey. See, a couple of years back I ran into Jon and he wasn't in very good shape. He'd spent a few months up in Budoun district working up an abstract for his dissertation: something unusual about their local caste system.

"He would never say much about it, but when I met him he'd just fired his interpreter, thrown out six months' worth of notes and was half stoned on *deshi* moonshine. Said what he needed was a real heart to heart with good old Gunga Din. Wanna rub a little lower? Anyhow, it's been downhill ever since; tea wallahs, desk clerks, total strangers in terrilyn business suits—nobody's sacred. It's always *'Gunga Din kaha hain'* or, 'Excuse me, waiter, isn't that Mr. Gunga Din sitting over there?'

"It's amazing how many remember the name but can't quite place the face. Anyhow, it must have been a tough year for

Jon. Last night he stopped the rickshaw every time we passed anyone who looked like Sam Jaffe."

"How terrible," Anna said. "Half the old men in Delhi look like Sam Jaffe."

Berren snorted, "Yep, 'twas a long night."

"Ladies and gentlemen . . ." The thin electric voice cut into the fragments of Berren's dream. "May I have your attention."

He sat up, rubbing his stiffened neck, looking around as if to find the human source behind the voice on the intercom. It was a perfect British accent, but its Indian owner could be recognized by the slight singsong of his delivery.

"We are approaching the western coastline of the Indian subcontinent, and have received a message from New Delhi control that may affect your stay in our country.

" 'Recent political events in our capital have resulted in [the captain cleared his throat] a restive atmosphere among certain elements. Some street, uh, street action has been reported. It is therefore recommended that our passengers pay close attention to the advice of the authorities posted at your places of accommodation.

" 'This caution will insure your pleasant and tranquil visit. Thank you for your . . .' " The microphone was clicked off.

"Diplomatic fellow, isn't he?" the man sitting beside Berren suggested. "Suppose it's that damned language thing again?"

"Could be anything, this time of year," Berren replied. "Riots are kind of a seasonal event there."

"Like the Monsoon, eh?" The man chuckled nervously.

"Yep, something like that," Berren replied, and settled back to consider what effect, if any, this might have on his search for Anna.

eight

There were few outward indications of the unrest that had worried the airline. A newcomer might have thought the ride in from the airport uneventful, but Berren had a more practiced eye and found the signs of trouble increasing as they neared the inner city. Small knots of people were grouped around sweaty orators, while policemen in khaki shorts and cross belts strolled in cautious pairs around their periphery.

Slogans were plastered or painted on whatever flat surfaces were handy, often one over another, in conflicting opinions or more recent causes. The high red sandstone walls of one of the ancient Moghul fortifications had provided too great a temptation for the political graffitist—the six or seven feet nearest ground level were a blur of slogans, the most prominent of which read, "English nasty, down down," smeared over the others in huge whitewashed letters.

The taxi squeezed expertly through the milling crowds of

the Nier Bazaar with the driver pumping a steady rhythm of barks from a curled brass horn outside his window. Despite the slogans and the crate-top orators, most in the crowd were occupied with everyday matters, jostling and bargaining among the open stalls. In the midst of the noisy swell, in its smells and color, Berren felt a familiar and fleeting sense of bittersweet wonder, as if he had been granted witness to something of timeless essence.

Delhi was like that sometimes. And sometimes it was an impersonal refuge for those who dealt with remote projects around northwest India. There was always a friend or two to be found, and the liquor was safe. There were endless poker games in a back room of the Lodi Hotel, where the ceiling fan blew the money and cards around, and, of course, there were all those absurd revelries that had made the small group around Berren a recurring topic of conversation in both the Chandi Chawk Bazaar and the A.I.D. cocktail set.

The taxi was a tribute to mechanical ingenuity. It was held together with bailing wire and riveted plates of rusty metal. The left door, opposite the driver, was roped shut, and the meter rattled off most of its numbers at impossible intervals.

The driver was a talkative Punjabi whose tightly wrapped blue turban swiveled back and forth as he watched for weak spots in the multitude.

"Ah, yes, sahib, it is the time of foolishness. This week they are rioting and killing over the use of the English." The auto jolted through a series of potholes, the driver jerking the car up and down through the gears, cheerfully uninterested in the strange new vibrations emanating from the front wheels.

They rattled out onto a wider avenue, leaving the hawkers and the bargainers behind. A light wind lifted the humid air that had greeted him when he arrived, and set to waving the fernlike leaves of the trees that lined the boulevard.

"Next week they will be demonstrating over high prices, or the killing of cows, or maybe even the use of Hindi. I tell you, sahib," the driver looked back at his passenger for a dangerously long time, "it gets worse every year. Not like when you English were here."

Berren laughed. "I'm American," he reminded him.

"*Hun-ji.* Same thing."

The lobby of the Ashok Hotel was the same as ever: vast and dark, hushed by the thick red carpeting, still threadbare near the brass revolving doors. Berren wondered again at his predisposition toward these colonial giants as he signed the register. He left his passport with the desk clerk and followed the dark old man in the neat khaki bearer's uniform who took the bags and struggled with them off toward his room.

They had no sooner rounded the corner out of sight (Berren attempting to relieve the aging bellboy of some of the weight and the bellboy steadfastly refusing) when a chubby man in a wrinkled and sagging blue suit put down the newspaper he had been hiding behind and left his place on a nearby sofa. He went to the desk and said something quietly to the clerk, who replied with an arched eyebrow and an icy stare. "Ah, well, then . . ." the man mumbled, and fumbled through his jacket until he found his identification. He opened it and took out a tattered, yellowing document as well. It took a moment to unfold, but the wait was worth it, for the change in the clerk's demeanor was immediate.

"Ah, yes. *Inspector* Gupta, is it?" he said, and hastily produced the forms and passport Berren had left behind.

With the clerk hovering over him, the chubby man perused the documents, searching through his pockets as he did so until he found his note pad. He smoothed his pencil-thin mustache with a pudgy forefinger, then shook his fountain pen until a few blue-black splotches appeared on the carpet. He made a few notes and then nodded toward the phone beside the clerk's elbow.

"Oh, of course, Inspector, sahib," and the clerk stepped aside. Gupta tried his number twice, and after several minutes of helloing and threats, he slammed the receiver down and walked off toward the revolving door, muttering dark curses against the government phone system.

Berren swung his feet off the bed and bent his head to his knees to clear it of his jet-lag dozing. He went to the door and sent one of the bearers in the hallway for a pot of tea, then to the window, stretching and scratching as he checked the progress of the day.

The heat of the early afternoon that had the distant buildings near the center of the city shimmering in a white glare had given way to the cooler shades of evening. Throughout the city thousands of cooking fires, stoked with coal and cakes of dried cow dung, formed a blue-white blanket of smoke that clung close to the ground. The ancient domes of the Moghul tombs stood like somber sentinels above the haze.

He took a cold shower, put on a comfortably faded pair of jeans, and was pulling a soft, loose-fitting Indian cotton shirt over his head when his tea arrived. He doused it heavily with the grainy sugar and drank it loudly, stuffing his mouth between slurps with sweet biscuits. That would hold him until there was time for a real meal.

Interesting, he thought as he headed for the door. For some reason he was feeling better than he had for a very long time.

The desk clerk looked up from his crumbling paperback and

noticed that the foreigner who had aroused so much interest earlier was now dressed in *mufti*. The sight didn't please him.

"Mr. . . . uh," he ran his finger down the register book, "Dr. Berren, may I speak with you a moment?"

"Hm? Sure." Berren paused at the desk. "What's on your mind?"

"Dr. Berren, I note that you are, let us say, casually dressed." He said it without hiding his disdain.

"So?"

"We have been asked to instruct our guests to confine their activities to the areas outside of the more, ummm, the more traditional sectors of the city. And, mmmwell . . ." he tugged at a button on his crinkly terrilyn shirt, "your unfortunate choice of attire indicates what one might call, in your country, a, um, Bohemian interest."

"Very observant," Berren replied flatly.

"You do not understand, Mr. . . . Mr. . . ." But Berren had already pushed through the revolving doors into the tepid evening.

The Chandi Chawk was the ageless hub of the old city. It was the quarter that harbored, in its Casbah-like narrows and alleyways, the resentment of the poor and the desperate, side by side with the very elements of piety and tradition that had enriched India's heritage since its origins. In the hands of the demagogue it was a volatile mixture.

It was a perfect setting for the trouble that the city was awaiting, so it was only natural for the driver to try to dissuade his passenger from his course, listing all the reasons he could think of to turn back and offering a few perfectly good alternatives.

They had left the wider avenues and were threading through the twisting streets and sharp, blind turns. As the jumble of buildings began closing in, the slogans plastered over their distempered walls turned from politics to virulent slander. The taxi had almost reached the sienna red wall that marked the boundary of the Chandi Chawk when the driver pointed out a disturbing observation: There was no other motor traffic, only themselves.

And there was something else: The mood of the crowd, surging and knotting among the shouting agitators, had become tense with a sullen malevolence. They were increasingly less inclined to let a taxi push them aside.

At last Berren abandoned the taxi. After a smile of apology for the glowering man his door had nudged, and a generous baksheesh for the driver, he began pushing his way through the gathering crowd and into an alleyway.

Mochies, members of the caste of cobblers and shoeshine boys, who traditionally plied their trade in this alley late into the night, were packing up early, sorting out their tools and rolling them up inside dusty rattan mats. A very old man recognized Berren and wrinkled his face into a toothless greeting.

"Salaam-ji," he nodded.

"Salaam-ji-gi." Berren's reply was warm, but there was a feeling in the air of energy and haste so he passed on by without their usual small talk and moved on up the alleyway at a brisk pace, trying to remain inconspicuous by keeping close to the walls of the buildings on the left.

At the end of the passage were several makeshift stone steps that bent the dirt path toward a winding street. The street, in turn, doubled back sharply to his left, where it ran along the foot of the annex to the high red wall that enclosed a still older sector of the city.

It was within these walls, in the days of Victoria's reign,

that the Indian sepoys celebrated their mutiny by performing the grisly slaughter of the city's entire foreign population. The British, in the fields just beyond, turned revenge into butchery by tying any Indian they could catch over the muzzles of their field cannon.

On a night like this it could all have happened yesterday. The great wall reverberated with the sounds of a gathering mob, with its sporadic chants and the harsh, maddening monotony of hands beating a staccato on hardened leather drumheads.

They're whipping things up for a good one, Berren thought. He'd seen it all before. Inside the wall, signs and placards were being passed out. Next it would be portable loudspeakers and the chanting of the latest diatribe would begin. After that, anything. A protest march, a riot, a mob acting out a concert of mindless destruction. There was a fever in the air, Berren could smell it like an approaching rainstorm. Somewhere in the city, something had happened to move the events beyond the bounds of human design, and something terrible was brewing.

Berren made a quick exit from the alleyway and crossed the street to the wall. Again he kept close to it, hoping to escape notice. If this was another anti-English language thing, he didn't want to be the only English-looking foreigner in sight.

Beyond an archway a few blocks to the north he caught a brief sight of four green army trucks roaring through the intersection, heading west, toward the only other gate into the troubled area. They were riot-control troops, and they were well prepared. Two of the trucks, their canvas thrown forward and secured, revealed dozens of cap-helmeted soldiers, some armed with oversized Enfield rifles and others with long, wicked-looking *lathi* clubs. They showed no concern for those who were forced to scramble out of their way. The unmuffled engines, as sure a warning as any sirens could be, momentarily drowned out the noise of the nearby mob.

Berren took advantage of the distraction to slip through the stragglers who were making their way up from the street, and headed for a sign that read SHALIMAR GARDENS CAFE, hanging out over a converging street a few hundred feet away. The sign was suspended from an iron pipe fastened to the roof of a deep, open porch that fronted a three-storied building set well back from the street. A few scraggly *sappon* trees fringed the walkway in front.

It was an old building with a certain flamboyance in its Asian rococo design that included a sturdy iron grillwork of floral ornamentation that barred each of the windows on the lower two floors.

Berren had spent a lot of time in this aging landmark, but he'd never gotten used to the ominous effect that occurred when the green metal shutters had to be closed tight behind the grillwork.

As he stepped up to the porch, he found three bearers in dirty brown shirts involved in the task of rolling the circular tables through a door that looked too narrow to accommodate them, and into the dining area within. From inside a familiar voice was exhorting them to greater speed.

"Ram Das," Berren called. "Hey, Ram Das!"

A bony face appeared in the doorway. Its mouth opened round with surprise.

"Mister Tommy, sahib," he cried, and leaped out past an oncoming table.

Ram Das was head bearer, and as such was allowed to wear his trademark, a red plaid shirt whose tails hung low over a pair of dingy white trousers.

"Mister Tommy!" He grabbed Berren's hand. "It has been a long time, sahib, where have you been?"

"A long way from here, Ram Das. You look in good health, yes? Getting a little fat?" It was wishful thinking. Ram Das was a short, wiry man, and though he'd always wanted the look of the prosperous plump, his leanness had remained the same for thirty years or more. "Where is that thieving Agorwal boss man of yours?"

Ram Das was shocked.

"Oh, Mr. Tommy, Krishen-ji is not a thief."

"I'll tell him you said so," Berren laughed.

"Tommy!" A huge man had squeezed his way past the rolling table and strode toward them. His smiling face was a perfect black ellipse with a ring of graying hair that circled his head like a monk's. His dark eyes sparkled with pleasure at seeing his old friend. He wore a pressed *kurta* that hung loose over a round belly, his girth made more graceful by the saronglike *lungi* that wound loosely around his hips and knotted in pleats at the front.

He padded to the American with his hand outstretched. "How glad I am to see you again, Tommy!" and took him by the hand. "But what a time you have chosen. Same as always, eh? Looking for trouble as usual—well, come inside. It will not be safe out here for long." He continued to hold the hand as he guided him into the fortified cafe.

"What could have brought you to us again like this? You know better than to come into the Chandi Chawk during such restiveness." Krishen had dropped the Delhi Hindi of their greetings and was now speaking his perfect English as he always did with his foreign friends.

He gave a few more directions to Ram Das, who hurried the process of fortifying the building by scurrying about, checking the street activity and giving orders to the other bearers with the appropriate gestures of his long, dangling arms.

"How's your liquor supply?" Berren asked.

"Please, Tommy," Krishen said in mock disapproval. "You know it is illegal in Delhi to sell firewater to the Indians."

Berren grimaced as if he couldn't bear to hear the joke one more time. Krishen had studied American history and the pun was as predictable as his renowned hospitality.

It was an unnecessary exchange anyhow, for Krishen had already opened the door to an upright closet behind the espresso machine. He moved his emergency hoard of bagged sugar to one side. "There is, of course, no bourbon," he said, "but there is . . ." and he pulled out a bottle of Portuguese brandy.

"Contraband from Goa," he said, and held it up for Berren's inspection. "You won't turn me in?"

His guest nodded his approval and the bottle was uncorked and poured into two tall, almost clean, glasses.

"I recall this same bottle from the last time I drank with you," Berren said. "You've become one of Gandhi-ji's abstainers?"

"No, Tommy, I've just had no reason to drink of it since." Krishen's reply held a note of sadness.

"Hasn't anyone been back?"

"Now and then. They came in for some time after you three went off to Bihar. But then they drifted off." His tone tried to brighten. "I can tell you it is all most depressing." He held his glass up in a salute to his guest, or perhaps to the old days, and they both took a swallow.

Ram Das and his helpers had finished their precautions and were hunkering in the corner of the room, ignoring the available chairs. They passed around a communal *bidi*, smoking it in turn through their fists, looking up anxiously at the occasional sounds of running feet and excited voices that sifted in from outside.

Berren answered Krishen's questions with an abridged version of the Bihar episode and of his exile, carefully excluding any reference to the Guild or his present affiliation. It was almost half an hour before he was able to wind the conversation around to the other purpose of his visit.

No, Krishen hadn't seen Josefs. No, there had been no news or gossip of him from the others. Well, yes, he admitted that he had heard (and here he tried to be delicate) something about Jason and Anna.

There was a stirring along the base of Berren's spine, which he thought was the brandy. He spoke with a deliberate calm.

"Have you seen her, Krishen? Has she been back?"

"No. No, my friend." Krishen shook his shiny round head sadly. "She, too, has left us."

"Left? Left for where?"

"No, she is here, I mean she is still in Delhi." The large man calmed him with a touch. He took a moment before he continued. "I think she does not come here for a reason."

"Reason?" The stirring had moved into the pit of his stomach, and he concentrated on the puddle of amber in his glass.

"I think she is sorry, Tommy, and I think she is ashamed."

"Ashamed of what?" He looked up at his host.

The large black face moved closer. Krishen searched the American's eyes as if he were looking for a way to communicate ideas that were beyond words.

"She should have gone home," he said. "You should all have gone home. What is it that holds you here? It is a dead end, this place. No, it is a trap. You and the others, Westerners who visit this land and cannot leave. They stay on, looking for things they will never find, struggling for things they cannot achieve.

"Then one day they find they are no longer really English, no longer quite American or Canadian.

"And even those who understand all this seem to miss a most important point. Just because they have lost their identity does not mean that they have found a new one. They will never be—*you* will never be—Hindustani."

He might have said more, but there were sounds of angry shouts and running feet past the front of the cafe; a scuffle, and then the crash of something metal. Leather boots could be heard, jogging double time, past the porch and continuing up the street toward the roaring crowd to the west.

"Where is she?"

Krishen wobbled his head, a gesture that could mean many things. It was out of his hands.

"Ram Das will show you," he finally said, and took a deep gulp of his brandy.

nine

The search had seemed safe enough at the outset. It was hard to tell, now that they were outside, whether the noise had subsided or had become confined only to the walled sector. But as Berren moved carefully through the labyrinth of narrow back streets behind a dauntless little Ram Das, he began to feel some misgivings. It didn't help that his guide was obliged to stop now and then and wave his American back into the shadows as clusters of agitated figures passed by. Some other passersby also kept to the shadows. They must have known well enough the dangers of the mob; they seemed frightened and confused, moving with painful caution away from the clamor.

Others trotted past in quick, quiet unison, at work on some mission of conspiracy, or just looking for some trouble to join.

The acid smoke from cow dung cook-fires that drifted out and into the street from boarded-up tea stalls and bakeries was overwhelmed when the breeze shifted by the unsettling smell of kerosene from the torches of the distant mob. Now and then a door or shutter would open a crack for someone to watch them pass.

A retreating waffle maker had overturned his cart in his hurry, leaving a soggy mire of rancid fish oil at the end of the dark alleyway. They must have been nearing their objective, for Ram Das stopped at last and allowed his foreigner to catch up. They were both beneath a makeshift wooden beam that buttressed the slab-bricked wall beside them against the stronger one on the other side. Beyond, the alley opened into a square with a small round green in the middle.

Past it, on the other side of the square, was a garishly modern concrete house, set back from the arabesque clutter of its neighbors that fronted directly onto the street. The lower level of the house was hidden by a high wall, topped, like many others in the city, with vicious fragments of broken glass imbedded in the concrete.

Ram Das was pointing a gnarled forefinger at the building. "She is there, Tommy, sahib, in the house of Ranjit Singh Bedi."

"She is living there?"

"Yes, Tommy-ji."

"She is this man Bedi's woman?"

The Indian nodded his sad bony face. Then, as if he read something in Berren's expression, he said, "I am thinking this isn't a proper thing." Then his face fell into a scowl, as if he shouldn't have voiced such an opinion.

There are times when rational thoughts outdistance their emotional repercussions; the hesitation as the laws of physics turn the jerk of a rope into the sting of a whip.

Berren had sent Ram Das back to the safety of the cafe

when he was struck by the meaning of his own questions. For a full minute he stood there, stiff with unreasoning anger, staring at the offensive house across the way.

Gradually, he forced himself to regain control. He tried to turn his mind back to where he was and why, details to drive some unformed but defiling image from his mind.

Then something changed in the lifeless square, something he felt that brought him back to his surroundings. There were signs of activity inside the compound of the house, and Berren's attention was drawn to a movement in the riveted sheets of galvanized iron that barricaded the driveway from the street. It was a recent construction, still shiny and unpainted, and with a clever practicality to its engineering. As Berren watched, it began to open, not on hinges as was more common, but sliding aside on what must have been heavy-duty rails running behind the wall.

It opened only a foot or two, just wide enough for a tall Sikh, wearing the blue turban of his order, to step out. He looked up and down the street, then, seeing no signs of immediate danger, he pushed the barrier the rest of the way open with a surprisingly light shove.

Scattered about the pavement were signs of an earlier clash; a few crumpled and ripped placards, a general litter of clubs and long sharpened stakes. There was an unraveled strand of red turban cloth draped over the bushes of the green, and here and there, lost in some closer scuffles, lay a number of cheap rubber sandals, each looking somehow silly and alone.

The peculiar assortment of debris and the unnatural quiet could mean only that this had been one of the streets chosen by the troops to disperse the crowd, or force it back into confinement behind the Moghul wall.

Berren wasn't quite sure what to do from here on, so he

decided simply to present himself to the situation and let events take their course. He stepped out of the alley onto the covered walkway and followed it around the perimeter of the square toward the open drive.

The Sikh had turned and gone back to shout something at a deep-voiced Alsatian that was barking from the compound behind the shiny barricade.

Berren paused when he reached the spot where he could see the steps in front of the house. A black Dodge, an expensive relic from the days of the tail fin, was parked below them with the back door open.

So that was it. They were getting ready to leave the troubled sector of the city while there was still a lull in the violence. No telling when they'd return, so he left the corner of the walkway behind and cut diagonally across to the barrier.

Something was overturned at the far end of the street. Whatever it was crashed loudly to the macadam and rolled away with a raucous metal grind. The mob was beginning to spill out of the back streets into the square again.

Things were getting risky out here and Berren had no sooner decided to take his chances with the Sikh and the dog when the door above the steps opened, and there she was.

He recognized her the instant she appeared, and yet, at the same time, she seemed a stranger. The woman he saw, picking her way down the steps toward the car, could hardly be that other Anna. She was passive and drawn. She moved with a vague slouch, and her face (though he couldn't be sure in the dim, reflected light) seemed flat and expressionless.

She was descending the steps as if each move were held in check from the next by the men on either side of her. The nearest was the one Berren had seen at the driveway entrance. The other was also a Sikh, but this one was *puka*—proud statured with a tightly wrapped gray turban and a well-tended beard. He was a fiercely handsome man, whose attire showed a sophisticated Western taste for understated elegance.

It was a refinement unexpected in a man who could own such an ostentatious house, for Berren knew at once it was Ranjit Singh Bedi.

Everything was wrong: the increasing noise of the rioters, the ugly rush of events closing in. But in another moment she would be gone—so he stepped into the compound.

It was Ranjit who saw him first. He stopped short, dumbfounded at the audacity of the intruder. Anna looked up, as if to question the hesitation, then followed his stare to where Berren stood. Her face went dead.

"Tommy!" It was not a greeting. It was the unhappy cry of a child whose dark secret has been discovered.

Ranjit reacted to the name before Berren could respond. He shouted an order to his subordinate, who left the girl's side and leaped the remaining length of steps. A second shout brought another of his goons on the run from a side door.

Luckily the newcomer hesitated, an almost comic caricature of villainy with a wild, scraggly beard and the eyes of a madman, trying to understand what was going on. It was only for a split second, but it was long enough for Berren, who had been frozen in amazement at such a drastic reaction to his appearance, to check the square behind him. It was rapidly filling with groups of demonstrators, and yet the way back to the alleyway was still relatively clear, so he turned on his heels and took off toward it.

He'd covered a quarter of the distance when he ventured a glance over his shoulder. The first goon was in hot pursuit, while Ranjit remained at the entrance, waving angrily at the other, still inside, to join the chase.

The square had become an obstacle course. The mob was pouring from the streets and passageways nearest the wall, pushing ahead of it a vanguard of angry troublemakers and frightened bystanders, almost hysterical in their search for an escape.

Berren was in full flight. He was large enough to crash through the smaller bunches or push them aside, while his pursuer met with more determined resistance. Berren was able to maintain his lead until at last he reached the alley. Now he was really in a bad spot. His only escape plan had been to return by the way he had come, but he found the alleyway packed solid. A few yards into its confines a fight was going on. Someone was getting a deadly beating from several others, amid the confusion of torn awnings and screaming women.

In his fear and dismay, Berren felt a rush in his bowels, and his legs trying to wilt under his weight. With the alleyway blocked, there was nothing left but a headlong sprint down the street ahead of his pursuers, and, most of all, ahead of the mob.

He looked back long enough to see the first Sikh only a hundred feet behind, scrambling through a large group of chanting rioters. At the same moment, the second wild-eyed goon emerged from the drive on a snarling foreign motorcycle. His appearance added a terrifying new dimension to the chase. Berren could probably outrun the first Sikh, and with luck be through the crowd before they had time to consider him as a target for their fury, but a motorcycle could maneuver through it all and cut him down.

It was enough to give Berren his second wind, and he found himself running for his life. His heart pounding with exertion and fear, he raced down the street, now avoiding the knots of people who were beginning to react to his presence.

With the urgings and harangues of Ranjit's goon, the curious were becoming hostile, and some had begun to break off from the crowd to join the chase for "the Englishman." With a new target for their hostilities they became a mob once again, and were close to his heels by the time he rounded a corner into the wider roadway beyond the square and spotted his deliverance.

A gaily canopied motor rickshaw had foolishly driven into the troubled area. Its little Vespa engine crackled loudly as the driver, desperate at the sight of the rushing mob, was attempting to execute a sharp U turn.

Berren was on it at the apex of its turn. He grabbed the canopy strut and swung aboard. The terrified driver hardly noticed the added hazard that was now riding in the seat behind him.

The mob was almost on top of them when he finished the turn and twisted at the throttle handle. There was a cough and an awful hesitation before the engine caught and they roared away, up the dark narrow street.

Two things happened to squelch any relief Berren might otherwise have been allowed. The mob, now falling behind and giving up the chase, parted in the center to allow the black foreign motorcycle to squeeze through into the open.

At the same time, a blond, athletic-looking foreigner appeared under a light on the street ahead. He was bouncing on the balls of his feet like a prizefighter with his open hands held out before him as if to fend off the speeding rickshaw. At first Berren thought he was trying to avoid them, and then he realized, at the same time as the driver, that he had something else in mind. As the rickshaw bore down on him, he leaped directly into their path.

Berren grabbed the chrome handle in front of him and braced himself as the driver slammed on the brakes and cut the handlebars to the left. The tiny vehicle bounced and skidded, its rear end broke traction and began to swing around. By the time the driver was able to correct the slide, they had slowed sufficiently for the foreigner to run along beside them for a few steps and sprawl into the back seat on top of Berren.

He sat up and slapped the driver on the back.

" 'Op it, mate!"

The engine strained for speed under the additional weight, but by the time it had regained it, the motorcycle was alongside. It was a heavy, ugly machine, and its burly-faced rider, his hawklike features distorted by a vicious sneer, showed a discouraging expertise by sideswiping his crashbar against the rickshaw's tinny metal body. It had no apparent effect on the stability of the marauder, but the ungainly rickshaw was driven out of line by the blow, and its driver had to fight hard for correction.

Berren watched what was happening with helpless disbelief, while the cycle maneuvered in and away again, as if toying with its prey. The rider reached under his *kurta* with his left hand and pulled out what looked like an ivory cylinder; then bent low, his beard almost touching the handlebars.

With his right hand twisting at the throttle, he dropped the left below his knee, and flicked the cylinder toward the rushing pavement. It was instantly a knife.

Its blade was heavy enough for a Bowie knife, yet he held it with a deft balance, and swung his machine hard toward the rickshaw. Berren flinched, but the lunge swept past him. The target wasn't Berren, but the driver, who yelped and swerved in time to avoid the attack. The rickshaw veered to the left, barely missing a street-side fruit cart.

No sooner had they regained their course than the madman was upon them again. This time he leaned in with the lunge, and his blade found a mark.

96

It opened the driver's arm below the elbow, and blood streamed back and spattered into the rear. Again they were forced dangerously close to the stalls that lined the street.

The intentions of the Sikh were clear. Even at this speed they hadn't escaped the mob. If they could be forced to crash, it would be only a minute or so before the riot overwhelmed them. Berren had seen the remains of victims of other riots, and was ready to try something desperate.

When the motorcycle began to close in again, Berren prepared to grab at their tormentor. There was a slim chance that he might be able to get a handhold, and, in spite of its heavy weight, throw the machine off-balance.

He was spared the attempt when the other passenger first shoved him back harshly against the seat. Then he wrapped a pair of hamlike fists around the chrome handle that ran the width of the vehicle and with two sharp jerks had it free.

The frightened driver was jerking the machine back and forth in an attempt to avoid the next attack, but the foe had the maneuverability, and easily compensated for his victim's antics as he began to pull up from behind again.

The stranger knelt over Berren's feet, filling the narrow floor space completely as he worked the metal bar into position. As the cyclist came abreast, he leaned in for another slash, giving the stranger the target he sought. He thrust the rod out, beneath the outstretched blade, hub level, into the spinning wheel. There was an almost musical ring to the snapping spokes. The Sikh realized what was happening and struggled to lean his mount away from the attack. His response was too slow. The rod suddenly grabbed and held, jammed behind the fork that supported the front wheel. It yanked from the stranger's hands and bashed another deep cut in the rickshaw's body.

Forward motion seemed to carry the speeding motorcycle

along miraculously, despite the now spokeless front wheel, and then it toppled forward. The rear wheel, still spinning at full power, lurched high into the air as the front hub, now free of its wheel, ground into the macadam. Its rider was clawing at the air when his scream was cut short as the back end of the machine completed its high sweep by smashing him against the street.

Machine and rider fell away from view. Berren looked back in time to see each somersault separately into a roadside tea stall in a dusty explosion of brass pots and burning coals.

The rickshaw continued bouncing down the street, putting welcome distance between its passengers and the mob, but its course had become a violent slalom back and forth through the yellow pools cast by the streetlights, careening insanely toward a certain rollover. In the front, the cloth-wrapped head of the driver was bobbing and nodding with each bump. Control was beyond him now; he was blacking out.

The stranger made a grab for the man and held him upright by the shoulders while Berren stretched over the front seat and yanked the choke knob up from the control panel.

Blue smoke poured out of the rear as the engine backfired once and lost power. The compression of the dead engine worked against their forward motion and they ground to a stop.

The stranger held the driver upright until Berren was out and examining the wound, then he came around to see for himself.

"Come on, chum," he urged. "No breaks while the meter's runnin'." He gave the driver's face a few light slaps and turned it roughly toward the streetlight to check for any signs of consciousness. "How's i' look?"

"It's a pretty ugly gash. Lost a lot of blood, too." Berren

ripped a clean patch from his *kurta*, folded it, and pressed it to the flow. "He needs some stitches, but . . ."

"Sh!" the stranger cut in. "He's comin' around." The driver was glaring up at the square-jawed Englishman, whispering hoarsely in weak anger. "Wha's he say?"

Berren had the driver's dirty headwrap off and was winding it around the forearm, binding the cleaner cloth against the wound. "He wants to know what we've done to his machine."

"Ha! Game li'l bastard, i'n 'e?"

Berren began to laugh. "You think *he's* game." He tried to steady himself as he tied off the rag. "Wait till you see me try to drive this piece of junk out of here to a hospital."

"You?" The stranger was laughing, too. There seemed no end to their sense of relief. "You're going to drive this thing?"

"You'd rather wait here for a cab? Come on. I'll even drop you wherever you're going, free of charge. How's that, mister?" He wiped his hands on a pants leg and offered it to the stranger. "What did you say your name was?"

"Not even a guess, Dr. Berren?" The stranger eyed him wryly. "The name is Michaelson. Ian Michaelson. And from now on I'm going wherever you are."

ten

Ian Michaelson was not at all what Berren had expected from the cunning Mr. Sharma. He was a tall, broad-shouldered man with a boisterous charm and a quick, loud laugh that often broke into their conversation awkwardly. He had bright, darting eyes that seemed to see everything at once, and a nose that Berren guessed had been broken for him a few times.

He wore his yellow hair short, combed to one side and back from his low forehead while his bushy white eyebrows bristled out every which way.

"Am I boring you, mate?"

"What? Oh, sorry. I think the old jet lag has finally caught up with me." Berren suppressed another yawn. "I'm afraid I didn't catch all that. You were saying how you just kept checking around the hotels that catered to foreigners till you found my name in the register. You were lucky in that. There's a lot of oddball *farenge* around who'd never stay at a hotel like this old monster."

"And lucky that fag at the desk didn't like your tailor," Michaelson laughed. "He's the one who figured out where you were goin'."

"The Chandi Chawk's a big place," Berren offered.

"Na' with a mob like that. I just followed along behind all those coppers, assuming you'd have done the same," Michaelson chuckled. "A great bloody romp wa'n' i'? Took the stuffin's ou'a you, though. I can see that from 'ere."

"It's not that so much. I just got to listening to your accent. I do that sometimes when I hear one I can't place."

"Oh, that." Michaelson probably smiled, but Berren couldn't make out much of his face anymore. One of the small alcohol patio torches had gone out, and the other one, sticking up out of a nearby flowerbed, was behind him and lit only his hair and his frosty white eyebrows.

"Most think it's cockney," he said, " 'n I leave it at that. I'm told, however, that I learned the Queen's English in the colonies."

"Sounds it."

"Right. Rangoon. Just in time to say bye-bye to the ruddy Nips in '39. Cockney, is it? Well tha's how things were after the war, wa'n' i'? What the Nips left, the Labour party back in the Motherland handed over to the coolies. Nothing but the dole for them that lost it all, so, Junior, here, went out on the streets to earn his bread as soon as 'e was able—and as soon as 'e was able 'e got his seaman's papers and back he went to get what was 'is.

"The old man couldn't see it, the old sot. I told 'm the end of his empire wasn't the end of the world. Without the

British paper shufflers to hold things down, it was like opening the jailhouse door. Every man for himself, and plenty of money for those in between."

Berren was watching him carefully. "And did you?" he asked.

"Did I what?"

"Get what was yours."

"Ha! Well, I'm workin' on it."

A door closed behind them and a waiter passed through the circle of torchlight, bearing their coffee on a wide wooden tray. It was a pleasant night, and Berren listened for sounds of the city outside the garden walls while the waiter cleared their dishes. He heard none.

There was an arbor in the dark beyond the pool and something was flowering there that gave the air a delicious fragrance. In Berren's exhausted state, after Anna and all the rest that had happened a few hours ago, it all seemed unreal and out of place. How strange to be in the midst of all this, listening to the earthy tales that this Michaelson character delighted in telling. He'd grown more expansive with the coffee, joking and weaving yarns of his escapades that told Berren more than he'd ever have thought to ask about. Michaelson appeared to be a man of brash good humor who maintained a knuckle-hard attitude toward the people of post-colonial Asia.

He told a good story, but try as he would, Berren could not imagine this barrel-chested Englishman punching those stubby fingers of his into the keyboard of a typewriter. Whatever use Sharma's wire service put him to, the only impression Berren could arrive at was of a boyish, international roughneck in search of the next bit of action. One more variation on the soldier of fortune theme.

Berren, for his part, was cordial but reserved. He liked the guy, but then he usually liked those he found entertaining, and trust is too welcome an indulgence when you're tired. So when the subject of their endeavor was at hand, he was reluctant to divulge any more of its details than he had to, despite Michaelson's pumping. Whatever course they were set upon together, he was determined to hoard his options.

"So tell me about this bird of yours," Michaelson suggested as he took a cigarette from Berren's pack.

"Bird?"

"This Anna. The one you risked both our necks over." He struck a match, which flared and went out before he could use it. "She know where your friend's at?"

"I doubt it. She was with him for a while, but he left her behind."

"Just like tha'," Michaelson said as he tried another match. "Well, he's your friend. But from here it sounds like he took your woman away just for a bi' of a lark."

"Yah, well . . ." Berren reached for the cigarettes and noticed there were only a few left. Good time to quit, he thought for the hundredth time. He'd never find Gauloises in this part of India. When he looked up, the Englishman was leaning forward with one elbow on the table, waiting for a reply.

"It's nice out here," Berren finally said. "It's a long way over those walls and into the real world. How many, you suppose, were killed in that mess we were in a couple hours back? How many lost everything they'd ever have? And now it all seems far away. In the real world there are places like the Chandi Chawk was tonight, and last year's Bihar. There's violence and famine, and those who profit. Then there's people like me who get stuck in the middle, so crazy frustrated they end up trying to punish anybody they can get hold of.

"Oh, yah." Berren shifted uncomfortably in his seat. "I got

to be a real bastard. You know the kind—the ones with a cause? How she stood it as long as she did is beyond me. I must have been taking it all out on her." Berren jammed a Gauloise into his mouth and reached for the matches. "She wasn't running off with Jason, you see; she was running away from me." He struck a match, which sputtered for a moment without producing a flame. "Funny thing about Indian matches. You never know what the next one will do."

"Still not ready to blame this Jason bloke, eh?" Michaelson's tone was not very sympathetic. "Don't think there was a little hanky-panky goin' on?"

For a second Berren thought of the girl he had seen in the Chandi Chawk, of the walls and the tail-finned car. "Doesn't matter," he said. "She couldn't stay, and she couldn't bear to be alone again. So when Jason left, Anna probably just picked up and went along with him." He shrugged. "As for Jason, maybe he'd loved her all along. Or maybe he thought that making his disappearance look like the old triangle was safer for all of us."

Berren found a match that worked and put it to his Gauloise, dragging out a harsh, bark-smelling puff and blowing it skyward.

The Englishman watched him steadily. "Where does that leave us, then?" he asked. "Any idea where he is?"

"Well, one thing's sure: He's no place around here," Berren replied. "If he were, Anna'd never have . . ." The same ugly image flashed through his mind but he shook it off. ". . . never have made accommodations with the likes of Ranjit Singh Bedi.

"I'd guess all the assumptions are right. If the smugglers are up in the mountains, then so is he."

"Could 'e last up there this long? I mean, it's been almost

a year—suppose he's dead?" Michaelson asked.

"Suppose he is? What choice have we got? Anyhow, let me explain something: Those are the Himalayas. Whole civilizations have been swallowed up in the second, the high range. And if he had to do much searching around—terrain as remote as that—how long could it take?"

"So you're not so sure 'e's alive either?"

Berren shrugged. "All I know is we've both spent a lot of time up there. With me, it was strictly the *Tibetan Tribals* study and long treks to get away from it all. For Jason, it was where he belonged. The more rugged, the more inaccessible, the more he liked it. Whenever he'd get sick and tired of the real world, he'd go trekking into the hills, off to some private Shangri-la he had found for himself up there. He told me once he had even been adopted into a Brahmin family someplace way up near the frontier—formally, I mean. Ritual and all. Said it was the only place he felt at home anymore, but he'd never tell me exactly where it was. Another *farenge* would have spoiled the place, I guess."

Berren could picture Jason, sitting on some mountaintop, laughing down at him. He smiled at the thought and noticed the Englishman eyeing him quizzically. "Hell, he could get along fine up there," Berren said. "Wherever he is."

" 'Wherever 'e is' doesn't help us much," Michaelson said. "You don't think the bird knows anything?"

"I didn't say she doesn't know anything," Berren corrected. "She obviously knows where he left her."

"Ah-ha. And maybe wha' direction 'e'd left in." Michaelson snubbed the butt of his cigarette in his saucer. "That means all we have to do is pry her loose from that furry-faced bastard."

"Yep," Berren said. "That's all."

The phone seemed to have been ringing for hours. At last Berren stuck out a hand, searching in vain across the nightstand. Damn, he thought, that's right; India. Where else would they put a phone but at the opposite end of the room from the bed? He jackknifed off the bed and cursed again as he stepped on the rolled map that lay on the floor.

He'd spent a long ugly day at the state cartographer's office, sweltering among the racks and security act strictures to find that crumbling yellow tube and now he'd crushed it.

He found the light and stumbled over to the phone.

"Berren here," he said. "Speak."

"Tommy, this is Krishen here."

"Krishen," he managed a laugh. "When did *you* get a telephone?"

"Ah, Tommy, you know what a poor man I am. I use the phone of a friend."

"Yah, poor Krishen. You own only half the Chandi Chawk."

"Well, that is why I have telephoned to you. The man who owns the other half is in my café."

"So?"

"So, with him is the girl, Anna."

It took a second to register, then Berren was wide awake. "Who else is with them?"

"A large, unpleasant-looking fellow."

"Another Sikh?"

"Yes."

"Okay, Krishen, now listen. Try to keep them there, all of them. We'll leave right now and be there in twenty minutes."

The receiver had barely reached its cradle when Berren was in his crepe-soled walking shoes and rushing toward Michaelson's room. There was no answer to his knock. He checked his watch—eleven-thirty. The whole town closed at ten. Where the hell could he be? He was about to try again when the elevator door opened and Michaelson appeared.

"What's up, mate?"

"Where've you been?"

" 'Avin' a drink. Spent a rotten day straightening out my visa."

"Come on." Berren turned him back to the elevator. "We've got some more business in the Chandi Chawk. I'll explain on the way."

They moved swiftly through the covered walkway. Its white-washed pillars reflected the light of a hissing kerosene pressure lamp sitting on the ledge of one of the reopened tea stalls. Closer to the cafe's porch, several betel-chewing old men squatted to discuss the tumult of the night before.

A light hung from the ceiling of the open porch. Its glow quivered in fluorescent uncertainty over a solitary figure sitting near the door, nursing a light brown glass of steaming tea.

Berren stopped to inspect him for a moment from the shadows. He was a plump man with a pencil-thin mustache, dressed in a rumpled blue suit. Berren took him to be some kind of a clerk whose interest was limited to the pages of the notebook that lay on the table before him.

His presence probably didn't mean anything but Berren was still leery of bystanders from the night before, so, as they approached the door, he kept a cautious eye on him.

They were still there, sitting beneath one of the heavy, kettle-shaped lights that hung from brass chains near the center of the room. Anna was bent forlornly over her tea, a matted lock of her auburn hair dangling over one eye. Beside her sat Ranjit, stirring his tea with his spoon handle, his eyes fastened to the table but with a certain expectancy, as if he were waiting for an excuse to leave.

Krishen was behind the bar, busying himself worriedly with some little job. When he saw them standing at the door he did a double-take. Then, getting hold of himself, he rolled his wide eyes to one side in a silent signal. Berren nudged Michaelson. A patch of cloth, a long strip showing past the edge of the doorsill; the shirt-sleeve of someone leaning against the wall, hidden on the other side of the door.

Michaelson nodded with a grin and reached in with both hands. There was a roar of protest as he wrenched the man into view. It was Ranjit's goon, his forearm braced against Michaelson's throat while with his other hand he struggled to pull a revolver free of his pocket.

Michaelson checked him with a blow to the stomach that doubled him over and sent him careening into Berren so that the three of them crashed into the table where the man in the blue suit sat. Berren jumped to his feet just as the chubby man tried to leap to one side. Not knowing what he was up to, Berren shouldered him against the wall and held him there with the heel of his hand against his chest.

"No, *please!*" The man flung his hands up. "I am but passing by!"

Berren pushed him out of the way and barged on into the room. Ranjit was on his feet but standing stock still. Whatever he might have done, he must have thought the better of it and stopped himself short. He stood half crouched, with his palms spread flat on the table. He showed no surprise, only a smoldering rage.

"Hold it, *Sidar-ji.* Just relax," Berren ordered. "I came here only to talk. I have something to say to your girl friend."

Michaelson was still grinning as he came into the room,

dragging the goon behind him like a sack of potatoes. "Bloke's got taste," he said, holding up the captured weapon. "Webley-Smith's a hell of a gun for his like."

Ranjit paid no attention to the Englishman, his eyes were fixed on Berren.

"That's good," Berren said. "That's real good. Now, you just stay that way and don't make Michaelson, here, nervous. You can have her back again, if that's what she wants.

"C'mon, lady." Berren pulled a chair out of her way. "It's better outside."

Anna looked fearfully at Ranjit, then stood uncertainly and came around the table while the Englishman straddled a chair and rested the arm with the revolver over its back.

Berren gripped her arm and led her outside, passing but hardly noticing the pudgy man trying, at the same time, to gather up his scattered notes and watch what was happening. Berren would have liked to have led her farther from the others, but by the time they had gotten a little way into the shadows, Anna was beginning to hold back.

"Tommy!" She had controlled herself long enough. "Tommy, what's happening? Why did you have to . . ." Her voice sounded shrill and timorous. She was like some saucer-eyed night animal.

Berren had never seen her this way before. For a moment he was unsure of who she was or who she had been. He held her arm roughly as if to immobilize her at last, to hold everything about her in place for a moment or two.

"Anna, listen," and then he didn't know what to say. Like an actor who had "gone up," he had rehearsed the scene so many times that the desire for fulfillment had overwhelmed the words to attain it.

"Oh, God, Tommy, what are you doing here?" Tears were

glistening on her cheeks. "Why can't you just leave me alone? Last night, when I saw you . . . last night . . ."

"Listen," he was saying, "listen, dammit!" He shook her until she fell silent, biting hard on her lip, her eyes shut tight in a painful grimace. It was useless anyhow. Whatever there was to say, she'd never get it out right.

"Okay? You okay?"

She opened her eyes and nodded slowly.

"All right then." He loosened his grip. "Look, I don't know what you're mixed up in with this Ranjit character," he jerked his head toward the café, "and I don't want to. And going off like that with Jason, that too. It's okay, see? I figure you know your own mind, and whatever . . . well, it's just that I want you to know that I understand."

"You understand?" Anna's eyes opened wide. "*You* understand?" She swung at him, striking him hard across the face with the flat of her hand. "You bastard. You self-righteous bastard." She'd have hit him again if he hadn't caught her hand. "You've no right to condescend like that to me. Not after the way you treated me. I used to love you. I had no life but the one you gave me, and you ended up by treating me like that." She slumped back against the wall. "Oh, God, Tommy, why did you come back?"

"I'm trying to tell you," Berren said. "I know all that now. I *do* understand."

Anna gave a tired sigh. "Then you understand what I'm 'up to' with Ranjit Singh."

And suddenly he did. He grabbed her wrist, pulling her arm out straight, and ripped back the sleeve of her *cameze.*

"I don't see any tracks," he said bitterly.

Anna pulled loose and shrank back. "Between the toes,"

she said, with a poor show of defiance. "The leg, sometimes. Ranjit gets it for me, but he doesn't like it to show."

He stared at her in shock. It was a long time before he could speak. "I've got to find Jason." His voice sounded terse and brutal when he found it. There was no reply, her attention seemed to be drifting. "I said I have to find Jason. He's gotten himself into some trouble, something big, and I've . . ."

"I know," she said absently.

"You know?"

"Of course. You're always involved in something big. Both of you," she said, and looked over at him as if in resignation. "Yes, I know; that's what he said when he left me."

"He told you that?"

"He *had* to say something, didn't he?"

"All right, lady." Berren leaned over so that his eyes were directly in front of hers. "Now you listen to me. We've all made a mess of this, and I'm sorry. But just because you've opted out and gone back on the shit is no reason to treat the fact that somebody's out to kill Jason as if it were fair game for your renowned sarcasm."

"Somebody wants to kill J. J.?"

"Yes, and we may not be all that safe either. The point is, I have to find him, so I have to know where you went together."

"I didn't know." Her voice was so small it startled him. It was as if another girl had suddenly taken her place. "You didn't tell me that. You didn't tell me J. J. was . . ."

"All right, all right." Berren wished he hadn't put it that way. He wanted to take her in his arms but he settled for stroking her hair back from her eyes instead. "Now it may not be as bad as all that. Just tell me. Where did you two go when you left, uh, left Bihar?"

"Up to the mountains," she said, holding her face between her hands, trying to remember it all. "We started for the Kulu Valley, but ended up in Dangra."

"Why Dangra?"

"J. J. kept looking for something. He was always asking questions wherever we went. Mountain people, mostly; Tibetan refugees, smugglers, anyone who'd been in the high mountains, he'd talk to them for hours. Whatever he was looking for, we ended up in Dangra. It was even worse there; I thought he was working on some new prospectus, but he'd never tell me about it.

"He put me up at that *bavan* next to Agorwal Cloth Shop, you know the one? Then he let me sit there alone while he went off for days at a time."

"Then what happened?" The talking helped, she was beginning to relax.

"One night he went off with one of the local smugglers who'd just managed to get over from Tibet. I think he was a Muslim, a hard, nasty-looking Kashmiri. When he didn't return I became frightened. First for J. J., then for myself.

"I had nothing of my own. No money—nothing. Nothing. He was gone for four days and when he came back he was all excited about something, as if he were close to whatever it was he was looking for."

"Did he tell you what it was?"

"No," she said. "No. All he said was that he had to leave me. He gave me a little money, enough to get back to you in Bihar, and said that would be the best thing. But I couldn't do that, you know, I was . . ."

"Where did he say he was going?" Berren interrupted. "Think!"

"He didn't. He just gave me the money and then he was gone."

They were silent. Berren's attention kept returning to her great, dark eyes. She was aware of it, and kept them averted.

From down the street they could hear hoots of laughter as one of the men at the tobacco shop danced a silly mime of one of the riot's victims. Anna had composed herself again. She stood straight, the way Berren remembered her, watching the clown with a vacant expression.

"Have you told anyone else about this?"

"No, J. J. told me not to. I may have said something to Ranjit, but nobody else."

"Oh, yah," Berren said, "Ranjit."

"I was in awful shape after all that. Awful. So I told him all my problems; I probably mentioned that, too."

"Sure," Berren said. "Where did you meet him, anyhow?"

"He was in Dangra. He has business there sometimes."

"He the one who got you back on drugs?"

"He knew what I needed, if that's what you mean," she said. "I guess it doesn't matter much to you anymore, but he used to be very nice. It's just that he's had problems lately, too, and, well, he's a terribly jealous man."

"I noticed. Well, come on. We've kept your 'nice man' waiting long enough. We don't want him getting jealous again."

"It never occurred to me that J. J. might be in trouble," Anna was saying as they stepped up on the porch. "If it had . . ." she stopped and turned to Berren. The light of the fluorescent tube made her skin look painfully thin, colorless except for the sickly blue tinge beneath her eyes. "There was something else. But he was acting so crazy and saying so many things, I don't know if it meant anything."

"A moment, please," someone called out. The rumpled man, who had been watching them from near the doorway, was hustling through the tables, nudging them noisily aside as he approached. Anna saw him coming and drew back.

"What did he say?"

"Huh?" She stared at the stranger, and Berren had to hold on to her to keep her beside him.

"What did he say?" he demanded.

"He said he was going home."

"A moment please, Dr. Berren." The stranger smiled with eager nervousness when he reached them and nodded respectfully to Anna. "My name is V. J. Gupta," he said. "I am with the investigative branch of the CID." He pulled a leatherette billfold from a pocket and began leafing through it. "See here, I have papers."

"I believe you," Berren said flatly. "What do you want?"

"Ah," the man began, slipping the billfold into a different pocket. "Some of us at Central Intelligence have been very anxious about your well-being, and, I must say, you have given us several unpleasant moments."

"You've been following me?"

"Um, we have been . . ." He pressed his fingers at his mustache, searching his English for a better phrase. ". . . looking out for you."

"Why?" Berren asked angrily.

Gupta glanced toward the doorway. His sudden appearance had been too much for Anna and she tried to slip away while his attention was diverted, but Berren's arm was around her and held her at his side.

"Let me say only that we wish you to reach your objective in but one piece." Gupta went on as if an alliance had been formed despite Berren's look of contempt. "Naturally, it will be much easier now. I am thinking you must have learned something this night, isn't it? Something that should be shared?"

"Go to hell."

"Please?" Perhaps the inspector had misunderstood.

"That means, Gupta-ji, that I don't know what you're talking about," Berren snapped. "And if I did, you spy-crazy sons of bitches down at the CID would be the last to know."

"Is it!?" Gupta was offended. He pulled himself back and struck a martyr's pose. "Well, of course, if you . . ." but Berren just pushed him out of the way as Michaelson showed himself at the door.

"There you are," he said, still waving the pistol in Ranjit's general direction. "Finished wi' your li'l tête-à-tête? Come on then, your hairy friend, 'ere, is waiting."

Without looking back, Anna slipped out of Berren's arm and went back inside as Michaelson backed through the door.

Michaelson kept the pistol, its heavy cylinder palmed lightly in his hand, as they trotted down the street. Gupta was already haggling over the price of his spilled tea by the time the two foreigners were out of sight.

They left the old city on foot, following the network of high sandstone walls of the mosque, dodging the platforms and canopy poles of the marketplace as they moved from shadow to shadow. Nothing was said until the Ashmeri Gate was behind them and Berren slackened the pace to a brisk stroll.

He had kept an eye on the empty lanes and alleyways behind, but there was no chase and no one following. In fact, the entire episode had gone off without a hitch. It had all been too easy, and he didn't like it.

"Well, mate?"

"Hmmm?"

"What did you find out?"

Michaelson waited for an answer, and when there was none, apparently decided the American was upset over the girl, so he didn't press it.

The streets were opening out into wider thoroughfares, straightening as they converged, like spokes, toward the hub of the colonial business district.

They paid no attention to the few shops and tea stalls that stayed open late along the wider streets, altering their course only when it was necessary to avoid stepping on the bodies asleep in the shadows. The hot nights had brought some of the local citizenry out from their stuffy rooms to find sleep in the cooler air of the walkway. Others had nowhere else, and home for them was whatever nook they could find for themselves. A decrepit-looking *sadhu* with shaggy white hair had made his bed out in the open atop a stone wellhead. Having shed his saffron robes, he lay in sweaty nakedness, smiling in his sleep as he gleefully exposed himself to the heavens.

The Englishman had a choice comment for that one, but he held it when a passing light revealed Berren's pensive expression. A horrid little ditty had found its way into Berren's head, wriggling through his thoughts and taunting him as he walked almost solely with the guidance of instinct. "Between the toes where nothing shows," it ran. "Behind the knees where nobody sees." He felt sick and ugly.

"Literature, sahib?"

A squirrelly shopkeeper slid out of his stall and was sidling along with the two foreigners.

"Most interesting Englesi literature, sahib," he offered with a conspiratorial hiss. "Recent *Playboy* magazines—"

Berren shook his head absently.

"Novels by Henry Miller?"

The disappointed peddler returned to the solace of his book-cases and bins while the two continued their walk.

"You've been broodin' for near half an hour," Michaelson pointed out. "She looks like a fine bird, all right, but not worth all that. I think it's time you told me what's what."

"You're right," Berren answered. "It's not just the girl, though. There's something about that whole setup back there I didn't like."

"What was wrong wi' it?"

"Well, that's what it felt like, a setup."

The Englishman frowned. "Righ'. I see what you mean. Maybe the girl got 'm to . . ."

"Nah," Berren waved the notion aside. "She goes where he wants her to go, not the other way around." He thought about telling Michaelson about the CID's interest, but decided to let it wait.

"Anyway," Michaelson said as if to change the subject, "at least you know where he is, right?"

"Wrong," Berren said, "but I do know where to start looking."

"Where?"

"A little town in the hills called Dangra."

"Righ'. When do we start?"

"As soon as I can con Krishen out of his jeep."

"That's good news. Now let's see if we can scare us up a drink."

There was still a nagging uncertainty pestering at the back of Berren's mind. There was a connection here he'd overlooked.

"Yah, a drink," he affirmed. "Hope they've still got that bottle of Jim Beam."

Michaelson was craning his neck in search of a taxi.

"You know," Berren continued as if to himself, "the worst

part of that sick scene back there was knowing that I had a hand in it."

"Tha' just goes to show you, one never knows, does one?" Michaelson had his hand up to signal. "Anyhow, they're out of Jim Beam at the hotel. I had the last of it this evening."

Before Berren could say anything, Michaelson had produced an ear-splitting whistle that pulled a passing taxi to the curb and awakened several nearby sleepers with a start.

One was shouting unkind things about foreigners as they drove off.

eleven

The *misri* looked all of eighteen years old. He had just finished bolting the valve cover in place over the gasket he had fashioned from laminated newspaper, and was shaking his head with uncertainty over the result.

"He doesn't like it," Berren said. "He'll want another day."

Krishen wrapped his arm around Berren's neck. "You are not to worry, my friend. He always wants another day," he replied. "I think he likes to keep my automobile in front of his shop. It is the only one here that is still in one piece."

"Yah, but he said the same thing yesterday and you let him keep it. You know what a hurry we're in."

"Ah, but yesterday he was sincere. It is not what he says, you know, but how he says it."

The jeep was a battered old beast, and Berren could appreciate the *misri*'s concern; it had certainly seen better days. It looked as if it were World War II army surplus, but it was actually of more recent vintage, made in India of outdated American castings. The unfortunate combination of adulterated metals and questionable quality control had left even its immediate future in doubt.

The crack in the windscreen had edged closer to the center since Berren had last used it, and one front wheel was starting to pigeon-toe under. Krishen loved to drive it himself, so he never employed a driver. That meant there was no one to tinker with the mechanical details or to clean the streaks of monsoon mud from its dull gray flanks.

But despite Berren's misgivings, the jeep was performing perfectly, puttering and bouncing its way north along the Grand Trunk Road through the confused tangle of the outskirts of Old Delhi. Beyond the shanties and *misri* stalls, the road became a straight line of crowned macadam that sped them along the same route that two thousand years of invading armies had used, north by northwest toward the Khyber Pass. The great plain of farmland stretched away on either side to the horizon, broken only by blue-brown stands of tamarisk and banyan trees.

The rectangles of fields, still greening from the recent monsoon, made islands of the tiny walled villages that looked as if they'd been there forever.

The hot sun sparkled down through the foliage of the trees that lined the road. Berren had gained confidence in the jeep over the last few hours and was driving with rough abandon. He knew the road and its hazards, from the plodding bullock carts, creaking heavily under loads of newly harvested cane, to the road-hogging big wooden trucks barreling down on them, forcing them off onto the shoulder, hub-deep in sprays of dust.

Ambala, Karnal, Patiala, each city with its hodgepodge of obstacles, its affable crowds thickening around bright-colored cloth shops and the awnings of fruit stands, and here and there, stately old buildings from the days of the British Raj, rich with Persian flavoring and decaying with dignity behind high, whitewashed walls.

They spent the night in Jagadri and left early the next morning to avoid the day's heat, creeping past the outskirts through a herd of bicycling workers heading for the mills of Jumna Nagar.

Their jeep was followed by an angry sweep of oily black clouds that failed to hide the clean morning sun. The patterns of shadow and yellow sunlight shifted along the cane fields and tamarisk until the clouds dispersed at last before some lofty wind.

By noon they were climbing the meandering roadway into the foothills of the Himalayas, which rose with startling abruptness from the flatness of the Indo-Gangetic plain.

Berren had left the driving to Michaelson that morning, content to relax and watch the passing landscape from beneath the brim of a slightly ridiculous tennis-looking hat that he'd found in the Jagadri bazaar the night before. He'd taken a lot of good-natured abuse from Michaelson at first, but now that the glaring sun was beating down again the Englishman had nothing to say.

For a long time Berren just rode along, savoring the drama of day-to-day life among these Punjabi villagers.

He took the wheel again after a while. The activity would relieve his growing melancholy, and anyway, the turns in the road had become tire-screeching hairpins. He kept the jeep to the extreme edge of the road, dropping the outside wheels back onto the shoulders to get out of the way of an occasional truck or bus which would heave around the turns with brakes smoking, directly astride their path.

Michaelson persisted in pointing out the infrequent telltale swirl of skid marks on the macadam, the only signs that remained of some past terror that had ended over the side and out of sight.

Berren sympathized, but he didn't slow down.

It was late afternoon when they finally caught sight of the little mountain town of Dangra. It passed in and out of view as they wound among the high rocks and outcroppings until they came to the top of a particularly sharp grade. The road swerved toward the north and gave them an uninterrupted view of crisp mountain ridge lines and a sky almost purple in the thin evening air.

The town lay along a level in the hillside opposite them by almost half a mile. Just above it the hillside paused in a green plateau of fields and pastureland before continuing its climb toward the nearest peak. From their view, the main part of town appeared neat and placid among the deep green groves of hardwood trees, while bunches of smaller houses were strung out along the base of a nearby ridge.

Beyond the town, to the north and east, the jagged peaks of the higher range stood in quiet majesty, their glacial snows bright gold in the late afternoon sun.

By the time the jeep entered the town, its streets were already darkening. A joyful crowd had gathered in the bazaar, and Berren was forced to give up pounding the horn and attempting to progress past the packed plaza near the town's center. He made a gesture of helplessness to Michaelson, worked his way to the side of the road, and flicked off the ignition.

The engine sputtered and was silent. In the near distance, over the shouts and horseplay of the crowd, the pounding drums of an approaching band could be heard. Trumpets and other brass instruments were experimenting with every third or fourth note, while a bagpipe fought to turn its hysterical whine into some long-forgotten British marching song.

"What the hell's goin' on?"

"Looks like a wedding," Berren said. "Might as well relax and enjoy it. We can't move for a while, anyhow."

A noisy procession chose that moment to turn the nearest corner into view and continue its slow course through the crowd. The tide of people spread before it to let it pass—but slowly. Brilliant kerosene pressure lanterns hissed from atop the long poles held by dutifully serious young boys in a less than tidy line.

Behind them swayed a draped and canopied palanquin suspended on two wooden poles, like a sedan chair, above the sweating line of men who held it aloft. Inside was a decidedly unhappy-looking young man, covered with glittering emblems of sequins and woven golden cloth.

"That the groom?" Michaelson had to shout above the din. "Yep."

The Englishman studied the figure on the platform again. "Not too pleased with the whole thing, is he?"

"Just a little anxious," Berren replied. "There's a good chance he hasn't met the lucky girl yet."

Michaelson shook his head sympathetically.

Beneath the passing rows of lanterns, the musicians went about their business with an almost grim sincerity, as friends and relatives in the line laughed and shouted to others who had been temporarily wedged aside.

"Tommy, Tommy-ji!" A hand was waving above the heads of the slow-moving crowd. The salute continued as its owner squeezed toward the jeep. "Tommy! It is I, Billum Singh!"

Berren used his grip on the wheel to hoist himself to a semierect position against the back of the seat. He twisted around, searching the crowd, and then his face lit up and he leaped from the jeep.

"Billum. Hey, Billum Singh."

The Englishman watched with bemused curiosity as a young man burst through the crowd. The two men fell on each other like long-lost brothers, embracing and shouting greetings unheard above the noise.

The young man was dressed in spotless white tight-legged *pajama* and a dark jacket with a vest sweater beneath, his white *topi* cap grasped in the hand that embraced his foreign friend.

Michaelson watched the reunion for a minute, then seeing that the others were occupied, he began to scan the crowd along the side of the street as if looking for a familiar face.

"This is Billum Singh Chawdri." Berren was leaning into the jeep so that Michaelson could hear the introduction above the din.

"How do you do?" Billum Singh said in a stiffly controlled English.

Michaelson took the hand and gave him a nod.

"Billum Singh worked with Jason and me on a caste study we did in a village near here. He was our chief cook-'n'-bottle-washer."

The title was delivered quickly, but Billum Singh caught the drift.

"As-soc-iate," he carefully inserted.

"Right," Berren corrected himself, and patted his friend on the back. "Our associate. Anyhow," he pointed to the palanquin that was swaying past, "that's his cousin up there." Billum Singh nodded proudly in confirmation. "It would make the family happy, and give the wedding big status if we went to the ceremony."

"Where's it at?"

"In the bride's village, up the hill, a couple of hours' walk from here."

"Not me, mate. Tha' bleedin' roller coaster ride wore me out. If you'll just point the way to our digs, I think I'll turn in. Weddings only make me cry, anyways."

"Okay," Berren said, "you stay, but I'm going. The family'd like it, and I need to find out a few things."

He was shouting now. The rear guard of the procession was passing, and its drums were pounding out an ear-splitting beat. Michaelson nodded, and Berren bent to Billum's ear to explain the decision. The young man nodded and pushed off to join his peers at the head of the pressing line.

It was nearly midnight, and the streets of the town were empty. The last of the revelers had gone off hours earlier to catch up with the rest.

The night air was a relief to the man who sat in the dark beneath the eaves of the tea stall. What a delight it was, after the muggy nights of New Delhi. There was a hardwood fire somewhere down the valley, lending a tangy smell to the breeze that stirred the *sheeshum* leaves against the low tin roof.

Behind him, deeper in the shadows, two other men sat on opposing twine-strung *charpois*, passing the mouthpiece of the gurgling brass hookah back and forth. It was pleasant to listen to the quiet mumbles of their Pahari dialect and the occasional rhythm of soft chuckles.

Every few minutes their conversation would lag and the stranger had the uncomfortable feeling that they were studying him, even in the dark. At last he shifted at his table and tried to catch a casual glimpse of them, but they remained only two dark shapes and their conversation began again.

When he looked back to the street he saw immediately that something had changed. He tried to scrutinize each detail he could pick out of the shadows until an unidentifiable motion caught his attention. There was a tall figure standing quite still in the shadows, watching the blue, moonlit street.

Gupta carefully set his cold tea back on the table and allowed himself the satisfaction of having his earlier deductions confirmed. The Immigration Section had Mr. Josefs's residence permit listed in Dangra district, so it was reassuring to see that Dr. Berren and this Michaelson fellow were proceeding with logic. The only place where they could stay was in the open courtyard behind the *bavan*, and Gupta had taken up his station in the tea stall across from its only entrance to wait for their next move.

Well, here was one of them at least.

Gupta pulled back the wrinkled sleeve of his blue suit to check his watch. It was too dark to make it out. He turned the face toward the street, and when he still couldn't read it, stood and stepped cautiously to the edge of the dim moonlight.

His knee struck a table leg. There was a clink, and something fell to the muffling dirt of the floor.

The foreigner on the other side of the street stopped at the sound and studied the darkness where Gupta stood. The inspector held his breath as he watched Michaelson step out into the street, his head cocked to one side with expectant curiosity as he ambled toward the tea stall.

This would never do. They must never know what he was up to. Chagrined by his own ineptitude and Michaelson's unexpected reaction, Gupta scurried off through the darkness of the eaves and awnings until he felt safe enough to chance a backward glance.

There was nothing to be seen behind him, but with his

next step he was bumped to one side by a large figure that seemed to have come from out of nowhere.

"Oh!" Gupta recoiled in surprise. He was looking up at the face of Ranjit Singh's bodyguard. "Oh, sorry," the inspector mumbled, and turned quickly away, hoping the Sikh wouldn't recognize him.

"Umph," the goon growled, and pushed past.

A very dangerous situation, Gupta decided. Whatever Ranjit's man is doing here, he's going to walk right into the man who beat him up at that café. In fact, he could see Michaelson still standing out in the street. What could he do if this fellow came out of the dark at him?

Gupta crept along behind the goon, wishing he had brought some kind of weapon with him. After all, if something happened to the foreigners now, after they'd come this far . . .

Somehow this Michaelson had to be warned, and Gupta patted his coat pockets for his change purse and pulled out a coin. He couldn't see the Sikh anymore, but he knew where he must be, so he tossed the coin ahead into the dark tea stall.

The clinking rang sharply in the quiet. Michaelson reacted instantly, springing backwards and bending to a crouch. He was sweeping something from his pocket just as the black form of the goon seemed to rush the last few steps—then everything stopped.

The inspector gaped at them in amazement.

"Oh, it's you," he heard the Englishman say. "Well, where is he?"

twelve

Dapples of yellow morning sunlight slid slowly down the white-washed wall of the courtyard, revealing in its wake a hollow niche holding a terra cotta figurine of a household deity smothered under layers of glossy paint, while tiny birds were bickering loudly over the property rights to a nearby tree.

The morning light moved over the *charpoi* cot where Michaelson was trying unsuccessfully to sleep. First somebody'd been snoring all night, and now those damn birds. He shifted onto his side and fumbled for his blanket. Then he remembered.

He sat up and rubbed his eyes with a beefy forearm. The next *charpoi* in the line was empty, and there was no telling if Berren had slept on it, but at least he'd gotten back from that wedding. His bedroll was at the end of the cot, rolled tight and bound on either end, slinglike, by a single leather strap. A similar strap lay across Michaelson's feet.

There were several other guests asleep in the shady end of

the courtyard. One of them was still snoring horribly and Michaelson gave the man's *charpoi* a kick as he passed.

"Shu' the hell up," he grumbled, but the man was oblivious. Michaelson stumbled over the flat stones to a rusty hand pump and worked the handle several times until the water began to spill. Then he bent to his knees under the freezing flow. Sputtering and shivering, he swept his hands through his hair and dried himself on yesterday's shirt. He didn't feel any cleaner, but he was certainly awake.

It was only about five o'clock and there wasn't much activity on the street except a moon-eyed cow that was strolling in the middle of the road.

Michaelson found Berren across the street in front of the tea stall. He was hunkered on the steps, holding an earthenware mug of steaming tea and wearing the same faded jeans and a pair of well-scruffed high-laced boots.

Beside him, in the same crouched pose, sat Billum Singh. He, too, wore a pair of much-abused jeans, which, judging from their size, had once been Berren's.

They squatted close to each other, the boy staring absently at the dusty street while Berren, his few camera accessories laid out on the jacket beside him, was testing the mechanisms of a battered-looking Nikkormat. They were conversing quietly in Pahari while he worked. Billum Singh nodded to Michaelson as he approached. The conversation came to a conclusion with their heads waggling in agreement, and then Berren seemed to notice Michaelson for the first time.

"Morning," he said. "Catch up on your sleep?"

"Some. Looks like you think we'll ge' to use this stuff," Michaelson said as he picked up a gadget he didn't recognize.

"If I get the chance," Berren said. "How're you fixed for a good pair of boots?"

"Boots? Well, I've got that pair of walking boots worked in. Why?"

"Hard soles? Thick?"

"Sturdy, you know. What's it all about? We goin' for a hike?"

"Going for a trek," Berren said. "A long one, it looks like. And we've got to leave right away, before the authorities can figure out where we've gone."

"So the wedding was a fruitful event, eh? You found out what you were after."

Berren sipped his tea and went back to his tinkering. Then he said, "Yep. That's why my maps didn't do me any good— at least not at first. The place would be too small; it'd be like looking for a needle in a haystack."

"But you found the needle?"

"No, but now at least I know which haystack."

Michaelson looked away in frustration, as if there were someone else around who would tell him what it was all about. "Right! Now tell me how we go about lookin' for your bleedin' needle. You really know these mountains well enough to muck about till you find it?"

"Nope. Not many do. Even this official map I got in Delhi is too sketchy," Berren said, tapping at the thickness in the pocket of his jacket lying beside him. "It just shows what the army learned in supplying the border troops—a few prominent landmarks and an approximation of the terrain, and that's it.

"Anyhow, that's why Billum Singh here is going along with us. He doesn't know any more about Jason's whereabouts than I do, but he's spent a lot of time in the high range, and between the two of us we should be able to follow up on a hunch I have."

"A hunch? We're going on a hunch?"

"Well, what else have we got?" Berren asked. They were going to share a difficult and dangerous few weeks together, and if the Englishman was subject to second thoughts in the matter, he wanted to know about it now.

Michaelson looked past Berren to his young friend. He'd been right the night before—the lad could be no older than seventeen or eighteen. And yet the foolish grin and childish enthusiasm of the wedding procession were gone. In their place was a smooth, calm face and deep-lidded eyes looking back at him with equal interest. Somehow they seemed too old for the boy.

He looked strong enough, though: long, wiry arms folded in front of a deep-chested torso like the Tibetan refugees Berren had pointed out on the road the day before.

Michaelson grunted. "He'll do."

"Damn right, 'He'll do'—Bi sahib . . . ?" Berren called to the tea wallah, who was bent over his fire, nursing his coals with painstaking economy.

The cow had sidled up to the adobied pillar near the brazier, pretending innocence while she watched for a chance to steal some breakfast.

Berren ordered tea for everyone, and some of the flat, doughy *parathas* soaked in buttery *ghee*.

When the tea wallah turned his attention back to the brazier, he found the cow with its muzzle buried in a heavy climb of bougainvillea that grew up the pillar to blossom in long trumpets of pink blooms along the eaves. With a cry of outrage, he leaped up and began cuffing angrily at the snout of the bewildered animal, until she backed away, drawing a spray of the trembling blossoms into her cud.

" 'Ere," Michaelson said with sober interest, "I thought they worshiped them things."

Berren smiled and emptied the remainder of his cold tea into the street. "Guy obviously thinks a lot of his flowers, too," he said.

The *parathas* arrived like pancakes in a steamy stack and Billum Singh, taking the first one, bit off a corner as he stood up and started off down the road.

"Billum's going to pick up some equipment I left with him the last time we went trekking up here," Berren said. "Had a couple Kealty packs, but Jason took one. Should be some canvas knapsacks, too, and canteens. He took the nylon line, so we'll have to make do with hemp. Wish I'd left my sleeping bag."

"Saw the bedroll," Michaelson said. "Looks comfy."

"Comfy here, maybe, but too heavy and not much for the kind of cold we'll get higher up. Got some tinned food left, Billum Singh says. I told his family to use it, but they just locked it away for my safekeeping. Not much there anyhow. Rice and lentils will have to do us for most of the time. *Dal bhat*, they call it."

Michaelson watched Billum Singh disappear over a rise in the road. "What'd ya tell him?" he asked.

Berren juggled the first *paratha*, testing its heat on his fingertips. "Everything," he said.

"You told him?" Michaelson was surprised.

"Of course I told him. Jason's his friend. Billum Singh and his cousin helped me figure out what we had to do, then Billum Singh wanted to come along. I told him it was going to be dangerous, and I told him why. Smugglers, trigger-happy frontline troops, and, who knows, by now maybe even the CID. I told him we couldn't get caught, or seen or even talked about."

"Ha! An' he still wants to come?" Michaelson laughed.

"Well, I told you," Berren smiled. "Jason's his friend."

They had been climbing the steepening path for three hours as it wound up along the meadow above the road. Now, as they stopped for breath, they could see the townspeople, tiny from this high perspective, filling the streets of Dangra, pursuing their affairs as if the wedding and the foreigners had never been among them.

The trekkers were not alone on the path. A line of four Rajput women in masculine black vests, billowing skirts, and balancing huge brass pots on their heads were on their way down to the town. Each younger than the one she followed, each smiled flirtatiously as they passed, their layers of silver bracelets and gold nose rings jingling merrily with their bouncing downhill gait.

Billum Singh never seemed to tire, but kept an eye on the two who followed. After another hour of steadily more difficult climbing, he allowed Berren to catch up long enough to have a private word with him.

"What's 'e say?" Michaelson was sweating heavily even though the morning air was still brisk.

"Billum Singh doesn't want to offend, but he says you look a bit tired."

"You don't look so good yourself," Michaelson said between gasps.

"I'm not," Berren said. "Want to stop a minute?"

"No."

"Good."

The pace never slackened from then on. The Englishman was tough, as tough as he looked. More important, he was as determined as the others, so they climbed on in silence while their straining lungs tried to accustom themselves to the thinning air.

It was nearing noon, and Michaelson was disappointed to find that what had looked like the crest of the ridge they were nearing was only the edge of a hollow between two steeper slopes that sheltered a ramshackle stone fieldhouse. It was a welcome bit of level path, but their climb would rise even more sharply a hundred yards beyond. An old farmer, prodding a lumbering buffalo with a long wooden pole, ambled slowly across their path. His bent back already matched his animal's slouch, but he managed to bow even lower in greeting. Later, when the path began to climb again, Berren looked back and saw him still standing there, nodding wisely up at them while his animal wandered alone into the fields.

Damn, Berren thought. He'll tell everybody he sees.

The sun had passed its zenith before the three finally crossed over the sharp ridge that curved down between the two nearest peaks. Most of the valley's farmland had been left behind. The slopes on the northern side of the ridge were too wet and too steep to support much of the elaborate terracing necessary to hold water and soil in place.

The sky was crystal clear, a dark blue unknown on the lowlands, and the sun was dazzling. The trekkers shifted their backpacks and moved off the ridge line, following a slender trail downward toward the sparse jungle of birch and elder that thickened into a lush green carpet along the valley floor. A rest was proclaimed when they were well within the cool, wet-smelling shade. The packs were dropped gratefully to the ground and the noon rations of leftover *parathas* and aluminum containers of an unappetizing green vegetable mush were sorted out.

"Try to enjoy it," Berren suggested. "It'll be mostly *dal bhat* from here on."

"I'll eat anything that doesn't bite back," Michaelson

quipped, and shoveled in a mouthful with a chunk of the flat bread, "and some things that do."

As he ate, Berren pulled a creased map from the pocket of his jacket and flattened it on the ground. Its ragged edges showed that he had ripped it carefully from a larger sheet.

Michaelson leaned close so he could read it over his shoulder. "Glad to see you bothered to bring one of these things along," he said. "All this time I thought we'd been flying blind."

Billum Singh lit up a *bidi* cigarette and drew a few puffs through his fist. Then he handed it to Berren, who took it absently and inhaled it the same way while he studied the map.

He was bent over it for a long time before Michaelson said: "You're goin' to wear it out, mate."

"Hmmm?"

"The map," Michaelson said. "I'm waitin' to hear how we're doin'."

"Oh. Well, we've got a couple of weeks or so of this; then we'll be in a position to start looking."

"Start looking?"

"Yah. I'm afraid these first few days will be the easy part. Billum Singh and I know this general area pretty well. It's up there . . . I'm worried about. Here, look for yourself." He pointed down at the right-hand corner of the map, then traced a meandering line through details toward the center. The contours of the terrain were delineated by precise curved lines, each showing an elevation of 200 meters. Between each line was a slight gradation in the color. The finger continued until it stopped and tapped the paper at a small area unlike the rounded forms surrounding it. It seemed to be an angular gash of brown an inch long among the almost-white ovals of the high mountains.

"There it is, somewhere in here."

"What is that thing? It looks like some kind of excavation."

"It's part of a geological fault that's supposed to run all through that part of the range, continental drift theory and all that. There's a lot more to it, of course. It might even connect with the one in eastern China, but nobody's been up there to chart much of it. Just that gorge, where it split apart. That's too spectacular to miss, even up there. There's no name on the map, but the mountain people call it Kaligarh."

The Englishman looked impressed.

"But how do you figure this has something to do with your friend Jason?"

Berren pulled his neckerchief off and used it to dab at a greenish blob in the middle of the map. "Remember I told you that he was adopted into a family in the mountains? He said it was up near the border; that's along here. Now I've always figured it must be northeast of Dangra. That's where we'd done most of our trekking before he started coming up here on his own.

"That night, at the Shalimar Gardens Café, when I got hold of Anna, all she could tell me was that he'd found what he was looking for. He was so upset by whatever it was that he took off without even waiting to see her off to Bihar. The only explanation she got out of him was that he was going 'home.' "

"So?"

"Don't you see? The only home Jason knows anymore is with his mountain family. If his search for the heroin factory took him home, then they must be one and the same place. See? No wonder he was so upset. And that place has to be somewhere in here."

Michaelson examined the few square inches Berren was indicating around the map's intersecting creases.

"Within that general area," Berren continued, "is the one place ideal for the purpose of the smugglers. Over the last two hundred years it's sheltered all kinds of clandestine activities, from rebellious rajas to tribal bandits. The terrain and geography leave it isolated, inaccessible, and now, smack in the middle of the no man's land between the Sino-Indian armies. . . . It's got to be here," his finger stabbed at the brown streak on the map, "in the valley of the Kaligarh Fault."

They set a fast pace that afternoon with Berren demanding the maximum distance over the several long stretches of level ground. Then they slipped down through the thickening trees to the valley floor. From above, the jungle had looked more formidable than it turned out to be. The foliage was beginning to show signs of the early mountain autumn and the undergrowth was already yellowing and dry, except along the banks of a slow stream. It was a brittle tangle that presented little resistance to their passing.

They followed the stream out from under the trees to where it sparkled in the sun, and when they left its course several hours later, it was like losing a friend, for the rest of the landscape was beginning to show its more inhospitable features.

What mellowing lush of green trees and thistle grass remained was becoming insignificant against the high crags of rock that reflected the sun's untempered glare.

They had pushed hard through the first valley and climbed over a low but difficult pass into another much longer and wider than the first. It had taken the major part of the afternoon to travel its length to where a sheer wall of rock seemed to bar them from any ready exit.

"I'm good for another hour or two," Michaelson said. "Maybe we should look for a way out."

Berren shook his head. "Billum Singh knows the way; he's been this far before. But it'll wait till morning. My guess is it'll be getting pretty treacherous from now on and twilight makes fancy footwork dangerous business."

So they left the path for the valley floor and the small thicket that grew a few hundred feet out on the narrowing plain of grass and rocks.

Berren knew there were others who occasionally used this part of the trail—mountain folk who would spread the gossip in no time—so they hid their fire in a culvert well within the grove where the smoke would be somewhat dissipated by the foliage.

Billum Singh found the rivulet of a spring among the boulders below the trail and brought the first canteen of cold, sweet water back to the others, who were too exhausted to believe it would be worth getting up for. It was.

The *dal bhat* was hot and spicy, and the tired travelers ate hungrily. When they were done, Berren found a small brown tin in his pack and tossed it to Michaelson, who was nearest the fire.

"Here we go; all the comforts of home."

"Nescafé Instant Coffee," Michaelson read. "So the sahheeb has a weakness, eh?"

"Hey, I brought that stuff all the way from Delhi." Berren laughed. "Don't tell me you're one of those limey tea-sippers."

"Na' me, mate." Michaelson was grinning as he put a pan of water on the coals. "Pleasure first, then queen and country."

Billum Singh was enjoying the exchange. He hadn't understood a word but the foreigners looked like they were having fun. Then something caught his attention from beyond the thicket. He cocked his head as if listening to something off in the southwest.

Berren noticed his attitude. "*Kya bhat hogia,* Billum Singh?"
The boy shook his head slightly as if he weren't sure. The
circle fell silent.

"I don't hear anything," Michaelson offered.

"These mountain villagers usually hear better than we do,"
Berren said. "I'm going for a look-see."

He stood up and walked softly into the grass. The stars were
out, though there was still some light in the sky. All was still
save for the whirr of crickets deep in the grove.

Something felt wrong. A faint disruption in the natural flow
of night sounds. Slowly it became more discernible, and then
he heard it. The rhythmic thumping of blades beating down
on the thin night air.

"Jesus Christ!" Berren whirled and ran to the fire. "Put
this thing out—there's a chopper coming."

He kicked the pan of coffee water over onto the flames and
all three flung handfuls of dirt over what coals remained, then
scrambled across the rocky grass to the cover of the boulders
where they had found the spring.

Their feet were in the mud, and they were crouched low
enough for the spring to trickle over Berren's unlaced boot
tops. He'd lost the sound in the noisy rush and began to doubt
his first impression. But from this point they had an unob-
structed view of the darkening sky, and if it was a helicopter . . .

Then they heard the sound again. The grind of the engine
grew louder, but the sky remained an empty dome. Suddenly
the rhythmic thumping became a deafening, sharp, rapping
noise and a dark shape jumped like a thing of prey over the
ridge directly above their heads.

It was an evil and alien thing, potbellied and insect shaped,
with no running lights nor any other link with humanity. With

139

a remarkable indifference to the dangers of its low altitude, it slid gracefully down the hillside below the surrounding peaks and continued its low course across the valley floor, sending the leaves of the campsite's thickets flying in its wash.

At first it looked as if it would surely crash against the opposite slopes, but at the last moment it lifted itself and leaped sharply over the rim of the valley and disappeared beyond.

No one moved. It was as though the thing could hear them, could spot their movements, though it was now out of sight. While Berren's boot filled with water, they waited until the engines faded entirely and the sounds of the evening had returned.

The Englishman was the first to speak. "There's a bloke who bloody well knows what he's doin'," he said.

Berren stood and shook his soggy foot. "Know anything about those things?" he asked.

"I do," Michaelson said. "That one's flown in 'Nam, I'll wager. The Indians fighting guerrillas up here?"

"That wasn't army," Berren said.

"'I' wasn't?"

"Nope. I didn't see any insignia, no running lights, and I'll bet he was flying low to avoid radar—if there is any up here."

Michaelson looked again at the spot on the ridge line where the helicopter had disappeared.

"Right," he said. "Well, c'mon, mates. Let's see if we can get that coffee heated up again."

The tin mugs were too hot to hold, even by the handles, but nobody seemed to mind. It was a matter of dexterity, lifting the shiny cup from the grass, taking a sip and putting it down quickly, before the pain set in.

"Ever flown in one?" Berren asked.

"Many a time," Michaelson responded with some pride. "Standard transport round the war zone."

"Oh yah? Tell me, how long could they fly like that?"

"This late at night? Let's see—low level like that, half an hour. No more. He's pushin' it thin, as it is."

"Sounds about right. Much longer and he'd have been in real trouble."

"How's that?"

"He'd have flown over the Tibetan frontier."

thirteen

There wasn't much to say once camp was broken the next morning, except a cursory comparison of stiff limbs and knotted muscles that managed to work themselves out after the first few hours of walking.

At the end of the valley the dwindling trail had edged up the steep wall and all but disappeared once it rounded an unexpected break in the solid barrier. After climbing to a higher pass they ran out of trail altogether, and chose what seemed to be the line of least resistance that rounded the mountainside toward the northeast.

By afternoon their options became increasingly limited by the rugged terrain, and Berren opted for the more dependable route furnished by the bed of a fast-flowing stream below them. Its course was straighter than the one they'd followed the day before, and it plunged through its deepening ravine with a roar that only occasionally abated where low waterfalls broke the rapids into quiet pools.

There was a heavy hush beneath the mossy overhangs and a damp, sweet smell to the motionless air, but it held no respite for the sweating trekkers. The bed of the stream was slippery, and sharp stones waited for them at every stumble.

Gradually the ravines began to close in and there were times when they could descend only by clambering down jagged out-croppings, grappling at any obstacle in reach to slow their slide. Now and then the cliffs were so close on either side that the dry bank disappeared and they had to hoist their packs above their heads and wade, waist-deep, along the flow. At last the stream grew quieter, and its eddies were almost completely covered by the strangely intricate water plants and strings of floating foam.

"I don't know which gets it the worst," Berren had a boot unlaced and was searching his insole for some foreign object, "the hands or the feet. You'll see what I mean when we start scaling this rockslide. Hell of it is, there's probably an easier way, this time at least. Around to the south, maybe. Oh, well," he flicked a tiny pebble into the water and began to relace his boot, "at least this way we're pretty well hidden."

"Something to consider, that's sure." Michaelson eased him-self down on the corner of the rock where Berren sat. He sighed in relief and wiped his brow with his sleeve. "I didn't think much of that chopper last night, either. Made me feel like me zip was open. Nothing shows, but it's a bit too exposed for comfort."

Berren gave a snort of tired amusement, then looked around at Billum Singh, who had begun to make his way up the steep slope behind them.

"It's not that I'm worried about," he said, getting to his feet. "It's the Gurkha mercenaries the army uses up here. We get a patrol of those guys on our trail and they'll make that copter seem like Tinkerbell."

Billum Singh led them in a slow, painful zigzag up the face where man-sized boulders clung in piles so sheer that footholds allowed no room for balance. The trekkers had to cling tight against the cold rock, grasping at whatever their fingertips could find.

"Yaha hain." "Here's one." "Got it," as each passed his hand-hold on to the next.

When at last the vertical eased and they'd reached the top, their hands were bruised and bleeding, Billum Singh had a cut below his eye and Berren was nursing a wide scrape across his palm.

"The perils of soft living," Berren said between gasps. He had his sweat-soaked hat off and was wiping the dirt from the wound with the neckerchief he'd wet with spit. "Now if I was still a working man . . ."

Michaelson had let his canteen go and it was sliding away from him. "Watch it!" and Berren grabbed it. He held it up for Michaelson and saw he was in no position to take hold. He was leaning back, his eyes rolling up at the sky, his chest heaving as he gulped in panic at the rarefied air.

"Try to relax—as completely as you can." Berren spoke in breathless phrases. "Your wind will come back—soon enough on its own. The harder you work at it, the worse it seems."

Michaelson scrunched his eyes shut in boyish obedience, but it was several minutes before he could speak. "I'm—all right." He sounded angry.

"Sure, but we'll be a lot higher in a few days. . . . And it'll get worse. So I'm telling you now."

"Hmmmmph."

The nearer mountains that rose above the smaller hills at their feet were themselves dwarfed by a spectacular panorama of the snow-capped Himalayan massif that stretched across the whole of the northern quadrant.

Berren had put his hat on again and pulled it low. It irked Michaelson that he couldn't make out Berren's expression beneath its rim; he wished he could see what the American was looking for. He brushed a few matted strands of hair back from his face and squinted at the rugged horizon.

"Looks empty to me," he said.

"Yah," Berren said, "empty."

It was late afternoon, and the texture and shape of the landscape were harshly delineated by the slanting rays of the sun. There would be several hours yet of usable light, but the lowlands were already lying in the shadows of the surrounding hills.

At first it seemed like the only other living creatures were a harrow of kite hawks that hung suspended in an invisible nearby thermal. Berren watched them for a moment as they widened their effortless circles. They were high out over the valley, yet below the ridge where the three men were resting. As his eyes followed the largest of the birds, which had just broken from the rest in response to some unseen event below, he noticed a thin line of dust along the mountainside far off to the northwest.

"That's odd," he said. He heaved the backpack around and began fumbling about inside.

"Wha's that?" Michaelson asked.

"Something's moving along that hill over there."

"So there are people out there after all. So what?"

"Probably nothing," Berren replied. "Ah, here it is." He'd managed to reach into his camera case without removing it from the pack, and pulled out a leather lens case. He popped the clip and slid a six-inch telephoto lens out onto his palm. There was a second pocket on the bottom from which he drew a smaller lens with an eyepiece.

"Wha's that thing?"

"Found it in a specialty shop in Tokyo a few years back." Berren fitted the eyepiece to the telephoto mount with a twist-snap.

He put the monocular to one eye and sighted with the other along its length while the flying forms of the kite hawks swept at abrupt intervals in and out of the magnified circle. With a twist of the eyepiece the hillside came into focus, but the images at the head of the line of dust were still too small to make out.

"Billum Singh?" Berren handed the monocular to his friend and reminded him of the focusing procedure.

The younger man accepted the problem with some formality and squinted comically through the eyepiece while steadying his elbow on a rock. He had to resight his arm several times before he finally spoke. "Horses, Tommy-ji," he said in Pahari.

"Army?"

"No. Only three or four horses. An army supply caravan would be more."

Berren translated for Michaelson, who reacted with irritation. "So there *is* an easier way."

"That one doesn't count. It's a pretty good trail but it starts from a long way west of here, near Hanli. The army used to use it to supply the troops along the frontier. It's not much good for that anymore. Most of it has fallen into the demilitarized no man's land."

"There's a reason why *we* aren't on horseback, riding along that trail, I suppose?"

"Sure," Berren said. "It would have taken us an entire week just to get to a place where we could pick it up. For another thing, while it's easier traveling, it meanders around in those hills. It would take half again as long to get to wherever it ends up.

"Most important," he emphasized, "is that we are here, sitting on a rock, several miles away, watching. . . ."

"Right," Michaelson said. "I see the point." He stuck his arms into the straps of his pack. "And where do we go from here?"

Berren paused from repacking the monocular. He searched the distance for a moment before aiming a finger at a group of particularly craggy summits on the northeast horizon. "Through them," he said.

"Through them!?"

"Yep, or around them, if we can't find the pass shown on this map."

"How far is it?"

"I'd only be guessing," Berren replied. "For every mile the crow flies up here, it's at least two on the ground."

"Well then," Michaelson shifted his straps over his shoulders, "let's get on with it." He bent forward against the pack's weight and stood up.

Billum Singh set a grueling pace and showed no particular admiration for the other two just because they were able to keep up. For him there was no other world than the never-ending slopes and obstacles that made up the land he called home.

The days that followed blurred over each other, each a feverish chore that dragged them from one campsite to the next. Their eyes were bloodshot, and the straps of their packs seemed to dig deeper into their raw skin each time they hoisted them into place.

Gradually they made their way out of the lower watershed, climbing steadily above the inarticulate tree line through a gap indicated on the map. And beyond it they found only another climb, another pass. But they pressed on, noses and earlobes reddening with altitude, headaches raging and tempers growing short as they tried to sort fact from fiction on Berren's disintegrating map.

Finally, after a long, bone-chilling hike across a bare, wind-swept cornice streaked with rivulets of powdered snow blown down from the looming glacier lands, they were brought to an irrevocable halt.

"Shit!" Michaelson snapped, stamping his feet to get some feeling back into his toes. "Shit," he said again. "Jus' look a' that. You mean that map of yours, that official bloody government map, didn't show this was waiting for us?"

Ahead of them, beyond what should have at last been the real pass, was an endless blanket of morning blue snow climbing skyward among ever higher crags of fissured black rock. It was more than insurmountable; it was a denial of the trekkers' very presence. Against all that, their efforts shrank to pathetic insignificance. Of course Michaelson was mad. It was humiliating.

"Well?"

"Nope," Berren finally said. "None of it." And he looked over at Billum Singh, who had already turned and started back.

They had to retrace half their highland distance, their toes bleeding from the nails and hamstrings inflamed from the erratic downhill pace, before they found a northerly breach. Bitter with the loss of precious time and its cost in provisions, they began a long, circuitous course around the base of the range.

It was several more days before they left the lowland again, and after that it seemed they never stopped climbing. Lank granite peaks were jutting skyward from close by on either side as the party moved on through muffling mists and ground fogs that looked like ominous copies of Chinese watercolors. Now and then thick blankets of clouds, heavy with late rains, flowed past through the depressions below them.

The birch and elder that had enjoyed the moist northern slopes of the first range had long ago been replaced by strangely resinous-smelling firs, increasingly misshapen and dwarfed by altitude.

They were working their way into the snow-capped massif Berren had pointed out in the distance the second day. The perimeter of its outlying glacial tracts, or at least the part that stood between them and the mouth of the pass high above, began with a remarkably sudden step several yards high from its own rock-strewn moraine. Its lower fifty feet were separated from the rest by an icy stream that tumbled out from deep inside the ice.

It was a dirty brown day and a dirty brown field of ice and snow that climbed up into a bank of cold, slow swirling clouds a few hundred feet above their heads.

Berren knew that to grapple their way up the ice and wet of the glacier was to risk serious frostbite, so they bound their hands in strips torn from an old shirt. It was better than nothing, but after a while the sodden cloth slid back from Berren's palm. The wet had loosened its weave and there was no way to retie and still maintain his grip on the slippery ice. He bit the edge near his knuckles and tugged it into place as best he could, then flexed his fingers painfully, one hand at a time, to keep the blood circulating.

At first they hadn't thought all this would be necessary. They had climbed over the foot of the glacier with little trouble, finding holes and footholds easily enough in the rotten ice. But an hour later they found the pass blocked by a tall icy barrier where the snow balled underfoot and the ice under it was glazed and wet.

When he was finally able to struggle over onto the top, he was relieved to find it a flat, even surface that molded solidly against the sides of the rocky crevasse.

Michaelson was right behind him, and sat huffing and puffing while Berren tossed a line down to Billum Singh and began hauling up the packs one at a time.

The mists had cleared and the ceiling had lifted somewhat. For the first time that day they could see far into the distance through the openings between the surrounding mountains.

"We've got to get out of these snow fields," Berren said, testing the line to see if Billum Singh had it tied off. "They're going to slow us down."

"Slow us down?" Michaelson was blowing into his frozen fists. "They'll freeze us solid. Can't believe they've got an army hidden up here."

"Two," Berren said, then called down for Billum Singh to use the line for support as he climbed.

"Two?"

"Huh? Oh," Berren said. "Two armies." He pointed with his chin. "One of those ranges over there marks the frontier with the 'Tibetan Autonomous Region.' That means the Chinese army."

He jerked at the line, helping Billum Singh free it from a snag, and continued hoisting it in until the boy was able to clamber up over the side.

"Yah, they're up here all right, burrowed away, trying to stay warm and hoping nothing'll happen to drag them out and fight."

"Like any good troops," Michaelson snorted. He was in better spirits now, thinking the worst was behind them.

"Speaking of burrowing away," Berren said, "remember that trail, the one we saw the day I pointed this place out? Well, it circles around through the base of those mountains. . . ." His hands were still occupied, so he nodded slightly to the west, " . . . and back below us, down there."

He stopped his adjustments. A portion of the trail was visible from where they stood, and he caught sight of an almost imperceptible glitter, and then a line of dark shapes.

"Hell of a detour," Michaelson was saying.

"Hmmm? Oh, yah." He looked down unhappily at the straps he'd worked so hard to adjust, then shrugged his pack to the ground. "Something's down there," he said as he searched for his monocular. His fingers were stiff and hard to manipulate. They seemed incapable of assembling the eyepiece. It was several minutes before he was able to put it to his eye and sweep its circle along the twists of the distant line. It was another minute before he spoke, and by that time Michaelson had risen to his feet.

"Down on the trail again?" he asked.

"Yah. Billum Singh"—Berren switched to Pahari—"how many horses did we see on that trail last week?"

"Three or four, Tommy-ji." Billum Singh had caught the drift of his friend's interest. "Why?"

"Because I think that's them down there," he said. "Whoever

they are, they're only a few days behind us, so they must be traveling hard, maybe even at night, to cover that much distance. That is . . ." he took the glass from his eye, "if they're the same three or four horses."

"Who else?" Billum Singh asked.

Berren explained the sighting in English for Michaelson and was surprised by his reaction. The Englishman was plainly upset. He turned away and screwed up his eyes in the direction of the other trail and then began pacing around, checking the view from various angles and mumbling under his breath as Berren handed him the eyepiece. It was as if he were party to some special foreboding that the others had been spared.

"Hey, relax," Berren said. "They're down there and we're up here."

"Right," he said. "That's right, i'n't it? They're down there." He took a minute longer, though there was nothing more to see after the first glimpse. Like Berren, he alternated his observation between the monocular and the naked eye as if to reaffirm the great distance.

"Any idea who they might be?" he asked. "Army? Locals?"

Berren shook his head. "I doubt if they're either one. Billum Singh says they're not likely to be army, and the locals don't keep horses. Not enough to feed them up here. But I wouldn't worry about it too much. They're approaching the demilitarized zone, and they'll be picked up by the patrol pretty soon now. When that happens, we won't be seeing them again."

"No? How's that?"

"Same as us. They aren't army and they aren't locals. That makes them outsiders, and outsiders are assumed to be either provocateurs or involved in some kind of espionage."

"Espionage!" Michaelson's face lit up with a wide grin. "A

bunch of spies? Oh, there's a bleedin' justice!" and he allowed himself a short burst of ironic laughter.

The joke was obviously his own, and Berren looked quizzically to his Indian friend, whose own face was creased with a pleased smile. It was nice to see his foreign friends enjoying themselves.

fourteen

Michaelson had been wrong: The worst was far from over. Berren tried to tell himself that's what was bothering the Englishman. He was just irritated by the prospect of more difficult days ahead.

Ever since the break on the foot of the glacier he seemed possessed by the dynamics of their mission. He had dropped any pretense of ambiance, and in its place had acquired an infuriating persistence in nagging and prodding the other two to greater speed and the risks it involved.

The way through the pass would have tested the skills of a mountain goat; it was the wrong place for this change in character. Beyond the glacial barrier was a deep gorge carved by the same stream that flowed through the ice and fell, unseen, into the ravine.

There was nothing for them but to follow the levels and shallow ledges that clung at a dizzy height just below the crest of the gorge's high wall. There was evidence, there, of a path. Almost hidden by years of disuse, it was often little more than an indentation in the sheer face, or a foothold where they could balance only long enough to jump to the next ledge. And through it all was the thick hiss of the glacial stream far below.

Despite his own insistence on caution, Berren was being pressured into risks that he considered unjustified. He didn't like it. And he didn't like the prospect of Michaelson needling him for the rest of the trek with his damn "Let's ge' on wi' it," or "Pick i' up, mate, can't you?"

He'd have had to put up with it, though, being pressed along the brink of disaster, but for an incident that put the fear of God back into the Englishman's heart.

It happened the morning of the third day in the pass. They'd spent the night roped to the rocks to keep from slipping over the side in their sleep, and, with no fuel for a fire, started off groggy and hungry in the morning.

After an hour or so the trail split; one part continuing along the face of the cliff while the other wove inland through a level in the sheer stone slabs.

"Straight line's always shortest," Michaelson said. " 'T's a matter of geometry. See there, that one doubles back on itself."

"Yah, but that ledge has been getting worse every step," Berren said. "This one'll have to straighten out eventually."

"Eventually isn't good enough, is it?" Michaelson demanded, and he started off toward the cliff before anything more could be said. For a while it seemed Michaelson had been right. Though it showed no signs of a path, the ledge was gradually widening and its grade seemed to be leveling slightly, when suddenly it all came to an end. Ahead was nothing but a chaotic tangle of rope and woven strands of fibrous vine.

"It's a sling." Berren leaned around Michaelson for a better look. "Kind of a combination bridge and scaffold that connects this ledge with another that must be just around that outcropping." He plucked experimentally at one of the vines. "Well, that's that. Let's head back for the path."

"Wha' d'ya mean, head back? You said yourself there must be a ledge around . . ."

"Are you blind? That thing hasn't been used in years. Look at that hemp, it's black with age and the strands are splitting. And those vines won't hold much; they must be as brittle as match sticks.

"On top of that you don't even know what it's like on the other side."

"Look, mate, this ain't a parish picnic; we've got to keep moving. It's sturdy enough. Look here, that hawser's as thick as me fist." Michaelson was adamant. "It was built here because this is the way, right? And if the rest of the path is around the bend there, that's enough for me. I'm not backtracking a day out of m' way just because you're afraid of heights."

"It's not worth the risk," Berren began angrily. "If you . . ."

"An' I'm tellin' you it is worth the risk. Now, if the Great White Hunter is afraid, he can just stay behind with his schoolboy chum and I'll prove it for him. If it'll hold my weight, I'm sure you'll find it solid enough for you two." And he stepped around the knot onto the supporting strand.

It seemed to be holding well enough as he bent low, grasping the hand lines as he shuffled cautiously along the heavy rope at the bottom of the V.

Berren was afraid to speak. It would do no good to point out the thirty-pound pack that Michaelson hadn't thought to leave behind, so he held his breath, listening to the groans of the aging twists and knots.

Michaelson had almost reached the outcropping when some-where in the structure a knot let loose with a pop and all three froze. He waited wide-eyed for a moment, but its impor-tance was not readily apparent, so he took another step.

It was this slight motion that made the damage show itself. From the other end, out of sight around the rocks, the raveled end of the heavy bottom cable snaked out into view and dangled in a limp swing beneath the Englishman. The entire flimsy web shifted abruptly, dropped, and caught. In the jerk, Michael-son's foot shoved the broken support rope away, and he lifted it instinctively and kicked it into the loose woven vines. It held, but with the shift of his weight his other leg split through the weave on the other side of the *V* and he slid through to his knee.

"Hold it," Berren shouted. "Don't move!"

"I *can't* move," Michaelson shouted back. "I can't . . ." and he leaned forward, only to produce another loud pop from around the outcropping. He didn't move again. He just clung there, staring down into the gorge.

Berren was cursing aloud as he ran his eye along the slope of the cliff above. Then he pointed out the irregularities in the cliff over the outcropping to Billum Singh, who nodded, picked up his pack, and started back.

Berren tried to sound reassuring. "Okay, now, just hold on and don't move; we're going to try to get you from above." And he turned to follow Billum Singh back along the path.

It was another twenty minutes before they reappeared. Berren was first. He'd left his pack behind and was hugging against the steep slope, agonizing over each toehold until he had passed over the spot where Michaelson dangled. He spent a moment examining the far end of the sling from above, and moved back again. Then he cautiously lowered himself down to the shelf atop the outcropping. While Billum Singh eased himself down beside him, Berren untied the coils of rope from his belt, wound one end around his wrist, and handed the rest to the boy. He lay down on his stomach, facing out over the gorge, wrapped his arm around a lump in the rock, and nodded to Billum Singh. The boy lowered himself, slowly skidding over the jagged surface until it was too steep to hold him, then let the rope tighten around his wrist. He lay facedown, trying to flick the end of the line back around the outcropping to where Michaelson could get hold of it.

"All right now," Berren called. "The problem is to free your leg without disturbing the structure too much. You might as well keep going, the sling is attached just the other side of the point, it's nearer to where you are. The hand lines look like they're still connected at that end, but keep hold of the rope anyhow; I don't know how strong they are. Billum Singh'll have to hold you till the angle's taken up and I'll be holding him. Got it?"

Michaelson didn't move.

"Now don't, *don't* try to climb up or you'll pull us all off."

Billum Singh needed a few more inches. He kicked until he had gained a foothold, then pushed himself forward for a cleaner toss of the rope, showering Michaelson with loose pebbles in the process.

"Okay, there it is. Right above you," Berren said as the line caught in a small furrow. "Look up. It's above your head."

Michaelson looked up. Then he forced his hand to let loose of the vines and reach up.

"Stretch," Berren called. "Stretch for it. We're as far as we can go."

Michaelson stretched and caught the line; there was a groan from the shuddering structure as he eased his weight onto the free leg and the strap and a ripping of cloth as he pulled the other leg free. He chose his next step and took it, pulling the boy painfully against the sharp corner of the outcropping. Another step and he was around the tip. Only two or three more to the safety of the other ledge—and they were the worst.

The rope straightened and lost the friction of the small furrow, putting most of Michaelson's weight on the boy and pulling him into an almost horizontal spread-eagle. The vine webbing had come to an end, and without the main foot rope there was no place for Michaelson's feet but the straining hand lines. He put his foot on the outside line and took a step. The structure twisted against this new center of gravity. Billum Singh gasped with pain as Michaelson fought for his balance by yanking the line. The angle was no good, so Michaelson let go and leaped for the ledge.

The pack struck the wall and tried to pull him over the edge, but his hand caught the sling's support knot, and held.

Billum Singh shifted his grip and his feet slipped out from under him, but with both hands he was able to pull himself to safety.

It was several hours before they found a new way around to where Michaelson was sitting. By that time, he had regained most of his composure; though, he remained diplomatically silent as they followed the ledge down away from the pass.

"Well, I was right in one thing, at least," he finally said, trying out his grin. "You must admit it was the fastest way."

Berren wasn't amused. He unslung his pack and sat down while Billum Singh moved on down the hill to look for an elusive landmark. "Takes a while for you to catch on, doesn't it?" Berren said. "You almost got us killed back there, and for what? You're not equipped to second-guess the way, and whatever's eating at you, it's not worth risking my neck or Billum Singh's. So from now on *you* do what *we* say and forget whatever record you're trying to break."

"You can quit the lecture." Michaelson was angry again. "It would have been the right way if you'd helped out in the first place instead of waitin' to play superman. Wa' ya' expect me to do now? Bow down and act 'umble just because I needed a hand from tha' wog chum of yours?"

Berren tried to control his temper. "I could stand up," he said carefully. "Right now. I could stand up and I could walk through that split in the rocks over there, and you'd never find us again. So don't you ever use that word again, and if you give either of us any more lip after what Billum Singh went through to save your ass, then count on it; we'll just leave you here."

Michaelson was avoiding Berren's glare. The wilderness that surrounded them was desolate and dangerous, the magnitude of the threat was clear.

Its position was clearly indicated on the map, give or take a few miles, a few uncharted obstacles, and they knew they would be able to reach it sometime this morning.

They had broken camp only a few hours earlier and soon found themselves moving along a narrow gap between the hillsides. There appeared to be no other route through these hills, yet what path they could pick out seemed to be strangely untrodden, constantly blending away among patches of grass, greened again at these lower levels.

Their pace gradually quickened with expectancy and with the myopic claustrophobia of the closing passage. At last the way became so narrow that the trekkers were forced to shed their backpacks and hand them through to Billum Singh, who was the first to accomplish the squeeze to the other side.

"Good thing I've lost some weight."

Michaelson had spent the last several days trying, with the restraints of pride, to ingratiate himself back into Berren's good graces. "Otherwise I'd have to strip naked to make it through this one, eh?" He waited, but there was no response from the two on the other side. "I said . . ." he began to repeat as he eased his way through the split. Then he forgot his joke and joined the others in their stunned silence.

It was awesome. A vast, yawning canyon whose sheer southern edge plunged into the void a few precarious feet from where they squatted.

The bright midmorning sunlight made the snowy peaks beyond a dazzling white against the impossibly blue sky; a blue that reflected up from twisting ribbons of water running through the otherwise dark depths.

Its vertical granite-gray walls fell away from a gently rolling plateau in a long, unnaturally straight precipice, as if hewn by some magical feat of intelligent force. Yet the fields on either side flowed north and south from its edges in a soft, lush green that the trekkers hadn't seen since they left the pasturelands of the lower range.

On either side of the great chasm were the first signs of man they had seen for several days—unkempt rectangles of abandoned fields, ruptured terraces, and a few derelict houses.

Their own side, lower than the other and lower still than the ledge where they sat, maintained a patchwork of fields stretching southward up to where they contoured into the steepening base of the surrounding peaks. Their tidy edges and the evenness of their distant textures showed the benefit of human attention.

"My Christ, what a gash." Michaelson was the first to break the spell. "So this is what you called the Kaligarh Fault. It looks like an old drawing I've seen somewhere."

"Dante," Berren answered. That had been his first thought. "As for the name, it applies to the whole valley, not just the gorge. 'Vale of Kaligarh, house of Kali, goddess of death and destruction,' " he said as he started searching through his gear for the monocular. "The British lost a whole punitive expedition in the 1800s. The few who managed to get here were thrown over the side by the local bandit raja. The name cropped up sometime after that. A little joke, maybe, by the locals."

Michaelson shook his head. "Strange humor, the locals," he said.

"And long memories," Berren replied.

"Anybody there, mate?"

Berren lay on his stomach, braced on his elbows, studying the details across the gorge through the monocular.

"Chinese," he answered.

"You can see them?"

"No, not them. But there're a few ruins over there that look surprisingly well made. They might be light artillery emplacements."

"That mean anything to us?"

"Well, no man's land or not, it sure as hell means there's something on our side worth shooting at."

Berren laid the eyepiece down long enough to puff on the *bidi* that Billum Singh handed him. They exchanged a few comments in Pahari, and Michaelson noted that the mountain boy seemed as impressed as the other two.

Berren turned his attention to the other side of the fault. After a moment or two he said, "Uh-huh, there they are," and handed the eyepiece to the Englishman. "Up there, above the terraces on that middle hillside. Looks like Indian army patrols. Probably Gurkhas. No wonder everybody's jumpy up here," he said. "The Chinese over there, the Indian army wandering around, both within sight of one another. I bet every time they let loose another volley in Ladakh, they all start arming their mortars up here."

"Still," Michaelson suggested, "it'd be a neat trick to charge across that canyon."

"Yah," Berren replied, "that's probably what keeps 'em holy."

When the line of sepoys finally filed away out of sight, the trekkers made their way down to the fields to search out a more secure hiding place. They found it in a dry creek bed that ran behind a single large boulder covered with a deeply chiseled Sanskrit inscription. Around it grew a clump of tall, broad-leafed plants that tangled together overhead in a shady tunnel.

In a few minutes they had caught their breaths, and Berren hunched close to Billum Singh for a quiet conference. They always left Michaelson out of these discussions, and when he asked for a translation he was given only a perfunctory summary. He had the feeling he was being kept in the dark by design and he didn't like it.

The huddle went on for a long time before both were satisfied. Billum Singh put down his knapsack and left the cover carefully. Berren watched as he rounded a boulder and disappeared over a nearby hillock, then crawled deeper into the foliage.

"He's gone off to see what he can find," Berren explained. "He stands a better chance than two white-faced foreigners."

"Took you two all that time to come up with that?"

"There were other things," Berren said. "Details."

It had grown late. Another patrol had passed, a rowdy bunch by the sounds of it, laughing and jostling within a few hundred yards of the hollow where the foreigners hid.

The sun was setting and the customary chorus of crickets signaled the night shift, and the nocturnal animals had begun their turn at foraging.

Two large animals came close, the first disturbing its way through the tall grass, snorting methodically as it searched. The second turned out to be Billum Singh.

"Well?" Berren asked. But Billum Singh was in a playful mood, smiling and refusing to say anything until prodded by his anxious friend.

"Here is Dev Lal Bahadur," he said at last, then realized he was standing there alone. He turned and waved to someone who appeared from behind a cluster of leaves.

The newcomer advanced with an air of caution, but despite his reluctance he was not shy in his bearing. He was a serious young man, fairer than Billum Singh and slightly Mongol in his features, with a topknot braided once on the back of his head. He was wrapped in a blanket patterned in faded brownish tones, which he had flung over his left shoulder so that it hung from him like a cape.

In spite of the roughness of the terrain, he was barefoot, and his hands were thick and powerful as he lifted them free of the blanket and placed palms together in a formal greeting. There was warmth in his dark eyes, but the face itself showed nothing.

"Dev-sahib knows our friend and will take us to him," Billum Singh explained.

"When?"

Billum Singh shrugged. "Whenever you wish," he said.

"Good! Thank God!" Berren was jubilant. "Billum Singh, you are a marvel," he said in English. "You've done it again."

"What's this?" Michaelson was ready to join the celebration. "What's he say?"

"He's taking us . . . oh, damn, we'll have to wait till dark. Ask him, Billum Singh, is it a difficult trail in the dark?"

Both Indians wobbled their heads noncommittally.

"It will be easy for him, Tommy-ji, he knows the way well," Billum Singh said. Then, as either an explanation or an afterthought, he added: "He is Jason's brother."

For the first couple of hours they climbed steadily along a zigzag path until it reached a shelf of sheer bluffs high above the terraced fields. At this point the path disappeared and Dev Lal struck off to the east along their rock-strewn base.

A crescent moon was beginning to show itself, and its glow combined with the brilliant clouds of stars to bathe the valley in a pale cerulean light.

The great fault followed their progress from below, an incongruous black pit amid the mounds of blue fields.

It was several more miles before the party found another path which wound along the top of a steep precipice, deeper into the shadow of the bluffs. Each man was forced to keep a careful eye on the small span of ground that would mark his next footfall, so it was no wonder Berren was startled when a tall, shadowy figure seemed to appear suddenly before them, motioning them to halt.

The stranger also wore a blanket. It was draped over his head with the ends flung over his shoulders to effect a monklike cowl that hid his face in shadow. The hand that emerged from the folds gestured for silence, then pointed up to the overhang of rocks above them.

As if on cue, the sound of voices reached them. Soldiers! They held their breaths, eyes round, trying to make something out of the dark. From above them came an exchange spoken in the harsh staccato of Punjabi; then blessed laughter.

They were still safe.

They waited for the footsteps above them to drift away, then hurried after their new guide, a phantomlike figure that was favoring one leg, though it affected his speed not a bit. For half an hour they seemed to be literally chasing the stranger until they reached a more gradual slope. There they left the path altogether, stumbling through the upper perimeter of the fields and working their way down the gradating terraces toward a small compound of stone and mud-brick buildings, hunched together within a low wall of loose fieldstones. It couldn't really be called a village. There were only two or three family groups, judging from the arrangement, each with its thatched main house and outbuildings.

They rounded the perimeter wall and crouched beside the gate while their guide moved into the compound alone, silently inspecting the area for signs of outsiders. The only sign of life was a dog that began to bark from the opposite end of the compound.

The phantom signaled them from a narrow passage past the first buildings. They moved inside and trotted over to where he had been, only to find that he was already at the end of the alleyway, hardly to be seen in the shadows.

When they finally reached him, he had his blanketed ear to the door, listening. A light that had showed through a small split in the planks was extinguished as the other two approached. The guide rapped quietly, and the door was opened from within. They stepped into the dark, smoky room and someone closed the door behind them.

A match was struck and moved to a small oil lamp on a table near the door.

"Sorry I had to meet you halfway like that. Broke my leg a while back, and it still tires easily." He spoke in stateside English while the wick caught the flame and filled the room with its light. "Should have known you'd show up somehow."

He unwrapped the blanket, and the cowl dropped back to reveal a dark, angular face with high cheekbones and eyes that glowed, coal black, beneath his heavy brows. His hair was long and curled in such a way as to almost hide the small black braid tied up from the back of his head.

"Hello, Jason," Berren said.

fifteen

Jason blew the wobbly oil flame from the lamp so that Berren could open the door a crack to let in some air. The moon had gone down, they had been talking for hours, quietly, to keep from disturbing the boys who were curled up together on one of the *charpoi* cots, and smoking *bidis* until Berren's eyes began to smart.

It was a strange reunion, spent untangling the intrigues that had led each to this place. And they spoke of Anna, of course, carefully neuterizing themselves in the name of objectivity, and leaving private insights unspoken. There was no way to allay the guilt they shared, nor did they try. When the talk turned to earthier things—to Cummings, to the riot, and the life in this pocket of the mountains—Anna was not mentioned again. But she was there.

It took a while for Berren to get around to a short account of the trek.

"Nothin' to i', eh?" Michaelson had propped himself up against the pile of backpacks on the nearest *charpoi*. "Why, you make i' sound like a ruddy stroll in the park."

"It was no stroll for me, I'll tell you," Jason said. "I headed up here with a bellyful of righteous indignation. Adolescent as hell, but beautiful."

"Very good," Berren said, without letting his amusement show. "So then you go and break a leg and screw everything up."

"Yah. Managed to pull a rockslide down on myself. Really dumb. I remember I thought it had passed, so I stood up and got hit by a chunk that was still airborne. Lucky it didn't take me over the side with it." Jason struck another match and warmed the end of a fresh *bidi* and Berren opened the door another inch. "Anyhow, I tried to make a splint, but that was ridiculous. So I just started crawling. I kept passing out, but I was only a day or so southwest of here. Luckily I was found by some valley people, and not our so-called soldier boys. My family here took good care of me, and I'd have been away from here months ago if the leg hadn't gone gangrenous. I was delirious most of the time, but I can still remember the stink."

Berren gave an incredulous half whistle. "Jesus, man, how'd they keep you alive?"

"Damned if I know," Jason replied. "I keep getting the feeling I wasn't here. . . . Anyhow, it was touch and go until a month or so ago."

"How are you now?"

"All right, I guess. There's still some pain, but for the last few weeks I've been getting around well enough."

"Noticed that. I had a hell of a time keeping up with you getting here."

"Sorry about that," Jason said, and looked for a moment out the door. "There's a sort of curfew in the valley, and the so-called soldier boys are pretty nasty about enforcing it."

"You keep calling them 'so-called' . . ."

"That, my friend," he lifted a finger and winked as if he were about to impart the answer to a remarkable riddle, "is because they aren't."

"Aren't what?"

"Aren't army."

"C'mon, I saw them!"

"What did you see?" Jason leaned forward for the answer.

"I saw, let's see . . . I saw their uniforms," Berren replied.

"What else . . . ?"

"Just the uniforms, come to think of it."

"Exactly. And that's all the proof these valley people need. Actually, they're a pretty ratty bunch, nothing like the *puka* sepoy the Indian army's so proud of. Punjabis, most of them."

"But that's unbelievable." Berren left the door and sat on his heels against the wall, his face vacant as he thought through the ramifications. "If they're not army, who the hell are they? And where's the real thing? And the Chinese . . . !"

"Ah, yes. And then there're the Chinese." Jason leaned back on his *charpoi* and folded his good leg in front of him. "Tommy, m'boy, it's a grand plot. But I'll have to answer it a point at a time. First, the Chinese. Well, that's easy. They'd assumed the territory north of the fault by the time the fighting sputtered out and that, as you suspected, is where they sit today, watching everything down on this side, no doubt, though nobody's actually seen them.

"As for the Indian army, they were told to give the *Chin wallahs* plenty of room so they couldn't claim provocation and start something again. That puts the Indians eight or ten miles that way, as the vulture flies." He pointed vaguely southward. "Dug into the second ridge of mountains past these; and it puts us in the middle of a no man's land." He paused to relight his forgotten *bidi.*

"There was no agreement, you understand," he said in between puffs, "it's just where everyone happened to settle in.

"Now you have a strip of land that's off limits to everyone," he said, waving the little smoldering cone for emphasis. "A vacuum. I don't have to tell you that nature, especially human nature, abhors a vacuum. So enter the bad guys who can use it best. Here's all this land with nothing but three or four hundred farmers and nobody else to bother them; where they can come and go at will. What a setup!

"All they need is a steady flow of experienced mountain smugglers who can run the gauntlet along the frontier from the Burma border with nine or ten kilos of opium cakes each. So it takes each porter a couple of months; that's okay. They're cheap, and there's plenty of time.

"Now, farther west of the vale it's a different story, but by then it's been processed down to a few ounces each, and even you or I could get that through."

"But what about these uniforms and the Chinese?"

"Well, let's see," Jason went on. "The smugglers had two big problems to solve. One was that it wasn't enough just to occupy and set up operations here. They had to keep visitors out—people like you and me—and they needed everything kept quiet enough so that the real army wouldn't be forced to risk coming in here to investigate. To accomplish all this they needed total authority over the valley and everyone in it. What better way than to convince everybody that *they* were the army! Who around here would know the difference? So they dressed their henchmen in uniforms, armed them to the teeth with

171

weapons also smuggled in from Southeast Asia, and declared martial law."

Berren stared back at him, unblinking.

"It may sound crazy but it isn't," Jason insisted. "These are simple people here; the uniform is enough to convince them. Even if it weren't, the real army is a long way away and it's worth a man's life to try to leave the vale. These guys are a bloodthirsty bunch; you're damn lucky to have gotten in yourselves," and Jason paused to relight his *bidi* again.

"Now then, the Chinese. Well, what are they to think? There's no reason to trust the unilateral declaration by India that created this demilitarized zone. Why should they, when nobody trusts theirs?

"The proof that this skepticism was well founded comes a few months after the fighting, when they start seeing uniformed Indians patrolling the southern side of the valley again. Still, they don't make a fuss. They just sit up there on those cliffs and watch.

"No doubt they're irritated as hell, but even if they knew what this bunch was really up to, they're not about to do anything about it. Any action at all could upset the balance and some Peking desk general might just issue orders that would send the People's Army over the edge of that fault like lemmings.

"No doubt the Indians feel the same way; they do their best to pretend this valley isn't even here. They don't want to know anything but it's artillery quadrants. Nobody wants to force the other's hand, so here we sit in the middle of limbo while those bastards have the run of the field."

It was daybreak and they began to hear the familiar sounds of village life. There was a well nearby and the women were babbling and laughing as they turned the morning chore into the social event of the day. The device that lifted the bucket from the water squeaked rhythmically under the strain of each turn.

"These villagers are probably already dying of curiosity," Jason said. "But we're lucky. Most of them are related to the Bahadur clan, so if we don't make ourselves too obvious, they'll try to ignore our presence here as long as they can.

"Just remember, as long as we're here they're all in danger. If we get caught, or if there's any trouble, you can kiss this whole bucolic scene good-bye. Some of the local villagers farther up the valley tried a local version of Gandhi's policy of noncooperation. Their reward was a couple of hand grenades in their meetinghouse."

"Nice bunch," Berren noted.

"And well armed, so watch yourself."

"This is all most interesting, I'm sure," Michaelson had had little to say until now, "but I work for Mr. P. K. Sharma, not the U.N., and he'll want facts and hard evidence before 'e makes his move. What I want to know is wha' about the 'factory,' where's the base of their operations? I can't go back without proof."

"Yes," Jason responded. "Yes, I was getting to that.

"An hour and a half northeast of here there's a sixteenth- or seventeenth-century ruin, sitting on its own rock right out over the gorge. It's quite a sight. No telling who built it originally; probably changed hands a dozen times between the Rajputs and the Gurkha warlords. When I first came to the vale, six years ago, it was a Lamaistic Buddhist monastery."

"That's odd," Berren interrupted. "I thought these people were Brahmanical Hindu."

"They are, but . . ."

"Wha' *about* it?" Michaelson urged impatiently.

"You can imagine I haven't been able to get around too much until recently. When I was finally able to scout it out, I found that it had changed hands again. The monks and *sadhus* are out, and the soldier boys are in."

"And you think that's it?"

"That's got to be it," Jason answered. "The damn thing just sits out there, all by itself, with the smugglers' trail running along the floor of the fault right under its feet. They can make the stuff up in the monastery, then send it back down into the fault where nobody can even get to them. They probably take it all the way to the western end, near Jagat-ki Dar and out over some of the old smuggling trails. You'll see what I mean. We'll go take a look at it later."

"Yah," Berren agreed. "Good idea." He felt exhaustion creeping in. "Later."

She was a delightful old woman. Or maybe not so old. It was hard to tell, for the wrinkles on her wide, reddish, almost Tibetan face showed the strains of her life, not her age. They also showed her joy, for it was plain that she smiled often. And there was something else, a surprising thing to find on such a handsome, friendly old face. On her forehead, from eyebrow to hairline, was a puckering pink scar. She was Jason's adopted mother and he introduced her with extravagant formality, listing her names and genealogy while the old woman beamed and chided him for his foolishness.

She uncovered a huge pot of curried goat meat she'd hauled in from the cook room and Dev Lal was sent back for a pile of heavy-grained rice while she stayed to fuss over her hungry guests.

". . . so I told Peta-ji that I'd put up the niece's dowry.

Of course he wouldn't hear of it. Not honorable. You listening?"

"Huh? Yah, sure." Berren looked up from his plate. "Her dowry, I heard."

"Thought you might be flaking out, like your friend there."

"Eh?" Michaelson came out of his private thoughts suddenly. "Oh, I'm just nervous, that's all. When do we get a look at this monastery place?"

"It'll be safe enough in an hour," Jason said. "Enough light to get there and take a look, and dark for a safe trip back." He was glad to drop the subject; he wasn't sure he liked this fellow. "Well, Tommy-ji," he brightened, "did I hear you mention a tin of coffee?"

sixteen

The carpet of grassy tufts swirled closer until the cold gust of wind was upon them. Those who'd thought to bring their blankets clutched them tighter.

There was a patrol below them. They watched until it was out of sight and then crept down the slopes to a knoll which was topped with a tall piling of weathering boulders.

The last light had gone from the depths of the gorge for hours, but the stolid walls of the ancient monastery continued, somehow, to hold their glow for some time longer. Jason hadn't said enough. It was much more than "quite a sight." It was a feat of construction as remarkable as the freak of nature it perched above.

Up to this point the massive gorge had been traveling in unnaturally straight runs, each varying only slightly from the next in an east-by-northeasterly direction. Below them now the course took an acute shift and angled suddenly back on itself, then back again, behind and to the right of the knoll where the foreigners lay, returning to its easterly course again as it closed toward the high northern massif, the last and most terrible barrier before the Tibetan plateau.

Aeons of erosion and geological tension had caused the tip of the easternmost promontory to break away from the India side and stand by itself, an abandoned spire of rock high above the riverbed. It must have stood that way a million years or more before some element of mankind, forgotten in the centuries since, sought safety or seclusion in its remoteness, and began the ages of labor that had at last crowned the pinnacle with an edifice of its own.

Berren had seen others of its kind before. Often enough they had been equally remote and serene within the majesty of the surrounding mountains. And, like the others, this one had served many purposes. It may have spent long periods of its history harboring holy men in monastic seclusion, but others had used its sanctuary to different ends.

While it was true that through the ages some monastic orders had been forced to fight for their survival, this was less a monastery than it was a feudal fortress. Its shape was harsh, yet its construction was anything but crude. Even with the distorted perspective of Berren's monocular, one could follow the subtle curves its ancient builders had wrought as the geometry of the walls adjusted at their base to the contours of the spire.

The outer walls of the structure towered above the rim of the fault with only a few narrow openings set deep in the thick stonework near the top of its otherwise featureless bulwarks. A squat battlement of round-topped merlons ran the length of its parapet, interrupted at the eastern end by two blunt, featureless turrets. At the center of the wall, between the turrets, was a wide-vaulted archway that must have been hiding the main gate in its shadows.

Beyond it, on the other side of the emptiness, its dark, smooth wall rising high above the monastery, higher still than the boulders where the four lay watching, was the China side, mute and mammoth—a quarter of a mile away.

There was another cold gust, and Berren tensed and stretched the muscles of his torso, trying to control the shivering that was disturbing his eyepiece.

"Now, take a look at that far side," Jason said, "the tip there, on the western end."

"Yah, I see it. Looks like the bow of a ship."

"Hm, guess it does at that," Jason mused. "Now, off to the left a little."

Berren shifted slightly as Jason dropped his head to compensate for the differing viewpoint. "See those uprights?"

"No . . . yes, wait a minute, I see something." The flat surface of the spire came to a point a hundred yards past the eastern walls of the monastery. Near the tip he could just make out a small construction of roughhewn timber clutching to the inside edge of the rock, holding two ten- or twelve-foot logs upright. Fastened somehow to the surface behind them were several strands of heavy rope that ran to the top of each log, then arched gracefully out over the abyss and disappeared into the darkness beneath the edge of the southern cliff.

"Yep, I see it. A footbridge."

"And a damn sturdy one, I'd bet," Michaelson added.

"You'd be right," Jason assured. "That's the first change in the place I noticed when I was up and around again. The monks had no use for such niceties. There's a trail that spirals down around the rock to the floor of the fault, and since they didn't have much use for the outside world, that's all they ever bothered to use.

"Of course before they acquired the place, the various rajas probably had some such configuration, too. So when I heard our smugglers had taken over the place, I came down for a look, and sure enough, they'd rebuilt the thing. I guess they use it so those damn patrols can get back and forth and control the people in the vale."

"What'd they do with the monks?" Berren asked. "Skip it. I guess that's a silly question."

"Yah, silly. I found some farmers who said they had once seen a pile of maroon-colored cloth lying at the base of the rock. No one could get down close enough to see if the owners were still wearing them.

"Anyhow, the trail runs along the riverbed, so the porters must use the spiral path up to deliver the opium and down the same way with the processed heroin. The light's bad, but you can just see it circling down under the bridge.

"Speaking of light," he continued, "if you're going to get your photos, you'd better do it now. Or is it already too late?"

"No, got some high-speed stuff. It'll work fine in this light."

Berren uncased his camera and adjusted the f-stop against the minimum shutter speed possible until the needle began to wobble at the right of the viewfinder screen. "All I have to do is note the film speed," he said. After a few shots, bracketing in the lay of the terrain, he disassembled the monocular back to its status as a telephoto lens, and twist-snapped it into the camera's mount.

He had just advanced another frame of film when they heard a loud *hssst*, from the boulder above them. Billum Singh had dropped to his knees, hissing and waving with his palms down.

When he'd caught their attention, he hurriedly pointed up the valley, then retreated from sight, back into his hiding place.

Michaelson had started to his feet for a better look, but Jason pulled him down again, and they tumbled back into the weeds.

"Here! What's this?"

"Shut up!" Jason said. "There's a patrol scouting along the edge down there to the right."

"So what? They're way down there. . . ."

"And there'll be another on a parallel search above us," he whispered fiercely. "I know how they work. Just keep back out of sight until they've both passed; and for God's sake be quiet."

Jason was right. This time there were no voices to warn them, only a few pebbles dislodged from the upper slopes rattled past them into the grass.

When they had passed, Jason leaned close to Berren.

"What's the time?" he whispered.

"Ten to eight."

"Remember that. If it's the same time tomorrow night, we can assume they've got a schedule."

They waited for a few minutes longer before returning to the edge of the knoll. Berren got a few more shots as the squad from the high path snaked down the hillside and joined the others. There was a moment more while the "soldiers" seemed to compare notes, then they moved to the edge and filed carefully through a small clump of scrub trees a short distance from the footbridge, and disappeared over the side. The last one hesitated, took a last look around, then allowed the trees to spring together again as he followed the others. It was as if they had never been there.

"Curiouser and curiouser," Berren muttered, squinting into

the fast-gathering darkness at the piny scrub.

"You won't find anything there," Jason suggested. "They'd be heading back toward the bridge. There's an inclining ledge leading to it underneath the lip of the cliff. That way the old rajas had plenty of warning of any intruders before they could get to the bridge itself."

"Yep. There they are now," Berren said and snapped off a few more frames as the line of men trod warily out along the swaying bridge.

They waited and watched late into the night, but, with no signs of any late patrols, they finally headed back to the compound.

The head of the Bahadur household was as weathered and ageless as his wife. His features were less Mongol than hers, and with his high cheekbones and a pair of quick black eyes, he could easily have passed for Jason's real father.

Jason was surprised to see him. He'd gone to Jagat-ki Dar, a tiny shamble of houses where his cousin lived at the farther end of the vale, beyond the point where the trekkers had found their entrance, and he hadn't been expected back for several more days.

The older man tried to behave formally in the presence of such important guests, but was happier to let his stepson host the occasion. It was enough to just sit and listen, though he didn't understand a word, and it was easy to see that the big yellow-haired man was not pleased.

"I just think you're all being too damn cautious," the man was saying, "that's all. It seems to me we could just sneak right in there and get what we need, and then run for it."

"Great!" Berren snapped. "Just wade right into 'em. Don't worry about a thing."

The old man didn't like the tone of the conversation and decided to do something about it. With a clownish look of intrigue he went into the storeroom and returned with a well-used pale green bottle corked with a whittled wooden plug. It was about half full of what looked like soapy water.

"Uh-oh." Berren took a closer look. "What is this? Raki?"

"Good old raki," Jason laughed. "How you've missed the stuff, right?"

"Actually . . ." Berren began.

"Don't tell me you're still on that bourbon."

"I don't even know anymore," Berren said wistfully, and held the chipped cups and glasses for the old man to fill.

It took only a few sips to ease the tension all around. The old man grew affable and elaborately cordial, so with a second cupful he tried, after a fashion, to toast his foreign guests. It started off well enough in rolling, rhyming verses and amusing asides, but suddenly his adopted son interrupted him. There was an excited exchange and Jason turned to the others.

"He says he was pleased and surprised to find you were staying at his house when he got back, but his biggest surprise was that you got here so soon."

"So soon! How could he . . . ?"

"Listen. Apparently word had reached Jagat-ki Dar while he was there that three travelers—he assumes that means you—had been seen nearing the fault."

"That's impossible," Barren said in amazement. "That last week or more there was nobody, *nobody* along that trail."

"You're right," Jason said. "There was nobody along your trail. You see, Peta-ji wants to know where you've hidden your horses."

From where Berren lay the distant figures hardly seemed to be moving. Yet over the last ten minutes they had traced along the line where the azure shade that stretched across the floor of the fault met the bright, sunlit base of its northern wall. He cursed at them under his breath, swearing at their slow, steady pace, he wanted to know *now* who they were and why they had risked army patrols and the dangers of traveling at night to dog the trekkers all the way to the great fault. For there was no doubt in any of their minds that the purpose of that distant line of horsemen was somehow enmeshed in their own: no one, Jason had pointed out, traveled this remote gorge except by consent of those who ruled it from the monastery. No horseman came here but to climb its spiral path; no one whose business wasn't its own.

Berren had left the compound with his companions within minutes of the old man's revelation. Wrapped against the cold night air, they pushed hard through what was left of the dark to intercept the riders at daybreak.

Jason must have used this observation point before. It was a near-perfect location, lying as it did at the end of a waist-deep culvert on the very brink of the precipice.

"What do you think?" Jason was almost on top of Berren in the narrow opening, sighting over his shoulders at the minute figures below.

Berren had been trying to gauge their speed by picking out landmarks through the monocular and timing their approach to them.

"Not much," he said. "Too far away to make anything out yet."

"That's okay. They'll be out of sight in a few minutes behind that point. Then we'll have another hour while they follow

the trail around and end up . . ." He leaned over the edge
and pointed at a sharply lower angle, ". . . right down there.
That telescope gadget of yours ought to pick them up pretty
good. Until then, there's nothing to do but wait."

"Nothin' but wait," Michaelson muttered. He paid no attention to what was going on down on the trail; he just sat watching
the others glumly. "You two are good at that."

With the riders out of sight again the waiting seemed to
grow more tense and they chain smoked through it in silence.
Berren took turns with Jason scanning the fault floor every
few minutes in case their estimate had been wrong. Berren
was restless and edgy. He had taken the eyepiece back again
just for something to keep him busy, when the quiet was shattered by a thin, high-pitched scream. He almost dropped the
precious monocular in surprise. High above them on the China
side, a black cloud of screeching creatures wafted outward from
the face of the cliff, spinning and circling higher and higher
until it dispersed as quickly as it had formed.

"Bats," Jason said. "There're millions of them all along the
fault, nesting under the overhang."

"Something spooked them. Suppose the Chinese are watching our friends down there, too?"

"They don't miss a thing," Jason said. "Probably got an
eye on us, too."

Berren followed with his eyepiece along the crest where the
flight had originated, then turned his attention back to the
riverbed, and there they were.

"There they are!" he said, and the others scrambled to his
side. "Two, three, four horses. I can see them pretty clearly.
So that's how they got through the army patrols. They're in
uniform. The first one . . . Jesus Christ!" His breath caught
in his throat and his mouth hung wide in disbelief.

"What is it? What's wrong?"

"But why?" he was saying. "Why?"

"What's going on? Here, give me that thing." Jason took the monocular from Berren's grip.

"Second horse in," Berren directed very quietly. "Behind the Sikh."

"Oh, my God," said his friend. "It's Anna."

seventeen

Think, think. Berren pressed his forehead between his fists trying to squeeze out a different answer. It didn't work this time either.

The long hike back to the Bahadur compound had to be covered in painstaking silence and not a word about Anna was spoken until they were safely inside and out of sight. The family was off at work in the fields, so for a while the house was silent, too.

Berren gave up his pacing and squatted dejectedly in the corner, arms around his legs, his chin resting on his knee. Jason was the first to speak. "Well? What do you think?" he asked.

"What do you mean what do I think?" Berren asked angrily. "It's all pretty obvious, isn't it?" His voice was harsh after the long silence. "She told him. That son of a bitch Ranjit Singh is involved in this thing; it's his shit and she's a junkie. She'd do anything, tell him anything. She'd have to. And now he's up here after us. When I had hold of her in Delhi she said she'd mentioned you to him, right? So she must have been the one who blew the whistle on you in the first place. Then, of course, I come along and practically pinpoint you for them."

"Told her everything, did you?" Jason sounded skeptical.

"Yah, with those big eyes of hers and . . . yah, I must have laid the whole thing out for her. God, how she must have hated us. Just waiting all this . . . no, wait!" He sat up suddenly. "No, she told *me*. I didn't really figure it all out until later."

"Glad to hear you say that," Jason said. "I guess I noticed something you didn't. You know how well Annie can ride?"

"Yah. She had that little mare when she was making her rounds of the hill clinics. What about it?"

"Well, from where I was it looked like that Sikh was the one holding her reins."

"He was?"

"Sure. He had to lean way back a couple times to hold on. Can you imagine her ever letting herself be led like that? I think you've got it all wrong.

"I think our Anna's the one who's in real trouble. I think her hands were tied, and I think that turbaned bastard is using her for more than just a playmate."

Berren sat speechless, shaking his head slowly.

"Look, forget your battered ego for a minute and we'll try to sort this thing out." He waited while Berren took a deep breath, and then began. "From what we've just seen, we know that guy—what's'is—yah, Ranjit is somehow involved in the smuggling. Why else would he be up here, right? Okay, so a year ago he's up in Dangra on a 'business trip'—we can guess what his business was—and he bumps into this distraught but very pretty foreign girl who's got no place to go. We'll skip the details, but . . ."

"Thanks."

". . . but suffice it to say he inadvertently or otherwise learns from her that I've just left her and wandered off to look for some mysterious goings on up in the hills.

"Now this Ranjit's no dummy. He knows that could mean trouble, so he sends out his troops up here to look for me. Of course by then I'm just one of the humble mountain folk again, and what do his troops know? They're all Punjabi.

"A year goes by and nothing happens. They'd like to forget me, but Ranjit's done his homework and knows that somebody with my background wandering around loose up here could ruin everything.

"Then you show up. Now our bearded friend has two problems. First, you might steal his girl back, and second, you might go looking for me. That would put two of us up here to snoop around, so he tries to do you in during the riots. I mean, you only confirmed it for him the next night by asking Anna about me. Sound right so far?"

Berren was staring at the opposite wall.

"Well?"

Berren nodded.

"Okay. Now we're both in the picture, and he knows he's in trouble. He probably discovered, or figured out, that you were heading for the mountains, so he had no choice but to get back up here before you could, and protect his center of operations.

"And he knew he could do that because, I'm afraid, he still has an ace up his terrilyn sleeve."

"Anna."

"Right."

"He's brought Anna up here to smoke us out."

By now they were staring at each other in sickening apprehension.

"After all," Jason continued quietly, "you risked riot and the wrath of his henchman just to see her. What might you do if word got out that something terrible would happen to her if you didn't cooperate?"

The point was made, and neither man wanted to linger.

"Swell," Berren said bitterly. "That's just dandy. We can't leave that poor girl alone, can we? You know whom I'd like to get my hands on? Cummings, that . . . smug as hell, I'll bet. Sitting in his tidy office. I'd like to put him and that Sikh Ranjit in the same . . .

"Wait a minute! The last time I saw Ranjit Singh he was sitting at a table in the Shalimar. How'd he get here so fast? He'd have had to pick up the lower trail back near Hanli. Even with horses, and pushing it, it should have taken them weeks longer."

Michaelson had been coiled in a darkening corner of the room, his eyes narrow slits that shifted from one man to the other as they worked out the answer.

"The chopper," he said.

"The copter?" Berren jerked around. "Of course, the helicopter. That first night on the trek. Flew past us at almost ground level, trying to avoid radar. I didn't make any connection at the time; it was headed northwest. But they couldn't have landed it anywhere near the fault. If they had, both armies would have called off the war just to go down and find out what kind of nut had the balls for a stunt like that.

"No, what they'd do is drop into one of those discreet little highland meadows beyond the worst of the first range and have their cronies meet them there with the horses."

"There may be some comfort in that," Jason suggested. "If he took the copter in, he may assume he's arriving here before you."

Berren regarded Jason carefully. He'd had his say, and relapsed into a sprawl.

"You know what that means."

"Uh-huh," Jason said. "But let's hear your side of it."

"It means we've got to get her out of there. We have to make our move now. What time will they get to the monastery?"

"It's half again longer along the fault. They'll be there early tonight."

"We'll have to be there by then," he said, his stomach sinking even as he spoke, "and make our move before they can get organized."

"Now you're talkin', mate!"

". . . have to improvise around whatever we don't know," Berren was already going for his pack, "and take our chances. Sure as hell they'll kill her one way or the other. Oh, yah," he turned with an afterthought. "Maybe we'll have a chance at the lab, too. Ought to be able to smell it once we're inside."

"I was hoping you'd say that," Jason said, and twisted to his feet. "I'll get some supplies. We'll have to leave the vale in a hurry if we pull it off. Got your camera? Good. Billum Singh?"

The young Indian was up and packing, without asking where they were going. As they went through the door, Jason's arm hung lightly around the boy's neck while he talked to him earnestly.

" 'Ere we are, our first bit of luck." Michaelson was practically a new man now that the action had finally started. Too damned new for Jason. He wished he'd been on the trek with this big Englishman so that he'd know more about what to expect from him. With Anna in there the situation became one of life and death. They were frightened and desperate, and here this guy was treating the whole thing like a bar fight.

The four lay concealed within the boulders of the knoll where they'd been the night before, waiting with an eye on the time for the patrols to join up again. It was eight o'clock when they appeared, close enough to last night to assume there was a set schedule.

"Yah, luck," Berren whispered.

"Well, we know we have at least three hours," Jason said. "The moon'll be up soon and we'll want to be over the bridge before then." He turned to Michaelson. "You sure you know what you're doing?"

"Leave it to me," he grinned. "It's so' of a specialty."

"Hmpf," Jason grunted. Now he knew he didn't like him.

There was something vast and liquid about the currents of dank-smelling air that coiled and eddied slowly through the black chasm. The air was always moving, stirring the bridge so that the hawsers and lines were constantly groaning against their stays.

There was a sentry at its approach, propped against the cool face of the cliff. He was bored and he'd eaten too much. He began to nod, but caught himself as his rifle slipped, and tried to shake himself awake. He drew this duty too often; it wasn't fair.

From far below he could barely make out the faint sound of horses climbing the path around the rock. Another big-shot *babu*, he thought resentfully. They were the only ones with horses.

Then he heard another sound. One ear perked back slightly, involuntarily searching for its source.

Must be an animal. Even those stupid farmers up on the top never came near this place—not after they'd tossed a few over the side. He gave a gargling chuckle, then stopped. He was sure he'd heard something that time. Kind of a hissing sound. He strained his eyes up the inclining ledge to where it met the lip of the cliff, a hundred feet to his right. Then he saw it. A shadow at the very top of the path, a man bent over, waving.

"Sssst . . . sssst—bi sahib-jiii, idhir aho, bi sahib." The fool was actually calling him. There would be some fun tonight after all, and with a malicious grin he drew his bayonet and snapped it in place under the muzzle of his carbine. He had already decided to deal with the farmer himself as he moved up the path.

Even from where he stood, Billum Singh could see the vicious leer on the face of the approaching sentry, but if it frightened him, he didn't show it. He continued to stoop over the edge, waving, palm down, and cooing softly, *"Aiyay, bi sahib, aiyay-ji."*

As the guard drew near, his head and shoulders rose above the canyon's edge. He shifted the carbine to his left hand.

"Tum ao." He growled and lunged with his free hand to grab at Billum Singh's shirt front.

He was wrenched up short by the burly arm that snapped out of nowhere and clamped around his neck. His eyes popped wide with disbelief and he dropped the useless rifle to claw at the stranglehold. Gradually his writhing ceased as the buzzing blackness pushed consciousness from his brain. The arm let him go, and he toppled silently over the side.

All four stared after him into the black, listening with macabre fascination to hear the body strike bottom.

They couldn't.

"Holy shit." Berren hadn't thought it would happen like that.

Jason tried to read Michaelson's expression in the dark. "That's your specialty, is it?" he said.

Michaelson's eyes flared for an instant. "That's 'ow the big boys play," he said. "What did you expect?"

They worked their way carefully down along the incline and huddled behind the construction that supported the upright timbers, examining the length of the starlit strands of hemp and wooden planks.

"Can you see the other end?"

"Yah, but only the top."

"Don't see anybody, do you?"

"Nope."

"I don't trust it. If I was them I'd guard the other side, too," Jason said.

Berren shifted for a better look at the span. He was glad for the night that hid the awful emptiness below. There— see how the span shuddered in that last little gust.

Berren retrieved his camera from his pack and checked it out. He wrapped the strap around his neck and stuck the instrument itself into the pocket of his jacket, where he could button it in securely. The packs were left behind against the cliff for Billum Singh to guard. It was the only way they could keep him from going along.

At Berren's first step, the entire structure began to quiver. The interconnected ropes creaked loudly all along its length. Oh, this was going to be great fun. His next step made the bridge swing to compensate for the shift in his weight.

Damn Newton! he thought, damn his apple. And these support ropes aren't far enough apart. The thing's about as stable as a clothesline. He tried to ignore the warnings his senses were pouring out and, his heart in his mouth, took another step out over the void.

Easy does it; take it easy. The others must have felt the same way, for they tried to synchronize to his steps, to establish a predictable rhythm to the gyrations.

They were halfway out when a breeze sprang up, causing the entire jerry-rig to sway. They were forced to drop to the wooden planks and clutch at the support ropes. The darkness was not such a comfort after all. Berren could see no horizon to measure the frightening sway, no sight of solid earth below. At any minute he might fall into infinity.

He didn't. He held on, and when the breeze subsided, so did his stomach. He was about to get up and move on when Jason caught his attention and pointed to the base of the uprights ahead. Berren concentrated on the spot too intensely and it disappeared into the faceless gloom. When he shifted his eyes again he saw it, a speck of red that bloomed bright then died again. Someone was down there, on some kind of platform or ledge, smoking a cigarette. The flame must have night-blinded the sentry, too. How else could he have missed their actions on the span?

Now what? All three lay stranded, riding out another gust of wind. When it died again, Berren could see the silhouette of another figure.

"*Ey, Devan!*" It appeared at the end of the bridge, holding on to a support line as it leaned out and called angrily to the sentry, "*Machote! Yahan nehi pio!*"

He's right, Berren thought. That's a dumb place to smoke.

"*Upar ao, abi!*" And he moved back out of sight.

That's right, bring him up there and let him have it. Better yet, take him inside and report him.

"*Acha, acha.*" A disdainful reply and the butt was snubbed. Now they could make out the figure of the sentry, or at least his movements, as he followed an invisible shelf a few yards below the surface of the spire until he disappeared around the tip of its bow.

Berren got unsteadily to his knees. The surface of the bow looked empty, so he motioned to the others. They covered the rest of the span in a low, slouching trot, and Berren noticed again that his friend's leg was not all it should be.

At the end, they held up behind one of the uprights and waited for any signs of life to present themselves. When none did, they moved gratefully onto the solid bow of the rock, and dropped into one of the shallow crevices that scored its surface.

There was a pause while they collected themselves and took stock of their new situation.

"Okay. Now, remember, that bridge is our only escape," Berren whispered. "If we try that trail down into the fault, we'll be sitting ducks from above, so somebody's got to stay here and make sure nobody's in the way when we're ready to run for it. Michaelson, that's you."

"Me! Listen here, don't you think you'd better have me along?"

"Relax." Jason tried to mollify the big man. "Listen, Tommy's right. We know what to look for, and we can understand what we hear. On the other hand, you're better equipped than either of us to do, uh, whatever's necessary to keep the bridge secure."

"There'll be plenty of action inside there, too," Michaelson insisted.

"Your kind of action inside," Jason hissed, "and we won't last the second five minutes. You can have your fun out here, wringing the necks of any more of those guards. After all," he added, "it is 'sort of' your specialty."

The Englishman wasn't happy, but he acquiesced, so they left him there and moved off toward the foot of the westernmost walls.

The stars shimmered brilliantly in the spare atmosphere while the southeastern sky gathered light from the crescent that still hung back below the horizon. A vague silvery sheen added to the remoteness of the valley beyond the spire.

After the first few yards, the surface of the bow became thick with swatches of low weeds that crinkled stiffly beneath their feet. Nearer the base of the wall was a scattering of scrub trees, like those growing at the bottom levels of the fields. They were a hardy breed, full enough to hide the foreigners as a small group of "soldiers" moved past them around the corner.

They waited for a moment, until the squad sounded far enough away, then pressed through the prickly foliage and peered around the corner after them. The squad jostled in comradely fashion along the pathway between the tapering wall and the outside edge, then unslung their weapons and bent through the small door, hardly more than a chink in the huge stone bulwark.

"Looks like it's either that door or the main gate at the other end of the rock," Berren whispered. "And they left a guard outside."

"We'll never get past him this way," Jason said. "Let's see what's over on the China side."

The shadow of the monastery's north wall was utterly black.

If Berren hadn't had his hand out and touched the corner he might have gone over the brink. At first it seemed there was nothing at all on this side. The edifice had been built up from the very face of the spire, confounding their sense of perspective by leaning out over the fault like something out of the Brothers Grimm.

Then Berren discovered that the path the sentry must have taken from under the bridge was carved from a natural shelf that came around the bow of the rock, to his left, just a few feet below its surface. A ramp for the sentries had been built where it neared the surface, but the original thin shelf continued past the place where they knelt, and on along the sheer face where they lost sight of it in the darkness.

Neither spoke. The prospect was terrifying. The shelf was too narrow, they would have to inch along with their backs to the wall, and then there was no way of knowing how far it went.

Berren sat on the edge, and slid down to where he felt the ledge firmly under his feet. Without waiting for Jason, he let go of the surface and sidled away slowly, his head level with the foot of the giant wall, his hands and feet testing each crack for a handhold, each step for its firmness.

Everybody knows enough not to look down, but Berren was engulfed in the black shadow and sought reassurance by looking up into the lighter sky. The battlements were indeed leaning out over him, and their unnatural angle made him doubt his senses for a moment. Instinctively he looked for confirmation of his balance, and he found himself looking down into nothing. For an awful moment he felt as if he were already beginning his fall. He threw his head back and clutched the wall until the feeling passed. His heart was pumping madly, but he moved on.

The shelf grew steadily narrower until it disappeared altogether, but by then they were under the base of the northeast turret, and the surface of the great rock curved out from the wall. Berren had gotten one knee over its edge and was feeling for a better grip when he heard the sound of approaching voices. He hesitated, listening for another hint of the activity happening on the other side of the rounded stonework of the turret. He could make nothing of it, so he pulled himself up and gave his friend a hand.

From below came the sound of horses' hooves, clut-clutting against the resonant stone. A moment later there was a low rumble of protesting metal against heavy timber, and a huge brass-studded door swung slowly outward from the recessed arch. A single uniformed *chokidar* stepped into a pool of dull light cast from within, and greeted the first horseman climbing into view with a yawn.

The first one to make it up onto the surface was Ranjit Singh Bedi. As he neared the light, his features revealed little of the strains of his hard traveling. The color of his turban was still lost in the dark, but it looked as tight and as neatly creased as it had in Delhi. His beard was rolled back neatly under his chin, and with the turban framed the same piercing dark eyes—or perhaps Berren saw them only because he expected to.

The horse had not fared as well. Its head drooped low as the Sikh stopped and brushed some of the dust from his beribboned field jacket, then shied as he angrily jerked at the line in his other hand. The second horse struggled against the tether, then stumbled up over the edge to its place beside the steaming flanks of the first. In its saddle, huddled forward against the neck of the beast like a trussed bundle of wares, was Anna.

The sight was almost too much for Berren; Jason had to restrain him from leaping out and doing God knows what.

Ranjit took up slack in the tether and spoke a few angry words at his goon, whose exhausted animal seemed almost incapable of the last steps to safer ground. The girl looked around at where she was, and for a moment stared at the spot where her friends hid. Even in the poor light her face looked swollen and bruised. It was easy to see she'd been beaten.

Ranjit's goon looked even motlier than when Berren had last seen him, crumpled on the floor at Krishen's Café, and the flanks of his scrawny beast were bloody from his rider's whipping.

The observers had seen enough and withdrew around the turret, where Berren discovered that he was still holding his breath. At last they heard the hooves clatter on the threshold and echo on into the courtyard. The ungainly door closed with a solid thud. Another sound, a heavy latch, secured it for the night, and the foreigners were alone again.

eighteen

Jason leaned out for a better look at the door that had just rumbled shut. "Maybe we should have brought along our large limey."

"I just want in," Berren whispered. "I don't want the damn thing torn down." He was straining his eyes in the dark, kicking and looking through the litter of stones at the foot of the masonry. He picked up several and discarded them again before he found one to his liking. It was the size and roughly the shape of a large mango.

"What's that?"

"A weapon, maybe," Berren answered, and hefted its weight a few times.

"You going to tell me about it?"

"Simple," Berren replied. "This place is a monastery, right? And you're the nearest we've got to a *sadhu*, right? So okay. Go on up there and demand a little charity."

Jason retrieved one of the stones Berren had dropped. "If you don't mind," he said, "I think I'll keep one of these handy."

The vaulted arch that had looked much lower from the hillside contained a pair of doors at least twice taller than the intruders who stood before it. There was a dim line of light where the two halves joined in the center, and another to the right that outlined a smaller secondary entrance.

Berren pressed himself painfully against the brass studs, the smaller door on his left, and nodded to Jason, who gave him an I-don't-like-this look before hooding his face under the blanket. He chose a spot below the barred peephole and pounded at it with the side of his fist. It made hardly a sound.

"Ban choat," he muttered, and tried another target closer to the center.

The second attempt was only a little louder, but it was enough, for it was followed by the sound of footsteps on the other side. Jason hunched over into a pathetic pose and readied his routine.

A wooden flap behind the peephole slid aside and two suspicious eyes appeared so close to the opening that the accompanying nose poked out past the bars.

"Con hai?" The demand was muffled by the door that still covered the lower part of the face.

"Oh, babu-ji, bakshe-e-e-e-sh, babu-ji." Jason's voice crackled with the whine of a street beggar. "I am alone and poor. *Baksheesh dejiyay."*

The flap slammed shut, and there were some hollow sounds against the wood from within. Then the secondary door opened, and the disconcerted *chokidar* stepped over the sill. Jason had pulled back out of reach, and the man had taken only one angry step when something told him he'd been fooled. He turned in time to see the blow coming and reeled back as it struck, off target, at the side of his skull. For a terrible moment the victim and his attacker stood there, stunned. How did this happen? What have you done to me? Berren's resolve faltered. He almost dropped his weapon in his confusion, but the act demanded its own resolution, so he hit him again.

There was no resistance. The *chokidar*'s head bent with the blow and he buckled instantly to the ground.

Berren knew his first concern should be with the open door, but when he rushed back to it, all he could see was the face of his victim. It took a while before he could focus again on their situation, and search for trouble in the courtyard beyond the tunneled entryway.

Jason had dropped the stone he'd been holding, and was hunkered beside the *chokidar* when Berren returned to his side.

"How is he?" He wasn't sure he wanted to know.

Jason just shrugged. "Let's get him out of sight."

The large rectangular stones of the threshold had been rounded smooth by centuries of passage. Beyond them, the deep vaulted entrance, lit by a dim lantern hanging from a line beside the *chokidar*'s cot, opened onto a rough cobbled courtyard with low colonnades on either side, hardly visible in the shadows of the high, heavy outer walls. Each colonnade ended short of the courtyard's westernmost perimeter at a pair of ugly, squat towers that seemed to be peering out over the battlements, on guard against the outside world. Past them, silhouetted still higher above the towers, was the main edifice: the court of the rajas and the monastery's *bavan*.

It was a strange configuration, the details of its upper levels faintly visible against the light of the sky where they rose above the shadows of the lower fortifications. Modified through its history to the needs of each changing tenant, it had evolved into a hodgepodge of domes and blocks, of balconied tiers and firing slits, intricate even in this light, yet at the same time somber and austere in its bulk.

The cobblestones were slippery with the dampness of the chilly night, and they had to move with great care among the boxy pillars of the colonnade.

They drew up short at the sound of footsteps coming from the passageway to the right of the *bavan*. A man in a white undershirt padded barefoot between the shadows toward something that was stirring in the dark below the northern wall. A few confused hoofbeats, a leathery slap, and the man reappeared, yanking painfully at the reins as he led one of the horses back into the passageway.

The intruders traded a look of misgiving and moved on.

At ground level the facade of the *bavan* was a jumble of protruding additions. The largest was on the side nearest their wall, extending toward the courtyard almost to the foot of the tower. It had three tall windows, framed within a single-pillared casement, each boarded up tight. They could hear voices from inside, so they ducked into a black little alcove in the corner past the tower and listened.

Someone was speaking, but they couldn't hear what he was saying because he was being interrupted by loud bursts of raucous masculine laughter.

There was a crack in the poorly mitered corner of one of the windows. Berren started for it but had managed only a few steps when out of the corner of his eye he caught a movement along the north parapet. He turned and darted back into cover.

It was another sentry, pacing off his rounds along the toothy line of firing notches and it was several long minutes before the measured tread faded from overhead and Berren dared creep back to the windows. He put his eye to the crack and recoiled instinctively at what he saw. Everybody was laughing at him! He found himself doubled up below the window, but when nothing happened he got to one knee and peered cautiously through the crack again. It was a large anteroom full of lounging men in shabby khaki uniforms. In their midst, standing a little higher on the stone staircase, was Ranjit Singh. Everyone was grinning and poking each other and staring at the very spot from which Berren was watching.

This time there was something else; part of a figure could be seen very close to Berren's peephole, someone whose hand gripped the window casing and whose wrist was striped with nasty red welts.

". . . only for tonight," Ranjit was saying, as much to the others as to the girl. "An upper room, one with a view. You *farenge* women like such accommodations, yes? Come. There will be business I must attend later, so we have but an hour together." A snicker spread through the group. It must have been a long time since the "soldiers" had seen a pretty woman, and Ranjit was basking in their envy.

"Not to worry. You will be safe after that until I return. These men will not harm you, not"—he added for their benefit—"until I let them."

There was another round of bawdy laughter, and Anna hurried to the staircase. The man squatting at its base made a teasing grab at her ankle as it flicked by, and she fled up the stairs.

All eyes followed her departure hungrily, even those of Ranjit's goon, who looked up from the bucket of water he was dousing himself with and ended the little show with an obscene comment.

Berren had nothing to say to Jason. He sat in the dark, his thoughts raging with that same defiling image that had come back to him—this time, with stark, ugly clarity. She'd be alone again soon enough, he thought miserably. An hour or so longer to watch for some sign of life in the face of the *bavan*, watch for a room with a view above the anteroom and wait for his chance.

But gradually he became aware of where he was and why, and it dawned on him that if nothing else, it was just possible that he could get even.

Very quietly he whispered to his friend, "Ranjit's got . . ."

"I know, I heard."

"You heard? How?"

"Back behind the pillar there's a door."

"And you could hear what was said over here through a door over there? Show me."

Berren trotted behind Jason around the tower and moved back into the colonnade. They stopped after only a few steps, but Berren could see nothing in the dark. He put out his hand, and felt along until he came to the door, hung deep in a recess in the stonework. At his touch came the same harsh laughter he'd heard at the window, echoing distantly through the wall. "The wall's hollow," he whispered. "This door must lead from that entrance we saw under the south wall, the one for the patrols. But it doesn't just go through the wall, it's got a passage-way leading back to the anteroom of the *bavan*. That's why we can hear them so well."

"Right," Jason said. "And I found something else, too, while

you were playing Peeping Tom. Come here and have a look."
He led Berren back to the first pillar and pointed down at a
pipe sticking up out of the cobblestones near its base.

"You paying attention?"

Berren's eyes were fixed on the upper stories of the *bavan,*
where a shutter had just been slammed to close off the light
from inside. He was lucky to have noticed it, for now there
was no sign that the light ever existed.

"Yah," he whispered, "a pipe. What about it?"

"Not *a* pipe, a dozen of them. There must be one at the
base of every other pillar, all the way down the line. Maybe
down the other side, too." Berren still seemed distracted by
the light he had seen. "Don't you see? Ventilation."

Now he had Berren's attention. Handling opium was difficult
enough, but making the heroin involved the heating of morphine, and its vapor could be so caustic and volatile that it
required a constant exhausting of its fumes.

The pipe was close enough to the pillar for Berren to remain
in the shadows while he knelt and inspected it closely. It was
about six inches in diameter and capped by a metal cone. He
sniffed hesitantly under the cap, and the sharp, sour odor it
emitted was enough to make him wince. There was no doubt
about it now, and he set to work trying to dislodge the cap
by twisting and pulling at it feverishly.

He was so intent that he didn't notice the sentry returning
on his rounds until Jason caught him by the collar and pulled
him back out of sight.

Berren left little margin for discretion. No sooner had the
leathery footsteps passed than he was over the pipe again. A
few more twists and the sharp metal cone was free. The shaft
was only a few feet deep, so its field of vision was still wide

enough at the bottom to make out a well-lit tabletop below. As he watched, the bent back of someone in a dirty laboratory smock crossed his view, rolling out a spool of neoprene tubing.

When he looked back, his friend was squatting casually against the wall, imitating his own foolish grin and nodding beneath his cowl at Berren's melodramatic thumbs-down signal.

The heavy door was a tribute to its ancient craftsmen, well weathered and bound with wide iron strapping. Like a fine-tuned machine, its balance remained true as it swung back easily and silently. They stepped over the high sill from the dark into the black and closed the door behind them. There was not a sound inside, no sign of life at all, except, suspended in the cold atmosphere, an incongruous sweaty odor.

The door was at their backs, so the voices had come from the right. Berren turned and stretched his hands out straight, to intercept anything coming at him from the dark. At his first step his hands found another door. He pulled it open gently and felt for the low frame he knew would be there, then waited until he knew Jason had found it, too.

Hands out, his heart pounding in his ears, he measured off a few steps into the inky tunnel. One more, fine, another . . . the *bavan* was closer. Another step and his shin cracked painfully against a horizontal pole. There was the sound of heavy creaking as a body shifted on the woven twine. He'd walked into a *charpoi*, one that was occupied, at that. Somewhere just in front of him a sleepy voice grumbled, *"Kya bhat hai?"*

It must be some kind of barracks. There could be cots of sleeping henchmen all down the corridor.

"Eh?" the voice demanded.

"Nehi hai, bi sahib," Berren soothed. Steady now, don't

panic. Each step back the same. *"Kutch nehi hai."* Straight back to the door. *"Bilkul tik hai."* And they pushed the door shut again.

Berren kept his mouth open wide, to keep his panting as quiet as possible. His forehead was pressed against the cold stone wall. This wasn't the way. There was only the courtyard door of the *bavan,* or maybe something around the northwest end, where the horses were kept. They could spend all night looking, and in a place crawling with Ranjit's "soldiers."

He heard something. A sound, no, more than that, it was a voice, two voices. He turned to see if Jason had heard it, too, but there was only blackness. The voices seemed to be coming from deep in the wall opposite the sleeper's passageway, and from below.

Berren's hands were out again, feeling along the wall, testing each step, until he found stone stairs twisting downward. He gave a quick *hssst* to his invisible partner, and when he felt his reassuring hand on his shoulder he began to follow the stairway downward.

It circled twice before they saw scratchy lines of blue moonlight reflected across the passageway ten feet below. That must be the door at the base of the southern wall where they'd seen the patrols enter—how long ago? An hour? Two?

All that crumbling masonry overhead, and what of the guard? To hell with it. He and Jason still had the advantage of the darkness.

In the time it took for these fears to come and go again, the intruders had passed the crack of light and were moving farther into the passageway, guided by another voice and the distinct sounds of clinking glass.

They had almost expected the next door, after all the others, but this one was quite different from those above. It wasn't old and decrepit, but recent, smooth wood with tight seams and a rubber seal around its edges. Berren carefully turned a modern knob and stepped onto the landing of a stairway as old as the others but lit from the cellarlike recesses below with the same warm light he'd seen through the ventilation pipe.

Jason let go of the door, and it hissed pneumatically shut.

Now what? Here they were at last, and Berren only felt trapped. His charge of anger had left him, drained away completely as if someone had pulled a plug in his toe. He longed to be back up on top, waiting out the hour for a chance at Anna.

It had all been a stupid decision, coming down here; a rash confidence easily acquired in the open air, but down here, in the bowels of the monastery, there was only the cold sickness of his fear.

And the stink of the place!

Somehow they went on, creeping cautiously down the narrow stairwell until it opened onto a huge, dungeonlike labyrinth of stone arches that crossed and recrossed in an integral network of buttressing against the weight of the mammoth above.

There was no sign of the technician Berren had seen from the pipe, and the sounds of voices and clinking glass had disappeared, too. Berren had the uneasy feeling that the stillness indicated an awareness of their intrusion. Someone unseen was watching for their next move. But then the voices began again from far away, unseen among the grottoes at the *bavan*'s end.

"Whew," Jason made a face. "Smells like vinegar. Maybe this is the wine cellar."

The yellowish light came from a multitude of open oil lamps suspended within each of the areas enclosed by the arches. Secured above them in long white rows were fluorescent tube lights.

"There's a generator someplace, but gas rations must be tough up here," Berren whispered. "See that tank with all the pipes? I'll bet they recycle all their sewage for methane and use the tube lights for the morphine process, when they'd have to douse those lamps. And maybe they have some electric equipment, too."

"Okay," Jason said, "let's go take a look."

They moved silently off among the squat archways to the western end where they waited for signs of what to expect from the technicians. A shape, a fluttering of light, darted past their peripheral vision, and they ducked into a corner. But it was only a solitary moth, flirting with the nearest open flame.

"*Wahan hai,* Shanti?"

The call startled them. It came from behind a nearby pillar, much closer to where they were hiding than they had expected. The technician showed himself, a frail-looking fellow with thick spectacles bridging a hollow-eyed face. His shapeless lab smock rode high on his hunched back as he scurried among the long lines of tables and gleaming paraphernalia, studying the papers on his clipboard.

The stench was beginning to get to Berren. He longed for the clean air outside and suddenly thought of Michaelson out there on the rock, ready to defend the span against all comers.

How long had it been, how long could they leave him out there?

When the technician had joined his co-worker and their voices had died away, the two foreigners stepped uncertainly to the edge of the laboratory and blinked about, dumbfounded.

Before them was a myriad of sparkling glass and polished chrome gadgetry as intricate as a college science lab.

"Can you make any sense out of this?" Jason whispered.

"Yah," Berren said bitterly, "I can. They make dope here."
And he pointed out what equipment he could recognize.

"Precision heating coils," he said. "And there's an orbital
centrifuge. The red lights along this aisle are probably connected
to electronic sniffers." Berren freed his Nikkormat from his
jacket pocket and began fumbling clumsily at its adjustments.
"That's just a refrigeration device; there's another over there,
in the next section. Probably gas—runs off the same supply
as those Bunsen burners over there. They must bring in bottles,
somehow; too much for just that methane plant.

"Okay, now, you stay here and be ready if those two come
back." He wondered if his whispering was as loud as it sounded
in the cellar's hush. "Time for my act." And he crept out
into the laboratory.

So here he was, he thought, standing in the middle of a
jungle of condensing coils and strangely shaped beakers, like
a bull in a china shop. His hands trembled so badly he could
hardly focus, so he breathed deeply a few times to ease the
shakes and went to work.

He had to move fast now. Those technicians could return
at any moment and he didn't want anything to get in his
way when he finished. Not with Anna . . . Jesus! What was
he doing down here?

He shot the first frame, and cursed himself for forgetting
to set the speed. He opened the aperture and spun the dial
until the needle moved, ever so slightly. It would have to do.
Somebody would just have to soup it up in the darkroom.

The next shot made him feel better, and the next better
still. It was as if he had somehow reached into the heart of
the thing that had twisted their lives over the last year just
as it had twisted the lives of the thousands it had poisoned—
and he was doing something to it, something, anyhow.

Clack! The centrifuge. Clack! A profile of the first table. Clack! Then he moved on to whatever looked important. The condenser coil, the sealed venting motor, all lent their images to his film.

A loud clatter echoed through from the eastern recesses, and sent Berren scrambling on his hands and knees into the nearest archway. One of the technicians must have dropped something. It was safe enough, but he didn't stand up right away. He'd come to rest at the base of one of the buttresses, and beside him was a tall, neat stack of molasses-colored balls the size of cabbages, each one wrapped in cellophane like a supermarket display.

He pulled one loose from near the top. Its surface was somewhat sticky, but it was dense and hard. It wasn't easy, ripping a chunk free with his fingernails.

Berren knew what it was before he sniffed it. He'd found the opium, and not far from it another stack. This one was built from fist-sized bags of milky white crystalline powder.

Berren was eyeing the array of brown bottles on the shelf. They must be some of the additives or the stuff they were derived from. But before he could pick one he heard the voices again, and the urge to retreat overcame him. He covered the distance to Jason's side in an undignified crawl.

"Let's get out of here," he whispered harshly.

"What's that you put in your pocket?"

"Free samples. Let's go."

nineteen

"Him and us," Jason whispered. "You'd think there was nobody else for miles."

The lazy cadence of the sentry's footsteps faded as he neared the far end of the wall. A sliver of a moon had risen, lending a dim aura of unreality to their medieval surroundings. Berren glanced at his watch to confirm the sentry's schedule and turned his attention back to the balconied window above, where he'd seen the light an hour ago. The hour must be up by now, but there was no sign. That bastard, he thought. And he can't take her back to Delhi now, not after she's seen all this. He'll probably feed her to the wolves just for spite.

"Look, you'd better take these," he said, freeing the camera and the two packages of dope from his pockets. "I don't think my chances are going to be very good up there."

"Don't give them to me," Jason said. "I'm going, too."

"Hell you are," Berren said. "Once that guard is behind

the *bavan* there'll only be ten minutes before he's in the open again, right? Ten minutes to find a way up that tower, over to that ledge and across the facade to the center window there. That'll be tough enough for me, and I don't have a bum leg. And there's that jump from the tower to the ledge . . ."

"Yah, all right," Jason said. "I'd hate to try that jump, even with a good leg."

Berren snorted. "Just what I needed to hear," he said.

No sooner had the sentry passed from sight behind the *bavan* than Berren was on his feet and off along the shadows of the perimeter. Ten minutes, Berren repeated under his breath, then eighteen more to wait, then another ten to get her down.

He'd just finished the recitation when he found himself under the heavy stone molding that surrounded the tower. There was the doorway, a gaping hole, and then he was inside.

He hesitated for a moment, but the tower was only a hollow, empty thing that continued down below the surface of the courtyard, and the only sounds were those of the rats scurrying in the pit below. The steps were there, little more than slabs of stone protruding inward from the sides. In the center there was nothing.

He kept close to the wall, feeling his way up, around and around until he could no longer judge how far he'd gotten, how close he was to the open sky. With every move came the urgent awareness of passing time, and he began pressing himself carelessly until at last he could see light. Some kind of platform near the top had hidden it from view, and as he climbed up to it he could see a square of starry sky through an open hatchway. His first urge was to race up the last few steps and free himself from the gloom.

It was a good thing he didn't: The next step was missing. There was a fleeting moment of panic as he struggled for balance, then another long minute searching blindly with his foot until he found the next step. It was a long stretch, and he had to lean sharply toward it before he could hike himself up.

Safely on the step, he scrambled over the platform and raised himself slowly through the waist-high hatchway. Now the details of the tower top were easy to make out after the darkness below. Its roof was slightly domed to hold the weight of its stonework despite the aging mortar, and the stubby-looking battlements were tall enough to hide behind, as he surveyed the surroundings through its embrasures.

The circling mountains formed a jagged horizon against the starlit sky, and Berren wondered if there was enough light for some watcher on the high cliffs of the China side to be able to pick out his skulking form.

He moved immediately to the corner flanking the southwest edge of the *bavan* and confirmed his earlier calculations. It was a long jump, maybe too long to return with an exhausted and frightened girl, but the tower's open roof would be a safer target than the foot-wide stone ledge that awaited him now. Besides, he thought, as he grimly reckoned the distance to the ground, there would probably be no choice.

There were only four minutes left, so he hauled himself over the embrasure and stuck his heel solidly into the base of the firing slit. For an awful few seconds he stared into the emptiness below, then swallowed hard, and, bracing his weight on the anchored heel, he leaned out. When the other leg had reached full stride, he kicked off from the slit. For a moment he was free of all contact with the stonework, then his left foot landed on the solid ledge and he collided heavily against the facade. He clutched the masonry until he found a grip and clung in relief, like a human fly.

With his heartbeat still roaring in his ears, he set his teeth and began a crablike shuffle toward the balcony.

The face of the *bavan* was almost featureless at this exposed height, except for the windows near its center, which were bunched together in a grouping of three, like those down in the courtyard, with squat columns between each, supporting separate sets of blackout shutters.

Berren clung to the casement fluting with one hand and tested the first set carefully with the other. These were better built than those below. There were no little cracks to peek through, and no give at all to his touch. He shuffled cautiously on to the center window where he thought he'd seen the light earlier.

Sure enough, this window had been closed but not secured, and he pressed it very slightly ajar.

She was there, sitting on the edge of a Western-style bed, wearing khaki fatigues and a blue "Press" armband. She looked dreadful, her hair unkempt, one eye blackened, and what seemed like a drying abrasion across one cheek. Her attention was fixed on something to the right of his window, but he couldn't see what it was.

He waited and listened—nothing. She sat motionless; her face held the same dazed expression he'd seen at the gate.

He checked the other window for a better vantage, then the crack at the hinged side of the panel. Nothing. Still, he didn't hear anything, and the sentry was due, so he gave the shutter another little touch.

The panel hadn't been so well made after all. It was poorly aligned and the last movement caused its balance to shift so that it swung inward with a squeak that grated up his spine.

Something moved suddenly from the hidden corner, a shadow passed the crack below the panel. Someone pulled the shutters wide. Berren had turned too suddenly and was fighting for balance when a fist fastened itself to his belt and yanked him back against the casement.

"Well, look a' this!" the voice said in a loud half whisper. Berren looked up at the grinning face of the Englishman.

Berren was bewildered and sputtering with anger as he climbed into the room. ". . . hell are you doing here!" But then he saw the girl. She stood at the foot of the bed, her eyes enormous and her hands clasped uncertainly at her waist. The scene had become disjointed, the reunion unreal. She should be relieved to see him. She should have run to him as soon as she realized he was there, Berren thought. But instead she looked like a frightened stranger, just standing there.

Berren didn't try to understand. If he had he'd probably have done it all wrong anyhow. So he just spread his arms a little and stayed that way until she came to him, her eyes still very wide, as if she were unsure what her embrace had captured.

"Tommy?" she asked.

"See there?" Michaelson broke in as he gave the panel a perfunctory shove. "I told you he'd be along. Bu' I must say, mate, I didn't expect an entrance like that. What'd you do? Sprout wings and fly up?"

Someone must have once taught Michaelson how to whisper, but not what it was for. A whisper for him did nothing but add an unpleasant rasp to his normally loud voice, and it brought Berren abruptly back to reality. He kept an arm around Anna and turned angrily on the Englishman.

"What in God's name are you doing up here? You were supposed to be keeping that footbridge open for us!"

Michaelson held up his hands in mock defense. "That's all

taken care of. Time was weighin' heavy on me hands, so I thought I'd help you find the little lady."

"Taken care of? Say, how the hell did you get up here, anyhow?"

"Came through tha' little door under the side—the guard was no trouble—then up over the place where they keep the 'orses. Strictly a second-story man, m'self." He tried out his little-boy grin, but without effect. "Bit a' luck, finding the girl. This place is like a bloody rat maze. This was the only room up here with a light, so here I am." He glanced at the shutter, which hadn't quite closed.

"Wha' about your other business? You find what your friend was after?" His eyes held an edgy glint when they caught Berren's again. "Speakin' of that, will he be stoppin' round, your friend?"

Berren didn't answer. His mind was casting about, trying to make some sense of all this. "What I want to know . . ." he started to say.

He was interrupted by a sound that seemed to echo from down a long passageway beyond the door. It wasn't a very loud noise, yet it struck Berren with a note of certain finality, the signal he'd half waited for all along. Things were coming undone. Damn Michaelson! They could have been out of here, and the bridge . . . now somebody was coming.

The sentry would have reached the north wall by now, so the ledge was out. The only way was through the iron-cinched teak door set into the wall adjoining the one with the windows. They heard it again, a sound still some distance from beyond the door, a pattern of movements becoming distinct, the click-clack of footsteps on a wooden floor.

"You came in that way?"

Michaelson nodded quickly.

"What's down there?"

"Sounds like somebody walking this way."

"Damn it!" Berren almost shouted in frustration. "What's the *building* like down there?"

Michaelson shrugged as if it could hardly matter.

"Confusin'," he said. "Just a lo' of li'l rooms sectioned off from some bloody-great corridor. If somebody's out there, we couldn't avoid 'em. The staircase is off at the other end."

"Great." Berren was frantically searching the room for a hiding place when the steady tread paused; there was another sound, like the first, and it continued again.

The danger must have been more unbearable for Anna with its return. Berren could almost feel her slipping over into hysteria, numbly repeating his name over and over and staring at the door.

"Hold on, lady. You're all right," he tried to sound reassuring. "Whoever's out there is expecting to find you here. Now, what we'll do is hide someplace . . ."

The footsteps were drawing nearer, but once more they stopped. Again the sound, a metal mechanism, and they picked up again. Something was trying to occur to Berren, but then he saw a *sheeshum* wood dressing screen leaning against the wall. He stood it upright and spread its accordioned sections. Just in time; the footsteps were almost at their door.

Yet again they paused, and Berren heard at last the missing sounds. He stopped dead when he heard the creak of hinges, immobilized by his fascination; he waited for the pattern to complete itself. And there it was: the metallic slide and click of a bolt thrown home.

Déjà vu became present. The lock! The endless corridor of locks!

Berren pushed the girl aside, and in the same motion spun

in fury, his fist cocked to smash at the smirk on Michaelson's boyish face.

"You!" he spat, but he checked his blow.

Michaelson was leaning easily against the wall, with a look of disdainful amusement.

"Tommy, what . . . ?"

Then she saw it, too: the ugly blue snout of a Webley-Smith revolver pointed with casual confidence at Berren's midsection.

"An interesting little phobia our Mr. Sharma has, don't you think?" Michaelson smiled smugly. "Still, I suppose if I was a tycoon publisher and ran most of Asia's drug traffic at the same time, I'd jolly well keep me doors locked, too."

"Quite so." They turned at the sound of the new voice. Sharma nudged the door without taking his eyes off the three foreigners. "But 'phobia'? A harsh description, isn't it, Dr. Berren? We prefer to think of ourselves as cautious."

Sharma's spare figure was clothed in an updated version of the old colonial tropic whites. It was a strangely formal costume—trim and immaculate in sharp contrast to both the surroundings and the chromed forty-five automatic in his hand. It was an outsized weapon for such a slender man, but he held it as if he was familiar with its potential.

"We must say it is a pleasant surprise to find you here, Dr. Berren. As for you, Mr. Michaelson"—his demeanor changed markedly as he shifted his attention to the Englishman—"we thought Mr. Ranjit Singh Bedi released you of your obligations when you were still down in Dangra." He made it sound as if Michaelson's presence were a personal affront.

Michaelson was so stunned by this frigid reception that he stood gaping for the second or so that Sharma allowed for a reply.

"Dr. Berren," Sharma turned as if he expected him to be

more reasonable, "you are a most worldly and intelligent man. Certainly you will understand the difficulty someone in our position has in dealing with such a complicated business. What we are suffering from here is what you would call a 'breaking down of communication.' " Sharma smiled. It was a clever expression.

"We have tried," he went on, "to make it clear to Mr. Michaelson and to Mr. Ranjit Singh Bedi that they are of equal stature in our humble organization. Each has his own area of usefulness and expertise. Mr. Ranjit Singh's is, of course, the subcontinent, while Mr. Michaelson here is most useful in Southeast Asia, as our liaison with a certain General Lee.

"And yet," Sharma continued, "each dreams of greater things, each must play his petty games trying to assert himself over the other in our esteem, isn't it, Mr. Michaelson?"

"Well, I . . ."

"Or is it . . ." Sharma didn't even bother with Berren anymore, but fixed his flinty glare on the Englishman. "Or is it that you both covet the highest position?" Sharma's brows lifted, pretending the idea was a revelation to him.

Michaelson made as if to say something in his defense, but Sharma, who had hardly moved since entering the room, waved aside the attempt.

"You see, Dr. Berren, the problem was really quite simple. When your Miss Anna mentioned your colleague's presence in the mountains to her new, er," he coughed discreetly, "to our assistant, Mr. Ranjit Singh Bedi, we immediately realized the peril of having such a man, um, as you Americans would say, 'mucking about.' So we had our little army scour the countryside in search of Mr. Josefs. They failed, of course. We are surrounded," and he cast an accusing eye on the Englishman, "by incompetents. Not like your International Journalists

Guild. No, indeed. A small but impressively staffed organization. It was they, was it not, who commissioned your 'Anatomy of a Famine' series?

"Well, as soon as our inquiries revealed their involvement, we understood your connection. After all, men like yourselves, and so eminent an organization . . . well, a story about a small famine is a thin excuse, isn't it?

"Yes, and then there was the matter of your sudden departure at the onset of our inquiries. You can see how that would only confirm our suspicions.

"Does it please you, Dr. Berren, to learn how dangerous your reputation has made you seem to us?"

"Very flattering." Berren clung to the frightened girl, pretending to be interested in Sharma's condescending prattle. "Let me guess your solution." He spoke carefully to keep his rage under control. "You went to the Guild, told them your crackpot political motives, and offered them your services. What you wanted, of course, was for them to send *me* back to find my friend Jason *for* you. That meeting in Istanbul was arranged just so you could toss in this . . . this . . . " he looked Michaelson up and down, "this bastard without the Guild knowing. That way you'd have your own man on the spot, ready to—what?—kill us both when the chance came?"

"That's very close indeed, Dr. Berren." Sharma was almost benevolent in his appreciation. "We have told you, Mr. Michaelson, Dr. Berren is a very logical man. It is a pity he is on, as we say in India, 'the incorrect side of the wall.'

"Instead," and his voice rose a scratchy decibel, "we are forced to deal with such as yourself."

"Look 'ere, Sharma," Michaelson had finally found his anger. "You've no call to talk to me like tha'. It was my plan, getting Berren here, and Ranjit had no right to call it off. An' you can see it worked, even without the cooperation of that furry-faced . . . it more than worked. Look here, I've delivered them right to your feet."

"Have you?" Sharma raised a derisive brow. "We see only Dr. Berren standing before us. Your gesture was very dramatic, as we're sure you intended, but you've left it incomplete.

"No, we're afraid we are not favorably impressed at all. You should have followed your original plan and killed Dr. Berren as soon as you found out from him where the other one was hidden. Then at least he would be out of the way, and by using his passport for your own departure, everything would have been settled. We'd know where to find this Jason Josefs fellow; Immigration would tell the CID that they were at last rid of their unsettling Dr. Berren, and you could be back, carrying on your logistics assignment in Cheng Mai."

"Will you listen!" Michaelson was almost beside himself. "I *couldn't* get any information out of 'im in Delhi. 'E didn't know any more than we did. As for your precious Ranjit, 'e did nothing but make trouble. The first thing 'e did was try to kill 'm off before I could even talk to him. There's *his* loyalty. He knew ri' enough you'd agreed to my plan, but I even had to threaten him before he'd allow these two to get together and compare notes."

Berren turned as much as he dared toward the protesting Michaelson.

"So the meeting in the café *was* a setup," he said. "I thought it was too easy."

Anna was totally bewildered, and almost past the point of caring. Berren could see this, but she was standing beside him, and by talking directly to her he could keep an eye on the gun while he stalled. So he continued as if it were important she understand it all.

223

"See, I'd mentioned to Michaelson that you were the only one who could tell me about Jason's plans. He knew Ranjit had already tried to kill me the first time I saw you. . . . What was it?" He turned to Michaelson. "Was he trying to get rid of me so your plan couldn't get off the ground?"

"Right. He . . ."

"Whatever it was, Ranjit couldn't very well just invite me over after that, so Michaelson here somehow coerced him into making you available at a place where they knew I'd find out about it, at Krishen's Café. You were all just waiting there for me to break in and practically kidnap you.

"Then we discovered that you didn't know enough, either. So the only thing left for Michaelson was to follow me around until I tracked Jason down on my own.

"Tell me," he glanced down at the gun. Not a chance, not yet. "Was Ranjit really so pissed off back at the café, or was it all just playacting to make it seem we'd caught him off guard?"

"Both, mate. Oh, he was pissed, indeed." Michaelson managed to smile at the recollection. "Ranjit would like me out of his way. He'd love to see me and me plan dead an' gone.

"Fact is," and he drew the gun back out of Berren's reach. ". . . that's the reason I didn't just do you and Jason both in that first night at the Bahadurs.' As soon as I figured out it was Ranjit on that lower trail, I knew I couldn't show me English face around here without you beside me to prove my plan had worked. Just wouldn't have been prudent, that Sikh and his trigger-'appy soldier boys bein' the ill-tempered sort.

"And, as you pointed out, I couldn't very well get rid of you and still expect to make it back on me own.

"Now, that Ranjit bloke—his idea wasn't nearly as clever. Just to bring the little lady up here and wait for your friend to do something foolish about it. Bu' I had to ask him, what if he doesn't do anything foolish? After all, she's not much to do with him anymore, right? Well then, I told him, he'd have played his only card, hadn't 'e?"

"Splendid, Mr. Michaelson," Sharma inserted pointedly. "Mr. Josefs wasn't enough trouble, you had to bring Dr. Berren here, too."

"Well," Michaelson replied, "this one won't be dangerous much longer, an' 'is mate is probably wondering about the delay right now. These two are thick as flies." He indicated the window with a nod. "He'll be along soon enough."

Berren followed his nod to the center window and the split of moonlit sky between its panels just in time to see something move—an ill-defined form that withdrew behind the secured half of the shutters.

If Michaelson and Sharma were intending to lay a trap, their timing was off again; Jason was already here.

". . . Hope you are correct, Mr. Michaelson," Sharma was saying as he turned toward the door. "We'll leave it to you to dispense with Dr. Berren while we go down and tell Ranjit and the others. We're sure they'll be happy to know you're here, and they can seal off the rock and start their search for the other one.

"Oh . . ." he stopped at the door as if he'd remembered something. "And just to keep peace in the family, you'll leave the girl for Ranjit. We're afraid," he made a slight bow of deference towards Anna, "our Sikh has some perverted notions as to his intentions for her."

Anna buckled slightly against Berren's arm. This was it. No ceremony, no meaning, just the end. Stall! He doesn't want to watch it happen, don't let him leave the room!

"And the CID?" Berren heard himself say.

Sharma stopped and turned back again. The door behind

him was still ajar, unlocked, and it occurred to Berren that there was some sort of last chance here, if he could only make out what it was.

"The CID, Dr. Berren?" Sharma sounded bemused. "What a curious thing to mention at such a moment."

"I . . . yes, well . . ."

"Please go on. We are listening."

"What I mean is, you won't get away with this. There's an agent who'll be watching for me in Delhi."

"Ah, yes, well, Mr. Michaelson can make subtle adjustments in your papers, and your identity will leave the country with him. Didn't we mention that?"

Berren focused his attention on the latch on the half-open door. "Yah, well, what happens if you can't find them? Maybe I don't have them on me. Maybe I've hidden them somewhere."

"That's unlikely, Dr. Berren. Foreigners always seem to carry such things close at hand. They're such a bother to replace in India. And no doubt you had a swift 'get-quickly-away' planned, isn't it?

"Still, Mr. Michaelson," he conceded, "perhaps there is a point in what he says. It would be awkward if his papers were not on his person and he is not alive. . . ." Sharma was becoming uneasy with Berren's unbroken stare. ". . . uh, to tell you where they are.

"We will cover the doctor." He sounded as if he were making up some rules for a child's game as he directed the muzzle of the shiny .45 with greater care, "while you search his person for them."

Berren tried to concentrate totally on the tycoon's singular phobia, the open door at his back.

"While Mr. Michaelson takes care of his task, Dr. Berren, we should like you to know how sorry we are that you had to discover the true nature of what must have been a budding friendship. Few things are as tragic as a fickle friend, isn't it?"

Berren's unbroken stare was beginning to irritate the Indian, but he continued.

"Yet the Hindustani have an ancient proverb. It is that 'Business makes strange bedfellows.' "

Sharma was a keen and observant man. His face was becoming as tense as the American's. Without dropping his guard, he began to puzzle out the object of Berren's attention, trying to discern its direction from those strange blue eyes. That didn't work, so he risked a glance.

Michaelson was standing to one side of Sharma's line of fire, going through Berren's pockets with his free hand.

Something had to happen now; Sharma had discovered his neglect. Surely under these circumstances the precaution was more necessary than ever.

A trickle of sweat appeared on Sharma's forehead as he edged toward the offending breach.

"Politics," Berren corrected.

"What?" Sharma shifted the automatic to his other hand, leaving the right one free to work the door latch.

"Politics makes strange bedfellows."

"Ummmm, that, too." And Sharma turned and bent to the lock.

That was the moment Michaelson made his mistake. He'd found the tattered folds of the temporary residence permit in Berren's wallet, but there was nothing else. So, assuming that Sharma still held a pistol on Berren, he stuck the document into his shirt pocket and the barrel of his own revolver into his waistband, then began to frisk Berren from behind.

Michaelson's big hands had circled from under Berren's armpits to his breast pockets when Berren made his move. He slapped his bent arms to his sides, pinning Michaelson's forearms to his torso. The big man reared back and shouted in surprise as he tried to jerk free, but in the split second between instinct and reaction, Berren had crossed his arms and clamped his opponent's straining wrists in a maniacal grip.

Berren couldn't see it, but Michaelson's howl of protest had summoned Jason from his perch. There was a thump and the sound of the two or three steps needed to cross from the window, then a squirming commotion as Jason lunged and yanked the pistol from Michaelson's waist.

In a single motion, Jason had the revolver free and whipped it down with a sickening hollow thud over the back of Michaelson's head.

Sharma had turned and saw what was happening, but wasn't sure what to do. Then he recognized the big chrome .45 for what it was and fired it awkwardly; it was still in his left hand.

Berren heard the explosion, and saw the frail body jerk at the recoil as the shot struck wide and hissed away from the fluted molding of the wall beside them. He thrust himself away from Michaelson's dead weight and tackled Anna to the floor as Jason stiff-armed the revolver and fired back. Like some giant hand, the force of the shot swatted the man from his feet and flattened him against the heavy teak door.

The outsized automatic was still gripped in Sharma's hand and yet, try as he would, he couldn't seem to raise it. He continued to try as he watched the wet red stain blossom from beneath the white linen of his suit, then he gave it up as he slid down the wood to the floor.

The roar of the volley echoed off down the vale and the blue smoke followed, drifting slowly past the lamplight toward the open window.

For a moment everything was very still.

twenty

It took a second after Berren opened his eyes again for him to realize that they were trying to focus on the small patch of Anna's khaki blouse where his face was buried. The cloth was damp and trembled beneath his cheek.

God, he thought, I must be smothering her. He drew his weight to one knee and eased himself up from her back. "You still with us, lady?" He touched her shoulder awkwardly. Her face was pressed against the floor; she was afraid to move, to discover before she was ready the worst that might have happened. Then, when she realized who had spoken, she opened her eyes and peered up from under the crook of her arm.

"Tommy?"

"It's all right." He looked up to see for himself, and saw Jason standing behind them. The monkish cowl was a blanket again, draped loosely over the extended arm that still held the smoking revolver. Jason's expression was a mask of shock and dismay. He kicked free of the Englishman's body and walked over to the bundle of bloodstained linen that sat doubled up at the base of the door.

Sharma was still alive, frowning down at the hand that held the gun, his mouth working soundlessly as if commanding his useless body to defend him.

Jason tried to retrieve the heavy gun, but the dying tycoon held on with grisly determination. When Jason had finally pried it loose, a finger at a time, he glanced quickly at where Michaelson lay. "I hope they come back as a pair of worms," he said.

Berren was still on the floor with Anna, holding her carefully and patting her as if she were a child, and Jason tapped his arm with something hard.

"Sorry. I'm afraid we have to be practical," he said, and offered Berren the pearly white handle of Sharma's .45.

Anna's huge brown eyes were still jumpy with shock, but when she turned her face to his, Berren thought he could see its color returning.

"Tommy, where . . . how did you get here?"

"Me? *Jason's* the one playing Errol Flynn. Where the hell did *he* come from?"

Jason had wrapped his blanket into a cowl again, and was checking the cylinder of the Webley-Smith. "I saw that commotion at the window and came up for a look," he said.

"How's the leg?"

"Like the other one. They both want out of here."

"Right. Okay, lady," Berren tried to smile for Anna, "here we go. There's a ledge outside that window, and it's going to be scary. Think you'll be all right?"

"I guess I'll have to be," she said shakily as she struggled to her feet.

Jason doused the room's only lamp while Berren checked

along the top of the wall for any sign of the sentry. Then he went out the window and found a good grip on the sill. With the other hand he guided Anna out onto the ledge.

"Don't look down," Berren whispered as they waited for Jason to close the shutter and join them. "Relax and breathe easy. This is all nice and solid along here, and remember I've got hold of you."

She was repeating the advice under her breath as they moved off.

Life inside the edifice was beginning to respond to the noise of the gunfire. At first it had held its collective breath, listening for another clue to what was happening. Soon the very absence of developments became a warning in itself. Then indecision slowly became alarm, and alarm became a barrage of commands diffusing down through the ranks. A confusion of activity ensued, spreading through the halls and passageways of the *bavan* until its noise finally reached even the heights where the three intruders were inching their way along the brow of the facade.

Strangely, the tranquility of the courtyard below them was broken only once, when a pair of "soldiers" jogged through it on a diagonal from the barracks' door toward the stable side of the *bavan*. The three above had no way to hide themselves, but the "soldiers" must have had their orders, so they didn't bother to look upward.

The Himalayan night was cold and clear, except for a fortunate few high wisps of strata that shrouded what little moonlight was possible.

"I'm telling you it's easy," Berren was whispering fiercely into Anna's ear. "I had to jump from the tower to get here. Jason too, and it was easy." There was no time for coaxing and Berren was getting frantic. But the tower was close to six feet away and Anna still clung to the masonry in terror. "That tower is the only way down. You've got to jump." He took her face in his hand and turned it to his. "Understand? You've *got* to! All you have to do is get over there. Just hit the roof any way you can and I'll be there to catch you.

"Now watch me! Watch me!" He squeezed her chin and she opened her eyes. "Watch how I do it, okay? Okay?" She nodded.

Berren looked around the parapets one last time, searching for the sentry, then he swallowed hard and kicked off. His landing, this time, seemed instantaneous to his jump, almost as if he hadn't done anything at all.

Anna was next, and she must have taken heart from Berren's example. With Jason behind her, encouraging her and illustrating some suggestions with his long arms, she hiked up the waist of her fatigues and stepped to the edge. She hesitated, shaking with spasms of fear, but when the moment came she made her leap.

All time was frozen in that second that held her above the empty space. Then Berren had an arm and was grappling her painfully over the embrasure wall. He sprawled with her back onto the hard roof and was on his feet again before she could recover.

Jason hadn't waited for Berren; he'd already made the jump once, but this time he kicked off with his good leg, leaving the injured one to absorb the impact. It didn't.

Berren had leaped up just in time to see the leg buckle beneath the hurling body, and the look of incredulity on his friend's face as his body slammed against the sharp stone and began to slide down the outside of the wall as he clawed at its top.

Berren was on him in a flash. With the front of his thighs braced against the embrasure, he reached through the firing slit and grabbed handfuls of cloth beneath the blanket. It was enough to check the slide for the second it took for Jason to shove his foot into the slit and loop an arm over the top of the merlon. Then Berren had him under one arm and hefted him over the barrier.

"Thanks," Jason said as he gulped for air.

Berren didn't hear him. A light, showing again from the center window, had caught his attention. "I think there's somebody healthy back in that room," he said. "We've got to get to the footbridge before they figure out what happened. Still got that camera and stuff?"

Jason replied by slapping the bulge at his waist. "And you, where's your gun?" he whispered.

Berren produced it from the deep pocket of his jacket and Jason nodded as he rocked forward to his feet. "Let's get out of here."

One after another they dropped through the dark hatch, with Berren leading the way.

They held back at the opening to the courtyard as a squad of "soldiers" ran past them and into the familiar barracks' door. There was a growing commotion inside the *bavan*, but the way to the vaulted gate tunnel looked clear, so they sprinted to the far end of the colonnade. Berren went ahead to be sure the tunnel was empty. He peered around the corner, and seeing there was nothing between them and the high, studded gates, was about to signal to the others when he heard another kind of sound. It seemed isolated from the rest; a voice, maybe, or a groan that came from back in the shadowy structures near the base of the tower. Impossible, he thought. They'd just left that corner themselves and it was empty.

Berren ducked into the tunnel, and keeping close to the wall, had made the first few feet to the gate when the other two scrambled around the corner and almost ran him down.

"Somebody's sneaking around back there," Jason said.

"I heard it, too," Berren said. "Down by the tower. Did you see anything?"

"No. But I heard somebody go through that barracks' door and close it."

There were lights at the ground level of the *bavan* and shouting as the henchmen began to break into the open. Berren ran to the gate and had hardly slipped the latch on the smaller *chokidar's* door when Jason hit it full weight and it sprung open. He pushed Anna through it roughly and hustled Berren out after her.

"Here they come." Jason said it offhandedly, as if it no longer concerned them, and while he shouldered the door shut again, he nodded toward the wider path on the India side.

"Wanna risk it that way?"

"Nope. We go back the way we came, along that shelf on the China side," Berren said. "Those 'soldier boys' were headed for the side entrance and we'd never get past them."

Berren sent the others on ahead while he held back behind the outside curve of the turret to make sure their narrow escape path wasn't discovered. There were a few echoing shouts from inside the tunnel, the grinding of the heavy timber gate sliding over stone, then the first few henchmen, weapons in hand, burst into the open. In their midst was a smaller man, unarmed except for the holster at his belt, wearing the bloomer shorts of the British tropical uniform.

Berren pulled back around the turret. The little man was apparently the noncom in charge. His orders split the group into two squads. The first ran to the lip of the rock and with the beams of their flashlights dancing before them, began to descend the spiral path, while the others turned toward the India side and started off at double time around the opposite turret, back toward the footbridge.

The one who had given the orders lingered behind, adjusting the hardware attached to the webbing of his belt before starting off at a more deliberate pace.

The other two were doing well by the time Berren caught up. Jason was holding Anna's hand, signaling her with his touch as he tested each step.

The way back along the uneven shelf was less harrowing after the circus act they had gone through atop the *bavan*, and yet they maintained an unbearably cautious pace, groping their way along until they reached the shapeless clump of scrub trees that marked the westernmost corner of the wall. Jason parted the bristling branches to see what he could make of the voices coming from the other side of the rock. The foliage was too thick, so near the wall, so he crouched low and crept farther out toward the point until he disappeared from sight.

When Jason didn't return right away, Anna's grip tightened on Berren's hand. But he was more concerned that the voices were starting to die away. Maybe the soldiers had completed their search out here and concluded that their quarry was still inside the monastery. It had been quiet for several minutes when Jason crept back to the bushes.

"Good news," he whispered. "First, the bow looks to be clear. I can't see anybody up there."

"Forget it," Berren said. "They'd never leave the bridge

unguarded. Either there's somebody down under it, like before, or they're hiding up there, waiting for us to make a run for it."

"All right, then. Second, we can make it around the bow without going over the top."

"You sure?"

"Yah. We were right when we first found this shelf. It runs into the one that the sentry under the bridge used. The next few yards are its narrowest parts, then there's sort of a ramp up to the surface; you have to climb over that, so remember to keep it low. After that it's out to the point and back the other side until you're up under the bridge."

"What if it leads right up under another sentry?" Berren asked.

"It doesn't. I've just come back from there."

"We'll still have to climb up those timbers to the span. Gonna be all hell to pay when we hit the surface!"

"We have a choice?"

"Okay, let's go. One at a time, now. Give him a few seconds, lady. Then you."

"And keep down." A second later, his form could just barely be seen above the surface level, then it was gone behind the ramp. Berren whispered something in the girl's ear and gave her an encouraging pat on the behind as he sent her on her way.

Something pushed free of the scrub near Berren's ear as she made her first few steps—something big that rushed toward her along the edge of the surface above. Anna saw it coming. Turning suddenly to see what it was, she missed her step and stumbled over the stone ramp. She flung herself across it and was grappling at the surface when she was intercepted.

Her arm was nearly broken by the force of the grip that

hoisted her like a rag doll up from the path and dragged her back from the edge.

"Right, you two!" It was the bellowing of a madman. It was Michaelson, his arm locked around Anna's neck and twisted. "Come out where I can see you or I'll break it off."

Anna squirmed and kicked at the shins of her captor, but he just gave her another jerk. She gave a choked cry and stopped her struggle.

"Simple as tha'," he growled. "You know wa' I can do. It takes more than a couple a' half-wog bastards like you to put me away."

His fury had done nothing to diminish his cunning. He'd hardly begun his move when Berren was up over the lip of the rock, trying for a clear line of fire through the shrubbery. He was close enough to make out Michaelson's light hair, matted with dark blood, but it was no good. His hand trembled under the weight of the automatic, and Michaelson had dragged her back too far to be sure of missing her.

"One of you has me gun. Flip it out 'ere." He jerked Anna's head upward. "Now!"

Berren remembered what that same burly arm had done to the guard. Michaelson wanted a gun, so Berren threw him Sharma's .45. Now he'd know there were two guns, but maybe Jason could get him when he bent down to pick this one up.

It didn't work; Michaelson didn't release the girl. He just kicked her feet out from under her and held her against him as he crouched to retrieve the weapon.

"Very nice," he growled, "bu' mine's a revolver." He put the muzzle of the automatic behind Anna's ear. "I'm not waitin' for it! I'll blow her away and get you two anyhow."

The Englishman was so absorbed in his rage that he didn't

see the squad of "soldiers" move in quickly from around the far corner. In fact, he'd never have noticed them if he hadn't heard the metallic double action of a rifle bolt behind him.

Michaelson turned as if to greet his cohorts and found the rifle was aimed at him.

"Put the pistol to the ground, Dr. Berren." The order was given with a precise singsong delivery by the little man in bloomer shorts. "We wish no more shots to be fired."

"Me!" Michaelson laughed at the mistake. "See here, mate. I'm not Berren, I'm . . ."

"Put it down, Dr. Berren." The order was emphatic this time, and the rifle was to be obeyed however stupid the reason. Michaelson threw down the .45 and pushed the girl away angrily.

"Listen, you . . ." he was trying to control himself, his words tangling together in the attempt, "Berren is . . . I'm Michaelson. Ian Michaelson. Dammit, I'm one of you, on your side. Ask your boss, Sharma. Berren is right over . . ."

"Sharma-ji is dead," the little man interrupted matter-of-factly, and picked up the chrome-and-pearl automatic.

Michaelson looked around in confusion at the "soldiers" who were edging closer. The vicious hooked blades of their *kukri* machetes were stripped from their scabbards.

"However," the little man continued, "as usual, he left instructions."

Michaelson's lips were twitching. He was beginning to comprehend his absurd peril.

"Instructions? Then he'd have told you about me."

"He did. Sharma-ji had only a few words left to him, I am told, so he just said to kill Dr. Berren and the girl."

"But I'm not Berren!" He was staring at the rifle, almost

pleading, while the largest of the men moved in to pat at his pockets. "This man Berren: Sharma meant somebody else."

The little noncom smiled at such nonsense.

"Tell them, girlie. Tell them who I am!" Michaelson said. Anna only shrank back.

"Somebody else? We are looking for two foreigners. You are one, the girl is another." He shrugged.

The search stopped at Michaelson's breast pocket. The "soldier" pulled out the tattered folds of the stolen document and handed it over to his leader. Michaelson's eyes widened with dread.

"Wait, listen!" He started to turn, but his guard braced the rifle and he reconsidered. "I'm telling you, Berren is right over there!"

"Yes, yes. I know that one from your cinema. Ah, here it is." He had the permit unfolded, and called for a flashlight.

"Berren, Thomas Everett. Place of birth: Hartford, Kansas, U.S.A. Father's name, hmmmm," he scanned down the next few lines, "et cetera, et cetera."

He looked up at his victim with a nasty smile.

"I will take from you the girl." He took her by the arm and pulled her aside. "Ranjit Singh Bedi has some other plans for her." He turned her face away from the shadows for a better look at his prize.

"You've got to listen to me." Michaelson was desperate. "Those papers aren't mine. I know where he . . . she knows. Tell him, tell them." Anna looked away from the cocky little man and kept her silence.

Michaelson was suddenly frantic. "Berren!"

"Please, Dr. Berren." The little man was annoyed. "We do not wish to disturb our neighbors." He turned back to the girl. Then, as an afterthought, he jerked his thumb at the hapless man.

"Kill him."

Michaelson tried to say something as the first of the blades swept down. Anna saw it coming and threw her hands over her face. If she could have screamed she would have been spared the sound of the slaughter. From where Berren hid among the prickly leaves of the scrub, the chopping was enough to make him turn away, shriveling his groin and leaving him weak with nausea.

There was little left of the big Englishman when the gleeful henchmen had finished.

When Berren was able to look back again, he saw Anna lurching away from the offal as if to find a place to be sick. By luck or by design she was staggering toward the clump of scrub where he was hiding. The little man, strutting up behind her, paused long enough to give a last order to his satiated butchers.

"*Chello!*" he commanded.

A couple of them chuckled at his intentions as they hefted their various weapons and moved off toward the far end of the wall.

The stripes on his sleeve were those of a sergeant major. Berren could make them out now, as the little man puffed himself up and moved in on the girl. He was obviously pleased with his captive, who could only stand there stunned. Her eyes were downcast, and she seemed about to collapse. Yet, as he approached, she moved again, nearer the edge, nearer the clump of scrub trees.

"Stop!" he warned. "Please to do nothing foolish, miss. It

is unfortunate to lose one's, ummmm, one's lover. But to jump now would be a waste. Especially when there are . . ." he fiddled with the fold of his collar, ". . . so many others available."

He was a parody of colonial military bearing, circling slowly around the spot where she stood, tapping his palm with the heavy pistol as if it were a swagger stick. Anna kept her eyes on the ground ahead, scarcely acknowledging his presence, until she heard a sudden movement through the leaves and the dull crack that followed.

She did not even look up when Berren appeared and tossed aside the heavy rock he'd used. He quickly relieved the corpse of the .45, and when he had stuffed it back into his own jacket pocket, took hold of the body by its lapels and hoisted it into the scrub, out of sight.

Without waiting to see how the girl was taking all of this, he grabbed her hand and half dragged her along the brink to where Jason crouched.

She was convulsed with sobbing, sucking loudly at the air as if she couldn't fill her lungs, her fists tight to her eyes to blot out the horror.

"Poor kid," Berren whispered. "Treated you like . . ." he put a comforting hand on her shoulder but she pushed it away.

"I think I'm going to be sick."

Berren looked over at Jason's silhouette. "Me, too," he said, wishing it were true.

"Uh-oh." Jason had been watching the surface a few feet above the shelf. Several of the "soldiers" had returned from the other side, accompanied by a large turbaned figure.

"What?" Berren asked.

"Here comes the boyfriend."

Berren looked over the rim in time to see Ranjit say something to one of the men, who replied by pointing to the mound that had once been the Englishman.

Without a sound the three pulled themselves together and started off toward the bow.

Ranjit was in no hurry to see what his men had done to Berren. It was enough to know he was dead. But he still needed the girl for his original plan.

It had been a close call. That idiot Englishman had really bungled it this time. A born assassin like Michaelson, and he allows a professor to escape him in a little town like Dangra. And lets him get all the way to this place. Could Berren have made contact with the one they were after? And then there was the greatest puzzle of all: *How* had he found the girl?

Ranjit almost wished they had spared Berren long enough to wring some of the answers from him. Oh well, he thought, making his way along the base of the wall, he'd learn soon enough from the girl, and she was safer to deal with.

Where could she be? The idea of that little peacock of a sergeant major with his woman began to gnaw at him. He checked the recesses beneath one of the buttresses. Not there. They were probably in the bushes somewhere.

When he caught the little *banchote* (nothing in there either) he'd make sure he'd never enjoy his superiors' women again. That's right, he could do that. The operation was all his now. Now he could deal with that Michaelson in his own way, and he was smiling as he parted the branches of the last clump of scrub.

There he found the sergeant major, his head askew, his sightless eyes rolled back, still watching for the blow that had killed him.

The girl! The body was alone. Could *she* possibly have . . . ?
No, it made no sense, something was very wrong. Ranjit stumbled out of the branches and ran over to the other body. Perhaps the answer was there.

It was, but at first he didn't understand it. He unsnapped the flashlight from its clip and ran its circle over the bloody form.

Blond? The hair on the corpse was blond.

Then he understood.

"MICHAELSON!"

twenty-one

Ages of erosion had begun to heal the hand-hewn shelf and turn it back into the greater mass of the spire. Even now, as the foreigners crept along its path, a faltering step too near its rounded edge was enough to send an occasional chunk crumbling quietly into the depths.

When they reached the very tip of the bow, they had to stoop low under the overhanging surface before doubling back along the opposite side toward the span.

The upright support timbers were hardly distinguishable from the dark cliff they were anchored to. Only the bridge itself, seven or eight feet above their heads, could be clearly seen against the faded indigo sky, its hawsers sweeping out over the chasm to where their graceful lines disappeared into the blackness of the Indian cliffs.

Nearer the timbers the path widened behind the absent sentry's makeshift stone blind.

Berren was up in the timbers immediately, searching for footholds and wondering all the while about the Sikh up on the surface.

Suddenly they were startled by a booming rain of curses from above that must have been heard for a hundred yards. He's figured it out, Berren thought grimly. The results were immediate. The surface became alive with the unmistakable sounds of action with hard-heeled boots and clattering armaments picking up a rough cadence as the troops raced toward the spot where their leader was raving. His orders sent one group off to scour the spire while the rest turned from where Ranjit stood over Michaelson's body and started for the bridge just as Berren emerged to the surface. There was a cry from their ranks when they saw him that drew the others from their previous objectives and into the chase.

Jason hoisted Anna, foot in hand, up to the cross beam, where she grabbed Berren's extended arm with both hands. She struggled over the brink to the surface only to find herself facing the mob of onrushing henchmen.

In spite of his favored leg, Jason was up and beside the girl before she had time to move. Berren spun her around and Jason gave her a shove after him as they ducked under the support hawsers and started over the bridge.

The wooden slats groaned against the hemp lines that wove them together. They had barely covered the first twenty feet when the entire flimsy span began to undulate like a snake under its shifting burden. A few more steps and it was gyrating so violently that they had to drop to their knees and hold on to the rope web that slung the wooden path from the hawsers, losing more precious seconds to their pursuers.

It was this hesitation that saved them from the first barrage of rifle fire that ripped splinters of wood and hemp from the spot where they otherwise would have been. Berren was crawling on his knees and one hand, while, with the other, he ripped the heavy pistol free of his tangled pocket.

The nearest pursuer was holding a semiautomatic rifle at his waist, pumping off one wild shot after another. Berren put his weight on his left elbow and aimed round it to loose two quick shots of his own.

Fortunately the safety catch was off; he'd never have found it if it hadn't been. Fortunate, too, was the reaction back on the surface, for the "soldiers" hadn't expected return fire.

At first it looked as if Berren had hit the man with the semi. He hadn't. The henchman just dropped his weapon in surprise as he ducked. The others followed suit, scrambling for whatever cover they could find. Even those closing at a run on the bridge's approach faltered for a moment.

Berren had forgotten that these weren't Indian army sepoy, but just a bunch of thugs painted to look that way. The foreigners were probably the first of their victims ever to shoot back.

Berren stayed low until the span's sway eased, then fired another round to hold them for a minute, while the three of them crawled on.

There was another scattered volley. A fragment spun away from the hawser, and a bullet split the slat in front of them. The man who had fired the shot had reached the bridge, and with that shot had missed his only chance, for Jason had already rolled over on his back. Sighting between his feet, he fired once and sent the man sprawling against the uprights.

Once more they began to move, as the last exchange echoed off down the walls of the fault. Only a few more slats had been covered when, in a brief lapse between the thundering reverberations, they heard a strange and very distinct sound, a hollow *floop* that came from above them, behind the black rim of the China side.

All motion stopped. Even the strands of rope and wood held their sway while everyone, caught in an attitude of conflict, watched a thin streak of light curve high into the night and burst with a *pop* into a brilliant phosphorescent glare that lit up the landscape for miles.

"Shit," Jason said. "That's all we need. A Chinese flare."

Berren looked away, covering his eyes with his hands to salvage what he could of his night vision. When he uncovered them again, he found the entire scene drenched by the cold light, filling the shadows that had been spared by the moon, and giving form to the spire and the cliffs.

Everything was silent, except for the barely audible hiss of the flare swinging beneath its chute.

He looked up to see Anna's reaction. She had turned away from the source of light and had inadvertently looked over the side. The sight of what lay below had wiped away everything except her terror, had stolen even the ability to avert her eyes.

My Christ! Berren thought. Look where we are!

Empty until now, darkened from their view, they had gotten this far knowing of, but unable to comprehend, such space. Suddenly, with its enormity plumbed by the light of the flare, it seemed to hold them in a dreadful *gestalt*, terrified and unable to move.

No one on the surface behind them could move either. The secret fear each "soldier" had harbored since coming here, the shadow they had lived under by accepting the precarious geography of their lair, all was summed up by the single word that passed among them: *"Chin."*

Their shots had awakened a phantom. How soon, now, until the first incoming shells sealed the fate of those who lingered on the great rock?

Berren forced his eyes back to the plank under his hand, forced himself to think of it as a solid thing. The whole bridge, it was solid, too. Hadn't they gotten this far? And there was refuge. It lay in the solid ground at the end of the bridge, only a hundred feet ahead.

Come on, he said to himself.

"Come on," he called to the others, "come *on!*"

He grabbed Anna and pulled her into motion.

"C'mon, Jason. Move. Let's go."

Slowly, unsteadily at first, they began to crawl. They had gained a few more yards and reached midspan when the spell was broken behind them. Ranjit had come to his senses and was screaming threats and orders, lashing at his men with his fists, dominating the smaller men who had gathered at the end of the bridge, forcing them back into action.

Ranjit shoved the first man he could get hold of out onto the slats where he held back, trying to get off a shot while he waited for someone else to move ahead. It was Jason who fired first and crumpled the man where he stood.

The shooting started again, and the three on the bridge forgot the danger of the chasm and scrambled to their feet. They remained bent as low as they could so that, instead of running, their pace became a series of lurching staggers that caused the rolling sway to begin again and added to the frightened confusion at Ranjit's end.

His men were afraid. Afraid of the return fire, of the gyrations of the footbridge, and of the Chinese and their flares. Most of all, they were afraid of the powerful Sikh shouting and kicking at them from behind, forcing them to pile out onto the span.

A second flare went off. Closer this time, almost directly over the bridge. Berren was gripping Anna's hand fiercely, and had to shield his eyes with the flat of his gun. Billum Singh was still at the end of the span where they'd left him, lit starkly by the phosphorescent glare. He was dancing with excitement, waving them on frantically. And there were two men standing beside him; two strangers who didn't move, even when a shot ricocheted off the upright beside them. Whoever they were, they paid no attention to it, for they were watching.

They watched while Jason dropped another pursuer, who fell in the way of the others. By now they were strung out along the span with Ranjit in their midst, shouting and thrashing at them for hesitating, and when Jason turned to catch up, one of their shots bowled him flat.

Berren had to leave Anna where she was and squeeze past her to get back to where his friend lay, trying to support himself on one arm. Berren fired a couple of wild shots then hoisted Jason up to his feet. With his arms around his friend's chest, he began backing slowly toward safety.

The first flare had disappeared behind an angle in the fault while the second caught the current of breeze that channeled between the great walls and drifted closer. Anna was at the head of the line, moving in dazed stumbles, aware only that imminent disaster was closing in from behind. Then the flare passed overhead, and there were the men, waiting. A chubby man in a ridiculous business suit who held a gun, muzzle down, at his side, and the other, a Sikh in an officer's uniform, who stepped aside to let Billum Singh run out onto the span. He grabbed her arm in both hands and began hauling her unceremoniously back toward the cliff.

"Come along, Dr. Berren," one of the men said. "You also,

miss, come along. I cannot shoot while you are in the way."

Berren stumbled over the lip and fell with Jason back onto the ledge. At last he could make out the round face with the pencil mustache that looked down at him. It was the CID agent. Gupta.

The flare still gave an eerie cold light, and the line of fire was clear enough for Gupta to make use of the gun he'd brought along. His marksmanship, however, proved to be as bad as Berren's.

Beside them in a spotless pressed uniform, the Sikh officer shook his beturbaned head in a professional critique of their performance. Berren lay flat to the stones, trying to make at least one of his bullets count, while Gupta, ignoring the bullets and their stinging whine as they bounced off the face of the cliff behind them, stood at ease, spending shot after useless shot in the general direction of Ranjit's men.

Somehow, as the henchmen neared the middle of the span, the first in their line was struck, and staggered back into those behind him. The others, unable to fire past the ones who were bunching up in front of them, began to reel in confusion and in fear of the increasing fire power they now faced.

Only the imposing bulk of Ranjit Singh held them from breaking into headlong flight. He stood fast in the center of the tumult, kicking and flaying at them with his pistol.

One "soldier," finding himself at the head of the line, turned and tried to force his way back to the rock, but his struggling only got him to within Ranjit's reach. Ranjit pistol-whipped him across the face, then spun him bodily around and threw him back ahead of the others, where he stood paralyzed with indecision and abject terror. Another "soldier" near him took a round that kicked his leg out from under him and he slipped out through the webbing.

The first in line watched it happen; he could see the hands gripping the strands of rope, and surely he could hear the piteous cries of the dangling comrade, yet he did nothing to help him, for he was about to make a move that could only have been born of a mind gone mad with fear.

With a last look at his tormentors, he threw down his rifle, reached under his tunic and pulled out a gray, egg-shaped grenade. Before anyone realized what he was about to do, he closed the release lever and yanked the pin. There was no return to the rock, for behind him was only Ranjit Singh and the Chinese. No, the escape lay ahead, and in his upraised hand he held the only weapon capable of sweeping away the enemy that barred his way.

His face was lit with a mad exaltation as he started off.

At first Ranjit was gladdened by such a brave example. Then he realized what the man was about to do.

"No, *murkh!* No! The ropes!"

It was too late. The man was already beyond his grasp. Ranjit turned and sprang into the men behind him. They didn't understand what had happened, but the sight of their leader trying to push his way back to the rock was enough to turn the span into a twisting free-for-all, each man fighting his way over the bodies of the others to regain the safety of the rock.

Berren didn't see the crush, nor its first victims go over the side. He was watching the madman bouncing toward them with his deadly little parcel. There was nothing he could do except watch; the chrome and pearly .45 in his hand was empty.

Gupta remained calm as he fired off a few more wild shots at the charging madman. His uniformed companion shook his head slowly at such ineptitude. He kept his maddeningly dispassionate attitude until the very last second, when the man's steps began skipping against his forward motion and his arm cocked back for the throw.

Then the officer held out his hand for Gupta's weapon. *"Le-lao."*

Gupta placed the weapon in the hand and stepped aside. The Sikh shifted sideways, aimed precisely down his long arm and loosed a single shot that stopped the onrushing man mid-stride and flung him on his back.

The madman's arm was still outstretched, but now it was empty, as the grenade, alive and free of his grip, sputtered and bounced backwards along the slats. It hesitated on the brink, then caught, wedged between the wood and a line of the webbing.

The blast roared away down the fault, whapping back and forth against the immense echoing walls, repeating itself again and again into the distance. Shards of wood flew in all directions and the heavy hawsers snapped and whipped outward from the concussion.

Then, for a moment, nothing. It was as if the span were not subject to the laws of nature, that it would remain suspended despite its fatal wound. But that was only for a moment— then its structure began to disintegrate as its lines lost tension and snaked back from the mangled point of separation. The long tangle of rope and wood began a slow-motion downward arch.

The last in the line leaped to the safety of the rock, while those at the end nearest the explosion were blown free into the abyss.

The others, still enmeshed in their abortive flight, were already slipping away, some clawing for purchase against the yielding slats that were dropping from under them.

Ranjit kicked off from the bulk of the man he had just

scrambled over, and caught hold of the hawser, only to follow its inexorable rush until it smashed against the face of the spire in a shower of splintered wood and broken bodies.

Hawsers and lines shivered down to their dancing ends, then settled limply. A few more planks dropped away into the void.

epilogue

Jason was almost giddy with triumph and loss of blood. There was a meaty tear beneath his armpit, and as he lay facedown on the *charpoi,* he pretended to endure the attentions Anna and the old woman made as one might endure a persistent barber who kept interrupting a favorite story. The rest of the Bahadur household were gathered around the head of the cot, completely enthralled by Jason's version of the night's exploits, encouraging him when he faltered and praising him for his better turns of phrase as if he were a wandering storyteller.

It was all too much for Berren. There was so little of the dialect that he could understand that after a while the words began to flow by, layer on layer, too much for his tired brain to contend with.

He had been rummaging through his backpack and finally had to dump it out onto the floor to find the crushed blue packet of hoarded Gauloises that had worked its way to the bottom. There were only a couple that hadn't been too badly mangled. He automatically handed one to Billum Singh and stuck the other between his own teeth as he got up stiffly in search of a light.

Inspector Gupta watched Jason with wonder, unable to make head or tail of the language; he seemed fascinated by the theatrics involved. His military companion, a poker-stiff major named Swaroop, was less impressed. He was pacing the room carefully, inspecting it as if it were an underling's quarters.

"Boom—aaargh!" Jason's closing gesture had been too much.

"I told you to lie still, dummy." Anna cuffed him lightly on the back of the head and dipped a clean portion of cloth into the pot of boiled water that the old woman held. It was oily with herbs and the steam gave off a thick, camphorous smell.

"There's no way to tell if the rib is in one piece or not. So you can't go flopping around like some big bird," she said as she pressed the hot cloth to the edges of the wound.

"Ouch! Damn, lady. You must have studied medicine in a locker room." He managed to make it sound playful. "Anyhow, if Mr. Gupta, here, hadn't happened on to us at the right moment, we'd all be flapping around somewhere."

"Happened on to you?" The inspector was a little miffed. "My dear fellow, I have been following you, in a manner of speaking, ever since you started making those unsavory friends in the Bihar underworld. That was a year and a half ago. We, too, are interested in drugs and smuggling, you know, and we might have come to an agreement if you hadn't gone and disappeared like that."

"I doubt that," Jason said. A makeshift but tightly wrapped bandage was tied off and he settled down with his head on his arm to watch the inspector with bemused interest while the old woman turned her attention to the crusty black abrasions on Anna's face. She mumbled and clucked sympathetically as she dabbed at the wounds with the foul-scented water.

Berren was struck by the look on the girl's face as it was turned to the acrid lamplight. She looked pinched and gaunt like a Bihari starveling. Her complexion was ghostly pale and her dark eyes, drawn deep into their sockets, seemed to be swimming about the room as if the heavy atmosphere were closing in on her.

The major stuck the flame of his shiny Zippo under Berren's cigarette tip, then tossed it back into a pocket in his pack before he could acknowledge.

" 'Anatomy of a Famine,' " the inspector was saying. "A wonderful exposé, Dr. Berren. Imagine my surprise when at last I discovered that it was really your very own International Journalists Guild who arranged for the true embarrassing nature of your reportage to be revealed to us. But why should they do such a thing? And here is the same news service sending you back again but one year later. Furthermore it seems there is some sort of liaison between this Guild and our own mysterious and rather sinister Mr. P. K. Sharma, who, I might add, has a perfectly good news service of his own.

"We know all this because, as a licit opium-producing nation we maintain close ties with the policing efforts of others. The Turkish government has, therefore, been keeping watch over Mr. Sharma's corporate headquarters and gives us whatever they can learn."

"If you mean that little guy, Supka, I'm afraid Sharma had him fed to a pack of dogs."

"Is it?" The inspector showed only a passing interest. "Well, you will not wonder that I would keep you under scrutiny."

"Sure," Jason said. "You figured out the Guild's dope angle

and hoped Tommy'd do all your legwork for you. But how the hell did you manage to follow him all the way up here?"

"Ah, this is a long story," Gupta began, "involving your Dangra district residence permit and a long and, uh, rather unpleasant chat with Mr. Billum Singh's cousin. He was persuaded to reveal that you were headed for the war zone.

"Major Swaroop, here, is the General Staff's regional expert on mountain combat and, our good fortune, my old friend. I was able to convince him that all this could be a strategic problem, so he arranged it all."

"And the two of you just put on your hiking boots and . . ."

"Oh, my, no," Gupta said. "We took a Pushpa light aircraft to a small army base camp north of the first range. The major knew you were not equipped for the high passes, so we headed directly for the abandoned military supply trail.

"But, I must say, those two weeks with the good major taking every overland shortcut—we were sure you would be caught before we could reach you—well, it was all so strenuous." The very thought of it all had him mopping his brow with an oversized white handkerchief he'd drawn from the pocket of his tattered blue jacket. "That is to say, a man of my age . . ."

"You know," Jason interrupted, "I think Mr. Gupta is in need of a little stimulant. *Peta-ji?*"

"Please," the inspector said. "Local intoxicants are such a risk. I believe the major has something appropriate, isn't it, Major? A medicinal something from the Simla P.X.?"

"Of course." A man of action, the major was pleased to have something to do. He lifted his compact military pack onto the end of a cot and began unpacking its contents with meticulous care into neat little piles.

"So you figured you'd catch up easy once you'd flown over the hard part." Jason rested his chin on his forearm, smiling and shaking his head sardonically as the inspector continued.

"There was only one trail your friends could have taken," Inspector Gupta said. "It did not occur to us that they would be resourceful enough to acquire uniforms and horses. That made it all very difficult, indeed."

"It might have been worse," Jason said, tilting his head toward Berren. "These guys may not have been equipped for the high passes, but that's the way they came. You and your major may have been very logical and all that, but it was Ranjit Singh Bedi you almost caught up with."

"Oh, my goodness." Gupta exchanged a rueful glance with Major Swaroop and then began working away at his thin mustache with a pudgy finger while he considered this new idea. "What a surprise that would have been, eh? But in the end it is all the same, isn't it? There was nothing for us but to strike off on a more direct route across the fields and hope we would find a way down into the chasm ahead of them."

"Instead you found our monastery without monks," Jason said.

"Yes, and soldiers who were not soldiers," Gupta said. "We had to hide all day, the major was very irritated. When it was safe we went to the bridge and there was your Mr. Billum Singh, waiting with your packs."

Berren had been watching the old woman at work on Anna's face. The more she muttered and mumbled about her concern, the more the girl cringed under her touch.

"Too bad you didn't catch up with Ranjit," Berren said. "Anna's really been through the wringer."

"Mmm. Yes." Gupta considered the idea for a moment. "But that would have left things somewhat incomplete, don't you think? And wasn't it interesting that the Chinese were content to just shoot off some flares so they could watch? I'm sure that Major Swaroop, here, will be able to use this as an example of their restraint. Very reassuring when we again ask Central Government to let the army police the demilitarized zone. After all, so far as the Chinese are concerned, our sepoy have been up here all along. Smuggling will never . . ."

"J. J., please!" Anna suddenly shrank from the old woman's touch, clasping the wrinkled hand as if her attentions were unbearable. "What is she saying?"

Jason twisted painfully to see what was the matter.

"Easy, lady." He touched her knee with his good hand. "Take it easy. Talk, that's all it is. She's just talking." He traded a worried glance with Berren. "Meta-ji just likes to mother everybody she can. She thinks you've got a fever and wants to know if you're sick."

"That's all?"

"Well, you know. She's kind of nosy," he added. "She wants to know if you're my woman."

"Oh." Anna slumped forward and looked away miserably. "Oh, Meta, I'm sorry. I . . ."

"She knows," Jason said. "You've had a terrible time of it. She wouldn't understand what you mean to me"—she let him fold her hand in his as he spoke—"to Tommy and me. I'd like to tell her but she'd never forgive us for letting all this happen to you." He tried to turn enough to see her eyes but it was too painful. "Not sure I can forgive myself.

"Anyway," he smiled hopefully, "You don't have to worry. I told her you belong to Tommy."

"You shouldn't have told her that," Anna said with her eyes lowered. "See, I don't belong to anybody. Not anymore." She rose unsteadily to her feet. "Sorry, I need some air." And she left the room.

There was an embarrassed lull, with those she had left behind staring at the door or searching the faces of the others for some kind of explanation. Then Berren started after her.

The moon had set, and the first inklings of dawn were stealing the light from the easternmost stars.

He'd come out of the dim light, blinking toward the fields in front, but when the first shock of blackness passed he became aware of her form, quite near him beneath the thatch overhang, holding herself with crossed arms.

It was enough to know she was within reach, so he didn't say anything at first. Then: "You're cold, aren't you." Anna shook her head, but he didn't see. "Aren't you?"

"No."

"Sure you are. You must be. Wait, I'll get a blanket or something."

"It's okay," she said. "I'll be okay in a minute, then I'll go in."

"You're sick." He took a step toward her but she backed away.

"Sick?" she replied softly. "I guess you could call it that. It's withdrawal. I'm a couple of weeks into it now."

"Oh, damn. I'm sorry, I . . ."

"I think it's been two weeks. No . . ."

"I forgot. I mean, it never occurred to me."

"No, it's more. I started that night at Krishen's Cafe."

"But that trek. And back at the monastery, running away with us like that. And all the time . . ."

"You were the ones who did it," she answered. "You and J. J. dragging me along like that. I just stumbled through it all."

"That's not true," he said angrily. "You did it, too. You were terrific."

But she went on as if he hadn't spoken.

"I mean, I know what you and J. J. did for me and I'm grateful. At least I'm trying to be grateful. But right now, you see, I'm sick. It's all catching up with me. What I did to that poor woman in there . . . and the cramps and shakes will be back, too. Again and again. And no sleep, no rest. Only those dreams again. Oh, God, it's going to be bad."

"I can help," Berren said lamely. "We can do it again, just like last time."

"You still don't see," she said. "*We* didn't do it last time, you did. It's not just so much chemistry. You gave me part of your life to live when I thought I had none of my own, but then what you did . . . the way you treated me in Bihar, it was as if you'd taken it back again. Then I had nothing. If that happens again, it'll be the end."

Her shadow seemed to turn slightly, as if she were listening to the rustling of tiny wings in the hedges along the nearby field.

"No," she said at last. "I've got to start with someone I remember being a long time ago, and build her into someone that nobody can touch."

"Hey, you two," Jason was calling from inside. "Tommy, she all right?"

Berren ignored him.

"You've got to do it alone?" he asked.

"For now," she said. "No, please don't touch me. J. J.'s calling. I'll be in when this one passes."

"Tommy, bring her in here. I think this stuff the major's got is real bourbon!"

So he went back inside.